TIME TO FLY

– J.P. REHBINE –

2019 Plowshare Books & Media L.L.C.

USA

Time To Fly
Plowshare Media & Books L.L.C.
ISBN NUMBER: 978-1-7332396-0-8 (paperback)
Cover Design: J.P.Rehbine

This novel is a work of realistic fiction. Names, characters, places, and incidents are either products of the author's imagination, a product of author research and public record, or used fictitiously. All active characters are fictional, and any similarity to people living or dead is purely coincidental and are in no way a reflection or commentary on any persons, specific places, event, locales, or institutions.

Registered in the Library of Congress 2019, Case No. 1-7826420371
Published by Plowshare Media & Books L.L.C., 2019.

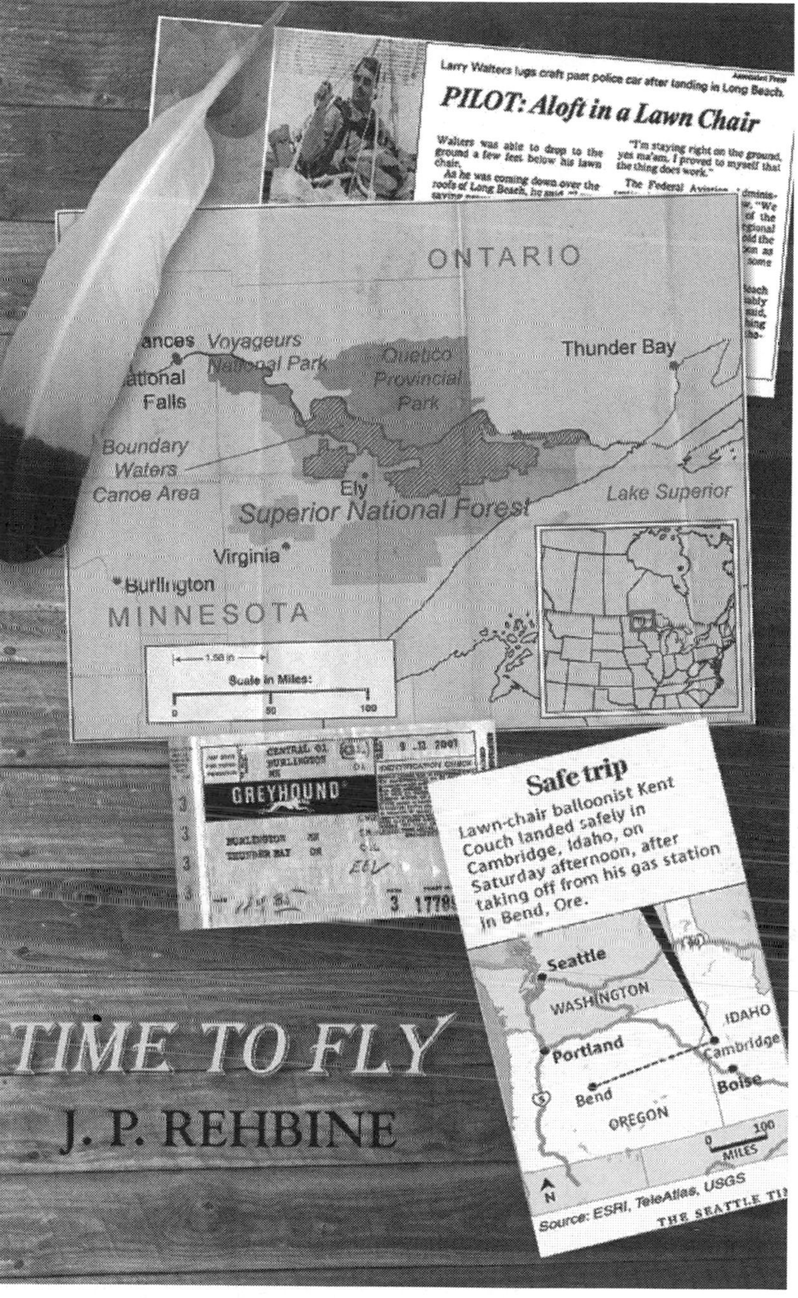

Larry Walters lugs craft past police car after landing in Long Beach.
PILOT: Aloft in a Lawn Chair
Walters was able to drop to the ground a few feet below his lawn chair.
"I'm staying right on the ground, yes ma'am. I proved to myself that the thing does work."
ONTARIO
Voyageurs National Park
Quetico Provincial Park
Thunder Bay
Boundary Waters Canoe Area
Ely
Superior National Forest
Lake Superior
Virginia
Burlington
MINNESOTA
Scale in Miles:
0
50
100
GREYHOUND
BURLINGTON
THUNDER BAY
Safe trip
Lawn-chair balloonist Kent Couch landed safely in Cambridge, Idaho, on Saturday afternoon, after taking off from his gas station in Bend, Ore.
Seattle
WASHINGTON
IDAHO
Portland
Cambridge
Boise
Bend
OREGON
MILES
N
Source: ESRI, TeleAtlas, USGS
TIME TO FLY
J. P. REHBINE

Dedicated to all my students

For all the adventures and goals that await in your mind

and outside your front door.

Acknowledgements

Many thanks to all those who were willing to use their skills to help me share this story with the world.

Editing and Review: Linda Hull, Matthew Hoey,
Lisa, Lilah, and Jane Rehbine
Cover Formatting: Vic and Charlie from Fivver
Map Page Formatting: Leah Tury
Malin Symbol Design: Marta Stachowiak @ martith.art

Contents

~ *The supreme happiness of life is the conviction that we are loved.*

Victor Hugo

–1–

Waking Up to Reality

Except for the sound of breathing, the dark room was silent, but he was not alone.

A young woman sat at the edge of a vinyl chair speaking in low tones to a shimmering wall of plastic. She leaned in so close to the barrier surrounding the hospital bed that tiny clouds of vapor appeared on it in front of her lips as she whispered. A slow procession of tears made their way down high cheekbones, soaking into long ribbons of raven black hair. Slender fingers lovingly pressed into the plastic attempted to hold the hand of the sleeping six-year-old boy fixed in the gaze of her deep brown Inuit eyes.

"Mrs. Windworth, you really ought to take a break and go home for a while," the night nurse coached as she swept into the room making her rounds. "His fever has come down and he appears to be stable. You've been sitting by his bedside for thirty-six hours now."

Meredith Windworth did not respond to her. She silently concentrated on the boy in the bubble as if she could somehow cure him with her thoughts.

"We can call you if there are any changes in his condition, and frankly, Mrs. Windworth, I'm getting concerned about *your* condition."

Sensing a stirring in the bed, Mrs. Windworth ignored the nurse, her nose now pressing against the plastic wall between them. "Dusty, I'm still here, and I'm not going anywhere without you, so just hang in there and come back to me, okay?"

Little Dustin began to sense light through the hazy layer that protected him from further infection. He squinted and focused with all his might, managing to see a blurred vision of his mother's face, her eyes now radiant with joy.

"Hello, my Dusty boy!" she said with a huge smile of relief.

"Mom ..." Dustin started, while turning his head to see her tear-covered cheeks through the foggy barrier, "I just had the most horrible dream. I dreamed you fell off the face of the earth!"

"Dusty, just lean back and relax. There's no need to get upset," she assured him as she offered her best attempt at a comforting smile. "We don't want you to start coughing again. Just lay your head back," his mother coached.

He closed his eyelids again and began to fall back asleep, feeling the sweet release of consciousness embrace him, but his head started to bob forward, causing him to briefly glance downward. However, instead of bed sheets, the earth itself appeared below him, beneath his body somehow which, after several seconds of staring down at a maze of autumn-colored broccoli, he came to his senses. He was not in his hospital bed. He was floating silently among fluffy, white clouds.

Dustin remembered where he really was. He was not six years old, nearly dying of pneumonia; he was thirteen, somewhere far above 12,500 feet and climbing higher, strapped into a lawn chair tied to over two thousand party balloons.

He assumed that he must have passed out again. The air was too thin at this altitude. He knew he was not getting enough oxygen. His research made him keenly aware of the atmosphere at this height, how it was causing him to feel light-headed, drowsy, blurring his vision, and messing with his brain, making him either faint or hallucinate. Although he was rather pleased with the memory of surviving his brush with death when he was six, Dustin could only hope the balloons would reach a point where they could no longer rise in the air. He knew the rising was slowly going to kill him.

He released the ratty seatbelt that held him safe, clenched his camping knife between his teeth, and considered climbing up the ropes that secured the aluminum reclining lawn chair to a large metal ring six feet above him—a ring connected to thousands of strands of fishing line glistening with beads of moisture from passing clouds, a shimmering web rising up to a giant mass of color. Reaching those balloon strings meant he could cut them, one by one, and finally bring his craft under control. But he no longer had the strength; lips purple from the cold, his body was shivering uncontrollably every few seconds, and his head infected with dizziness. He put down his knife and re-buckled.

The students in Mr. Wolcott's third-hour English class were glued to the monitor that hung near the front corner of the room. Half of a sentence was scrawled onto the whiteboard. Tony was frozen to the spot where he had stopped writing when they heard the announcement about what was going on. They all knew who it was on the screen up in the air. It was the absent kid from the third row next to the center aisle who had been called to the principal's office a week ago for stealing a bike—that new kid with the lost sense of fashion who came to school last spring wearing a braid to his waist. Mr. Wolcott had been staring from the back of the room with his arms crossed and his mustache twitching for nearly twenty minutes now, and Tony was still holding the marker in his hand. Fear, excitement, and nagging regret fluttered about the room like a trapped bat.

"...And now let's go to our own News 5, Eye in the Sky reporter Gurdeep Canary with an update on a most unbelievable story. A thirteen-year-old boy, identified as Dustin Tecumseh Windworth, has somehow launched himself into the sky in a lawn chair tied to balloons," a female reporter exclaimed on the wall mounted monitor. "We are still searching on the ground for his parents and wondering how he was able to acquire the contraption. At this point, however, he is so high up that he is barely visible with the aid of binoculars! Gurdeep, what do you have for us out there?"

"Well Darla, he has risen beyond the maximum ceiling our helicopter can fly. As you can see, we can get a view of him from our external camera, but the concern now is whether he has enough oxygen to breathe at that altitude. The word on the scanner is that the Canadian Armed Forces plans to send one of their CH-147 Chinook twin rotor helicopters up to see what can be done for him. It is the only helicopter of its kind that can fly above 12,000 feet, so it's being flown in from Thunder Bay and may take another half an hour. Unfortunately, any helicopter getting too close would increase the risk of complicating things for him, as the balloons he is using to fly his craft look like ordinary party balloons. But we all have very high hopes—excuse the pun there ... it was unintended. Regardless, we have high hopes for him as we all wait to see how this turns out."

"Additionally, Darla, an interesting tidbit of info just came in about a curious symbol painted onto the bottom of the chair so when you look up, you see it ... that is, if he were about 11,000 feet lower in the sky. It's in the shape of a figure 8 turned on its side with arrows of some sort shooting out of it. No one has figured out what it means yet, but we have a few interns working on it as we speak."

Great Aunt Myrtle and Uncle Donny sat bolt upright on the edge of a threadbare couch, clutching hands and staring at the screen in front of them on an old console TV. Myrtle's eyes were bloodshot from crying, which she now had under control. Meanwhile, Donny remained completely unaware of the way his heavy body made the old couch creak and whine at his constant rocking back and forth. He took a sip of peach soda from a can and set it back on the arm of the chair. The phone began ringing again. By this time, Myrtle had it set on the table next to her, ready to pick up.

"Hello? Yes, this is she. Yes, he's our son, I mean our nephew–well, my grand-nephew. No, none of us were aware of what he was planning."

Myrtle listened to the voice on the other end for a few moments. Donny, his eyes glued to the screen, reached over and felt for the pop can with his hand, knocking it over into the lap of his camo overalls and onto the floor.

"Dag-nab-it all!" he declared. The couch creaked as he lifted his wide body up and walked to the kitchen for a towel.

"No, we did not provide him with anything to make it! He just used stuff we had around here, I guess," Myrtle said.

"Yes, it just so happens that we sell balloons commercially and we probably happened to have what he needed in the barn. Yes, a barn. Yes, we stock helium."

There was more chatting from the other end of the phone while the news reports droned on from the TV speaker about the boy in the sky.

Myrtle's eyebrows lowered, and she began scowling at what was she was hearing over the old, corded receiver. "No, I do not think we are responsible! Sure, we did, but c'mon sir, how many kids do you see actually trying this kind of thing in real life? None! No, I would not like to be paid for an exclusive interview and I think our conversation needs to come to a close now. Have a nice day, sir!" she said as politely as possible as she hung up.

She looked up at Donny, more tears beginning to flow, "Oh dear, oh dear! Don, are we responsible for this?"

A hoboesque man with a three-day beard sat puffing on a cigarette at a diner counter outside of Fargo, North Dakota. Sipping coffee and leaning in, he began squinting at a small screen that was squawking away in the corner of the room.

"Excuse me, ma'am," he said. "Can we turn that up? I mean in a hurry! I think I know that kid."

He got out of his seat, cup in hand, and walked stiff-backed over to the corner to get as close to the TV as possible. "I *do* know that kid!" he announced to the nearly empty café, "Oh my ... what in the dare-devil? Now that's a stunt ... but kid, you gotta know that's probably a one-way trip ..." he muttered under his breath as the cigarette clung to his lower lip.

His mind raced to think of what possible thing he could do to help or save him, but nothing came to him because there was truly nothing he *could* do but stare in disbelief. He looked out the window at the massive sky backdropping a treeless landscape for a moment, contemplating. "That's right Teddy," he whispered. "You got nothing, and you got yourself in the wrong place at the wrong time, as usual." He locked his gaze back onto the screen, listening and puffing. The runaway carnival clown raised his coffee cup as if to toast an imaginary friend. "Godspeed to you Dust. Fly like the wind! I know what you're up to. Now you get this one figured out, so you can make it in time for her!"

Dustin gave a hazy glance at the vintage altimeter duct taped to the arm of his lawn chair. The red metal needle was still pegged at 12,500 feet. That was as high as it measured. He wished that the cluster balloon craft had finally reached its maximum height so it might level off or begin losing altitude, but now these thoughts appeared to be just a new set of empty hopes. *How could it come to this? How could I make the exact same mistake Larry the lawn-chair balloonist made back in 1989?*

The crippling feelings swept into his gut for another round, but they had nothing to do with being stuck in a lawn chair, lost in the sky. They were the voices of Zane and Harley, dive-bombing his brain again as they rattled around, trapped inside his head, "Dude, just admit that you're a lost cause, an idiot ... the local freak-a-zoid that'll *always* have it wrong and *never* get it right—the true definition of zero! Just give it up, Dust-in-the-Wind."

All their many choice words played on in repeat mode and raged in his mind, hot flames from a dragon's mouth igniting shame and fear as he silently sat, buckled into a reclining position rising out of control into an unknown atmosphere. He pictured himself lying dead in it, floating into outer Earth orbit—white, frozen, and forgotten, but faces of family flooded his mind ... how stressed they must be, now that the news choppers had found him out.

Still, in spite of the anxiety, he turned back to musing optimistically ... *if I make it ... if I can get to her in time, then it will all make sense. It will all be worth it.*

These thoughts were like medicine that soothed and healed the dragon's latest attack on his soul. His mind drifted to Uncle Asa's argument about unlimited potential. He could still picture Asa pointing at him saying that he was the type of person who could break through and tap into it. As much as that sounded like crazy talk, Asa wouldn't just say that to make him feel good. Asa never lied.

Am I that kind of kid? Or am I just a misled dreamer? The two conclusions about himself sparred back and forth in his mind like Athena and Aries fighting to the death in the sky, while Zeus tossed in shafts of lighting for confusion and Poseidon stirred up menacing thunderclouds for a convincing emotional backdrop. He had never imagined he would find himself riding the skies in his own handmade flying machine, suspended above the earth, floating among the clouds. Just two short weeks ago the whole idea did not even exist in his head, and yet, here he was.

Dustin could hear the whirring of another helicopter engine coming towards him from somewhere, and his vision blurred again in the sun trying to locate it. He needed to stay awake—alert.

Reaching for the cell phone, he checked for reception hoping to give his friend, Elise, an update on his situation ... no bars appeared on the screen. He knew that he was somewhere above the massive Superior National Forest, thousands of square miles of tree-covered wilderness in northern Minnesota. There was no reason to put up a cell tower there. *Who would use it, bears?* He pictured a big brown bear on a cell phone and chuckled to himself.

Flight time: 1017 hours. Dustin noted he had been in the air for over five hours now. He leaned to one side and hoisted up a gallon jug of water from a rope tied to one arm of the chair. Taking small sips, he looked off into the horizon. He could see the curve of the Earth before him. The view was amazing. It didn't seem real.

He grabbed onto the cord that held his bag of little plastic army men and dropped one into his lap. With shaking hands, he pulled out his black marker from a pocket on his fishing vest, yanked the cap off with his teeth, and scrolled out a message, along with his flight time, onto the plastic parachute that was attached to the toy soldier. Holding it at full arms-length, it dangled in the breeze below his hand, underneath which, billowy, white puffs moved slowly above a luxurious, rolling carpet of fall color.

"You have no idea just how far you're about to fall. Enjoy the scenery," Dustin announced in a shivering mumble to the silent, plastic man. Then in a deep, commander's tone, he barked, "Good luck on your mission, and may God be with you!" Switching to a munchkin voice he yelled, "Geronimo!" as he released the plastic paratrooper into a cloud below. He watched the chute open as the tiny green paratrooper made his way along the wind current, down toward the Earth, disappearing into a cloud. "God be with me too," he whispered.

These distractions helped him more than he knew. Feeling another wave of dizziness enter his head, a strong desire tempted him to give into it ... to just close his eyes and float off into dreamland, perhaps never to return. The feeling was so relaxing, so peaceful, but he knew he had to fight it. There was no way to know just how high in the atmosphere he had risen, and he realized there was a chance he would fly too high and simply run out of oxygen to breathe. But there was still some fight left in him, and until a better opportunity came his way to get out of this, he just simply had to hang on. He decided to try staying awake by breathing deeply and remembering as many details as he could about the past few weeks that led him to this crazy journey through the clouds.

2

Trapped in Burlington

"Get your balloons here! Straight from our own Burlington Novelty Warehouse! Get your balloons here. One for three or two for five ..."

Dustin hated balloons. When he was younger, he loved them. His Uncle Donny always had all the coolest new kinds he sold to fairs and circuses from his mail-order novelty warehouse, and every time Dustin went to see big Uncle Donny, he always walked out with a smile on his face and a fresh balloon in his hand. But life was so different now. He was no longer a little kid, and each time he looked up to pass one to another eager young customer he was reminded of how happy his life used to be before it all came crashing down.

"Get your balloons here! One for three or two for five ... hey, how about a little floating happiness for the little guy there?" A set of parents passed with a toddler in tow. Dustin knew which lines worked best. He had been working the Burlington, Minnesota County Fair selling toys and balloons since he was eleven. He'd learned from his uncle and father how to call customers as they walked past the entrance. The sweet smells of cotton candy, fried elephant ears, and hot dogs lingered in the air mingling with the occasional whiff of cigarette smoke and body odor, wafting from crowds as they passed.

Working the fair was always fun. During the past two summers, when his mother was sick in the hospital, Dustin's father drove him down from their home in Thunder Bay, Canada, leaving him to stay with Uncle Donny and Great Aunt Myrtle for most of the summer. He got to work at his uncle's warehouse, which was fascinating since it was always stocked with the latest goofy carnival toys, gags, and magic tricks, but the best part was selling at the county fair.

Each September, Dustin would go back home to Thunder Bay with a whole new load of stories and gags to lay on his friends and scout buddies, telling of his adventures, the odd people he met, and all the money he earned. He remembered the look of longing in their eyes to be in a small town out in the country, exploring fields, trails, woods, and fishing all summer. Living in town was nothing like that. Elise, his best friend from two doors down, always begged Dustin to talk his parents into bringing her for a week. The two hundred fifty-mile drive was long and expensive, however, so Dustin never got the guts to ask.

But the fun and magic were gone now. The adventures at his uncle's had turned into a dismal and depressing trap. It was another warm day in northern Minnesota, the final day of the Burlington County Fair, and Dustin knew that this was his last chance to earn some decent dough for a while. He stood on the matted, brown grass between the ticket gate and the concession area, wind blowing his nearly black, shoulder-length hair against his suntanned face—bracing his quickly growing frame against the stronger gusts, holding his giant bouquet of colored balloons which constantly tried to escape from his hands. Dustin, unaware that his favorite canvas cargo pants had become a little too short due to his growth spurt over the summer, stayed planted in what he called his "lucky spot," a money pouch hanging from his hip. Dustin's thoughts drifted to something hopeful. He was only seventy-eight dollars away from the bike he wanted. His mind began computing to figure out how many balloons it would take to get that money in his hand if he sold them in groups of five. A single sale netted him a dollar, but *three-for-five* meant less profit for him.

"Yo, Dusstin!" Zane Johnson crowed as he approached with his buddies. He was wearing a perfectly fitted T-shirt to show off his athletic, muscle-toned arms, a backward baseball cap with sports sunglasses perched atop the visor, and a winning smile forever plastered onto his face. It was the kind of smile that might melt a girl's heart, a grin which radiated a confidence that could always fool you into thinking he was genuinely interested in you each time you saw it. In Dustin's eyes, he was a guy who had it all going for him, including plenty of friends; something Dustin was in short supply of since moving to Minnesota. "Dudes, check it out. It's Dust-in-the-wind sellin' air in Mylar bags to the kiddies again."

Zane leaned in close to Dustin's face, "Hey Dust, what's your *wind* worth?"

The others glanced at Dustin and chuckled, or simply ignored him as they carried on their conversations. One of them, Harley, the big heavy of the group, rolled his eyes at the sight of the long-haired balloon salesman.

"That would be helium, Zane, and you sound kinda like you've already got plenty," Dustin replied in a barely confident voice, using minimal eye-contact.

"Ooh, Dusty, I wasn't dissin' you now, was I? I was just pointing out all the hard work that you do for your loser dad and uncle, so you don't all go broke," Zane sparred back as the trio of athletic prowess took their position in front of him.

Dusty noticed the smudge of dried chocolate ice cream still left on the tip of Zane's pointed nose. He wanted to comment on it and was surprised the others hadn't noticed. The nose resembled a ski jump, with two flaring nostro-caves on each side and a round muddy target moving ever-so-slightly above his big mouth, just like the tin-man from *The Wizard of Oz*. Dustin had a knack for noticing detail, and in stressful times like these, tended to focus in on it. "So ... I take it that you guys are standing so close to me 'cause you want some balloons, eh?" Dustin cooly asked with a smirk, not knowing what else to say. He was trying his best not to look nervous, even though his heart kept picking up pace in his chest.

"We're just standin' here waiting to see if you'll float away to where you came from," Harley taunted with a mild but firm push to Dustin's chest. "What do you think it would take guys, maybe five-or-so more balloons and a stiff breeze?

"I think his hair is the only thing keeping him grounded right now. Anyone got a pair of scissors?" Dante, the shortest of them tossed in.

Two of them tried unsuccessfully to hold back a snicker as they spied a few girls approaching to join them from the concession area.

"Later, Dust-in-the-wind," Zane sneered while walking backward, mocking a salute. He turned, and they sauntered off toward the girls, laughing and adding more ideas which Dusty couldn't hear. It made him feel even sicker about starting school in a week.

The name. The name and the hair were sore spots which got scratched, pecked, and poked at daily at school. What were his parents thinking to name him Dustin with a last name like Windworth? It started the day he came to

Wooddale Middle School last May after leaving Thunder Bay with his dad to move in with his uncle. Some kid who heard his name in the previous class walked past him in the hallway loudly singing the chorus to the 70's Kansas rock group song, "*... dust in the wind, all you are is dust in the wind ...*" and then several others who knew the song jumped in for the second line, "*dust in the wind, everything is dust in the wind ...*" walking off laughing. The idea of using his middle name crossed his mind once, only to be quickly shot down by the realization that his First Nations name, Tecumseh, a name he was once proud to carry, got mispronounced most of the time and only pointed out his native status all the more. Last year it had become a hallway tradition for some to sing at the boy with the windy hair.

The hair... *What to do with the hair?* When he arrived last spring from Thunder Bay, he wore it in one long braid, and it hung nearly to his waist. Back home, there were many other Ojibwe who still wore it traditionally, out of respect, and tribal elders taught how it was a sacred reflection of their strength, it connected them to the earth, to the flow of life, and the Creator.

Yet it was the long braid that started the fight. They kept pulling on it. Yanking it, saying things like, "ding-dong," and when he turned, he never knew which kid pulled it. He couldn't tell his father, he had enough to worry about. He couldn't speak of it. And it continued until the day he turned in time to face the puller. Dustin had no plan. He just wanted it to stop. But Harley took it as a challenge, and being surrounded by a small audience, decided to slam his arms into Dustin's shoulders, knocking him off balance. Instinctively, Dustin returned a push, not knowing it would lead to his bloodied nose. Not knowing it would lead to a suspension for a fight he never intended to be part of. But he needed one less stinging sore spot, so the next Monday morning he snipped it off and tried not to think about what all that meant for him. Since last spring it had grown back out, not long enough to braid, but long enough for the pecking to start back up. However, he just couldn't cut it. He knew his mom would be heartbroken to know it had all come off. He had to grow it back, regardless of the abuse; it was sacred.

He stared down at the worn grass, not noticing the many shoes and strollers scurrying by. He thought about all his old friends in Thunder Bay, Elise, and his mother. For a brief moment he could see his mother's smile. It felt like an arm suddenly reaching out of his heart and stretching for hundreds of miles toward Canada. But it wasn't long enough. She was too far away, and it had been too long since he had seen her in person. There was nothing he could do but wait and hope for a solution.

Dustin thought about the bike again, got his mind busy again ... this one would have a lock on it no one could break. He planned to engrave his name on the underside of the pedal bracket so no more kids like Harley could take it, repaint it, call it theirs and get away with it. He had a plan to solve this problem once and for all and he calculated in his mind that he was only seventy-eight balloons away from it. He refocused.

An excited little girl with brown pigtails walked up to him.

"The purple one, Mommy," she requested as she pointed up to the large clump of sparkling joy attached to Dustin's arm. Her mother picked out a shiny purple one and the girl giggled with delight as it was handed to her.

"That will be three, Ma'am," he politely slipped out as she reached for her purse. "Thank you and have a great evening at the fair."

Seventy-seven more to go, he thought to himself as the girl happily skipped away.

"Get your balloons here! Straight from our own Burlington Novelty Warehouse! Get your balloons here. One for three or two for five ..."

Off in the distance, he saw the purple balloon begin floating gracefully upwards, rocking gently side-to-side on its ribbon string. He knew what had happened. It happened quite often, and within moments a dull whimpering was heard among the crowd. Dustin watched the balloon begin to grow smaller in the clear, blue afternoon sky, floating off toward the northeast. That is where the wind always carried the ones that slipped away. Soon the whimpering began to grow into a rising weeping.

Northeast, Dustin thought. *I wonder if that little balloon will make it all the way to Thunder Bay,* he pondered to himself ...*to home—to Mom.* He pictured it floating over the hospital she had been in for nearly six months now. He glanced back up. The purple balloon was now the size of a dime and still rising.

The little girl with the brown pigtails continued to cry as her mother pulled her by the hand toward the midway rides.

Dustin imagined the purple balloon floating past the hospital windows, and his mother looking out, seeing it, and thinking of him standing out in the Minnesota prairie selling his balloons, so far away. He pretended she would wonder if it was one that he sold. He remembered her last smile for him, and it ached to think about it.

He looked up a third time. The balloon was now a tiny speck in the sky. He knew what he had to do, which is what he always did, to give one away. He knew it would cost him. His dad kept a careful count in case Dustin got tempted to give away freebies to friends. It would set him back exactly two dollars, but he just had to do it.

Dustin left his post near the front gates and began walking toward the sounds of sorrow. They were now mixed with the sounds of the Burlington County Fair, shrieks and loud music from the rides in the midway, the crazy whistle of Teddy, the hobo clown at the dunk tank, and the competition announcers with their cheap microphones. He walked past the trinket booths, past the livestock buildings, the Four-H building, and into the concessions area.

Suddenly he heard Uncle Asa call out to him from the window of the concession trailer he was selling food from, "Hey, Dust, did another one get away? You go Dusty! Remember to come by tomorrow to help me pack down!"

Dustin gave a quick wave. Uncle Asa knew exactly what he was up to because Dustin had given away at least half-a-dozen balloons that summer. Sometimes Asa would slip him a few bucks to make up for the loss. He was glad his mission was noticed by someone.

Carefully avoiding another confrontation with Zane, Harley, and their gang, he caught up to the little girl with the brown pigtails near the ticket sales booth, across from the Ferris wheel. She was still crying and nearly inconsolable. He tapped her on the shoulder.

"Did you lose something?" he asked with a concerned look and sad eyes.

As she turned around, he held out another shiny purple balloon to her. Her mother twisted her neck before turning to see what stopped all the crying so suddenly. "I'm sorry balloon boy; we can only buy one tonight, but thanks so much anyway."

"No charge," Dustin quietly said with a big smile on his face.

The little girl with the brown pigtails immediately started squealing with laughter again while doing little jumps in the line.

"That was so sweet of you. What's your name?" the mother inquired.

"It's Dustin ... Dustin Windworth," he quietly slipped out while tying the string on the little girl's wrist.

"Thank you ever so much, Dustin. You just made my baby girl's day!" she replied back, her eyebrows revealing grateful relief.

Dustin politely nodded and walked away. "Seventy-*nine* more to sell," he said to himself with a satisfied sigh.

"Get your balloons here! Straight from our own Burlington Novelty Warehouse! Get your balloons here. One for three or two for five ..."

-3-

Surprise Visitor

The sun was sinking low in the sky by the time Dustin and his father got back to the farmhouse. Dustin jumped out of the truck and ran around to the side door to the kitchen for a snack. After a few minutes, the familiar evening banter between his father and uncle could be heard from the family room.

"Donny, did you call on the Darby account today?" Dave inquired from a corner room he used as an office.

"Tried to ... they don't ever answer their phone these days. I'm starting to think I oughta drive over to see them, but that's a two-day trip there and back."

"Well, you're going to have to do something. They're our biggest account and we haven't gotten an order from them in at least six months. I'm afraid we're gonna lose 'em, Don."

"I know, Dave. I know. Them fellas are the reason we converted the barn into a warehouse years ago. They're still the biggest circus and fair company in the mid-west.

Where are they buying all their toys and gags from these days?"

"I know where," Dustin declared from the kitchen. He knew what they needed to do to make the novelty business take off again, but whenever he suggested the idea, neither man would listen. He couldn't help but try again.

"Dad, you and Uncle Donny need to get a website. You have to set it up so people can just use their credit card to order the stuff online! It's not a big deal. I bet that's where Darby's going to buy their toys these days."

"Dustin, all that fancy-schmancy electronic stuff is not for us. It's not the way we do business. Sales is a personal thing," Uncle Donny advised from the couch. "Always has been—always will be. You just have to meet the right people and then take care of them. We just seem to be running a bit short on the right kind of people these days, that's all."

"Times are different now," Dustin reasoned back. "Everyone's doing things through the internet. Phone calls and hand-shakes aren't working anymore. What people do now is text. Have you guys ever heard of Amazon?"

They replied with silence.

Dustin had mentioned this fact on more than several occasions, always to be shot down. It hurt him that they didn't think his ideas would work. Back in Canada, in Thunder Bay, he had friends. People listened to him there. His scout troop always loved his ideas. His mother listened to him there. Even though he was just twelve at the time, they knew him and respected him.

“Don,” his dad started again, “besides the money we get from leasing out our fields to Jeb Fischer next door, we aren’t getting any more orders for product and we aren’t getting any more income either. The fact is we are out of money and we have bills coming due at the end of the month. You said you had a plan two months ago. Now, where’s the plan for finding more customers, little brother?”

The truth was Uncle Donny didn’t have a plan. His uncle never liked farming and always had other interests he was pursuing while growing up. First, it was snake collecting. At fourteen, his uncle had over twenty exotic snakes he kept in the old chicken house. He would breed and sell baby pythons to folks in the tri-county area. This went well until a particularly cold Minnesota blizzard knocked out the power one night and he woke up to find all the snakes frozen.

The snake incident was a horrible blow for his uncle, but by the time he got over it he was selling a gag toy he found on a field trip to a factory in St. Paul. He started off by selling a box full of invisible dog-on-a-leash toys to a local traveling circus manager his father knew, then later, through the mail. Uncle Donny always wanted to join the circus, but would never directly admit it. His big dream was to be a large cat trainer and stand in the middle of the ring with lions and tigers jumping around him. He often told his Maximus Brother's Animal Act story to new people he met in the novelty selling business. Apparently, when his uncle was sixteen, the head trainer invited him into the act for a show once when they were in town. He always ended the story with the part about the Siberian tiger snapping its jaw closed a little too early after he had placed his head in the tiger's mouth. Then he would triumphantly end it by pointing to a tiny corner of his earlobe which was missing. He kept a poster of the Maximus Brother's Animal Act in a cheap frame in the living room.

Uncle Donny figured out how to make money selling gags, toys, and trinkets to circuses, county fairs, and anyone else that needed goofy stuff. Dustin's father, Dave, was good with numbers; while Uncle Donny did the sales and got new accounts, his brother would keep the books and fill the orders. The year after Donny graduated from high school, their father had a stroke and had to give up farming one of the last dairy farms in Burlington County. That was when they started using the big barn to store the products they were selling instead of the shed, and within two years they had set up a respectable mail order business. Eventually, Dustin's dad got married and left the business all to Donny to become an accountant in Canada.

Uncle Donny was a good salesman, but a lousy bookkeeper. He hired his Aunt Myrtle to help him pay bills and keep track of paperwork after both of their parents died. She was living alone, so she decided to move in to watch over Donny and help him keep the business going. Sadly, after fifteen years of using paper, pencils, phone calls, and Aunt Myrtle doing all she knew for him, the novelty business began to fall apart.

"Don, it's been what, four months now since I moved back here with Dusty hoping to build the business back up to what it used to be? All I'm saying is we've got to find a way to make this thing grow or it's not going to work."

Dustin never dreamed that his dad would end up working for his uncle Donny at the novelty warehouse. That was what his uncle and father had called it since they were teenagers. It was actually a large barn. It sat at the back of a row of barns and outbuildings on the farm his uncle and father had grown up on.

"Dave, your makin' me do something I can't. I can't make money just grow on trees for you, and I'm doing the best I can!"

"Well, if that's your best, it's gonna have to get better because your best isn't cutting it, now is it, little brother?"

This is when the silent awkwardness began as it often had before, the time of day Dustin really wanted to just disappear. He started quietly heading upstairs but was met by his great aunt halfway up.

"Hey there, Dusty boy. Did you reach your goal today?"

"Hi, Aunt Mertie. Nope. I'm still seventeen dollars

short. Almost got there but I got a little distracted today." Dustin tried to appear cheerful. He really appreciated how perky she always was with him; how she was always trying to look at the bright side of things and wanting to even out the mood in the household.

"Listen, I picked up the last of the broasted turkey from Asa's Tin Goose concession trailer today. He gave us enough leftovers to feast for a week. Asa asked me to tell you he'd pay you to help clean up and pack down his trailer for the season. That should be enough for you to meet your goal *and* get a good lock for your new bike," she said with a grin and a wink as she turned her portly body back down the stairs to the kitchen.

Aunt Myrtle knew about the whole bike theft incident. It burned her up to know that Harley Dumas was running around on Dusty's bike, but there was no way to conclusively prove it, especially with Harley's mother lying for him. But Aunt Myrtle had put it all together and figured out how he did it. Regardless, she was cautious to never show Dustin how she really felt. She was being careful with him, knowing the circumstances, and making sure he had someone in his life that treated him like a mother would. She rather enjoyed the opportunity to be a mother, since at this point, her hopes of ever having kids of her own seemed impossible.

"Well, Dusty. I bet you're thinking that's some good news, but I've got a better one for you. Are you ready for me to lay it on you? I'll give you a hint: someone special is coming to visit!"

Dustin's eyes lit up.

"Let me guess… It's Mom isn't it—she's coming! I knew it when Dad told me the doctors were reviewing her case again last week …"

"No, honey, but it is a girl though," she slipped in reassuringly.

"Elise? Is Elise coming?"

Aunt Myrtle nodded with delight.

"Who's bringing her? How is she getting here?" Dustin knew it was a long trip.

"Well, her parents called yesterday evening. They decided to take a trip to the states to see some old friends in Chicago, so they're dropping her off for about a week."

"When are they coming, Mertie?"

"They should have arrived already, so why don't you climb up the silo and watch for them? You can take the belt radio and let me know when you see them coming up the road, since I got a little busy getting the house ready, and I've got some primping to do before they show up."

Dustin grabbed the radio and tore out the door, his sneakers scattering gravel as he ran across the farmyard toward the big barn. He loved climbing the silo. It was one of his favorite things to do at the farm. It towered eighty-two feet high and it took him two weeks last summer to get the courage to climb all the way to the top. He slid to a stop in the loose pebbles, shaded his eyes from the setting sun with his hand, and strained his neck to look up at the gigantic cylinder-shaped building that stood three times taller than the two-story farmhouse. He remembered Uncle Donny telling him how they used it for years to store the feed for the cows during the winter.

Hugging the side of the silo was a spindly, round safety cage surrounding a skinny, steel ladder. It rose up the giant, blue structure and was so long that it looked as if it simply disappeared at the top. But Dustin knew that the ladder, as tall as it was, was the easy part, because when he reached the roof, he would have to claw his way on his hands and knees on an open catwalk over to the little platform at the peak, to the safety of the rooftop railing, which stood in a tight little circle around the hatchway door at the center of the roof cap. That part was always nerve-wracking, but he had gotten used to it—used to the height, and accustomed to the wind gusts that came and went when scaling the rooftop catwalk.

As he climbed away, Dustin imagined himself heroically waving "hello" to her car as it approached the farm. Elise had never been here, and she would not only be impressed with the place but might really be blown away by seeing him aloft this giant rocket-shaped object, greeting them from the sky.

Even though he could picture all this, Dustin still knew he was mortal, and that what he was doing was dangerous, so he had to be careful and think about each step, each hand grip and footing as he climbed the silo ladder. Approaching the windy top, heart beating fast, he reached up from the ladder to grip the steel mesh of the catwalk. It angled up and away from the stairs and sat, bolted to the roof of the colossal blue and white cylinder. He felt like an ant as he crawled his way along the narrow steel bridge. He glanced to the left for a second, and from the catwalk could see only sky beyond the edge. The farm looked miniature from this height; the cars and tractor were sandbox toys. He felt a wave of dizziness come over him as he considered the fact that there were absolutely no barriers protecting him from falling. Then he refocused, looked ahead and determined his way beyond his fears to the hatchway.

Being on top was a feeling like no other—none of the kids from his old neighborhood in Thunder Bay knew anything of it, like flying. Standing at the cap railing, the smooth, steel roof sloped down in front of him as a ten-foot circle below his feet, but beyond that, nothing but open air, sky, and land as far as he could see in any direction. Even the tallest trees stood a good twenty-five feet below him and looked remarkably small. A wind gust blew, but Dustin knew to keep a firm grip on the railing—always one hand on the railing, the way Uncle Donny had shown him to.

Dustin looked over the greenish-gold wheat fields to the north. The roads slipped out like thin ribbons into the distance. He knew exactly which road she'd be coming in on and he squinted at every vehicle driving its way south, toward the farm.

The top of the silo was Dustin's sacred space. It was far away from the problems and disappointments below; a way to shrink them down to size and pretend they didn't exist for a few minutes. He had named it Sugar Loaf, after the sacred 75-foot-high rock tower on Mackinac Island, a rock that points skyward at the northernmost tip of the mitten-shaped state of Michigan. It reminded him of other sacred sites he admired: Denali, the highest peak in North America; Mount Shasta in California, a powerful sleeping stratovolcano; Chief Mountain in Montana, the sacred tower of the Blackfeet Indians; Ship Rock in New Mexico, the sacred spot to Navajo and Hopi; or the Devil's Tower in the Black Hills of Wyoming, called Bear's Lodge by the Cheyanne and Lakota. You had to risk your life and work hard to get there, but once you arrived, it was a place of freedom and peace. This was his place to connect to the universe and its maker.

Scanning the farm below, he spied his own junk pile of inventions, partial successes and failures manufactured out of his need to forget his situation each day. The windcart's tattered sail had been left tied to the mast too long and now clung to its pole like a poor man's blanket. It was a triangular wooden frame on wheels, steered by foot stirrups, slowly giving up its red, white, and blue paint job to the weather. Next to the wind-car sat the high-speed lawn tractor, now covered in grime and weeds. It did win the annual Burlington Main Street Lawn Tractor Race last spring, but later blew out a transmission seal when Dustin tried to pop a wheelie, rendering it useless without the right parts. Then there was the ski-bike made from Myrtle's 1968 Schwinn, an old waterski for the front wheel, banana seat on the back, and chain wrapped around the rear tire to grip the snow. That idea was a true fail once he tried it out, but there it sat, hiding in the tall grass like a bad bicycle joke.

After waiting and thinking atop the silo for quite some time, he saw the red minivan. It looked so tiny and appeared to inch along the road. He waited until they were a half a mile away before he began his waving routine. Studying the vehicle as it approached, he could hear the sound of the tires tossing gravel chunks into the wheel wells. He watched for a response ... a horn blow, or maybe a flash of the headlights. Then it dawned on him; Elise had never seen the farm before, and there were a lot of farms that looked like his Uncle's around Burlington. He stopped waving, grabbed the radio and gave the warning to Aunt Myrtle that she had about two minutes left. He figured he'd better start the process of climbing down early since it took a while to back down that catwalk and descend the ladder.

The sound of the horn mixed with peacocks crowing as his feet smacked the gravel at the base of the silo. Dustin ran up to the minivan as it rolled to a stop. Elise got out of the car smiling from ear to ear and looking about, wide-eyed, taking it all in.

"Hey Dusty, I finally made it out here," Elise declared with a gleeful grin. "It's so good to see you!"

Dustin stood close to her with his hands in his pockets: too old to hug like when they were toddlers and too young to hug like ... like adults often did. "Good to see you too. I just found out you were coming a few minutes ago."

Dusty studied her for a moment. She had gotten taller in the last six months, and her face had grown a little thinner and more like a young lady than a little girl. He always remembered her as she looked when she was eight and they were playing in one of their backyards, imagining all sorts of silly things and sometimes getting into trouble. Now she was looking older. He didn't know what to think of that. She definitely looked pretty. He would be careful not to point that out. They were best friends, at least as of last spring, before moving away. What made the meeting even more surreal is the way she stood there holding a sketch pad, exactly like she always did since he first met her.

"So, I see you're still drawing the entire world like you announced when you were eight," he said to her with a grin.

"Yes, I am, Dusty ... up to my sixth book. Still a lot of things I haven't gotten to sketching yet," she said with gusto. "Did I miss the fair, or can we go tomorrow?"

"Sure, we can go tomorrow, and it will be just as fun as if the fair were still open," Dustin said with a knowing confidence.

Elise's dad came around the car with his hand outstretched. "Hello, Dusty. You're looking tall these days. I hope you don't mind a surprise visit. Oh, speaking of surprises, your mother asked us to haul down a little something she wanted you to have." Mr. Cambry pulled up the rear hatch, and sitting in the back were two large boxes with pictures of computers on them.

Dustin's heart skipped a beat. This was a truly amazing surprise, but it was not something his mom would normally do. He scratched his chin, lost in his thoughts for the moment. Where did she get the extra money to buy this? He thought she didn't like computers and the internet. What was she expecting him to do with it?

"Hello, Mr. and Mrs. Cambry, I'm Myrtle, Dusty's great aunt," she declared with a rosy-cheeked smile. "It's nice to finally meet you all. We've heard so much about you. Welcome!" Then she turned to the silent Dustin who was staring at the boxes with one hand on his chin. "Well, Dusty boy, are you just going to stand there, or are we going to take charge of those two boxes?"

Elise stepped in and placed her sketch pad on the stacked boxes, "We can do it together."

They grabbed them both and began lugging them

toward the front door while the adults got acquainted in the driveway.

"I saw you up there," she slipped out, "up on that giant cylinder thingy. How'd you do that? It's so high up!"

"I was hoping you'd honk your horn or something," he said.

"Oh, I wasn't about to say anything in the car. Are you kidding? It was hard enough convincing my parents to let me stay for a week. If they saw you up there, they might have turned around and headed for the interstate!"

"Let's just put them over on the dining room table for now," Dustin instructed, not knowing what else to say about the silo stunt.

"You know I got a cell phone for my birthday?" Elise reported. "I can't use it here because of international charges, but I bet we can email between this machine and my phone."

"That ought to change things a bit," Dustin cautiously said.

"Quick question for you Dusty: what are those giant, creepy birds doing roosting on the top of the farmhouse roof?"

"Oh, those are just Uncle Donny's peacocks. He raises them. They kind of act like guard dogs for the house too, making all kinds of noise when they see strange things."

They reached the table and Elise leaned on the box to catch her breath and glanced over at Dustin with a mischievous look. "We're going to have a whole ton of fun here, aren't we?"

She quickly scanned the open main rooms of the farmhouse Dustin now called home. Antique furniture and outdated, overstuffed couches and chairs sat hiding under a gentle coating of clutter and paperwork, knick-knacks, and a few books. Everything looked old and tired, except for a long folding table standing in the corner, backlit by a bay window. It was covered in colorful piles of little plastic blocks that surrounded amazing little sculptures. "I see *you're* still doing Lego. Are these the advanced kits you're into now?"

"I never built off kits, remember? Well, I may build a kit the day I get it for fun, but I need them for the rare pieces to make my replicas."

She recognized his art and imagination immediately: Dustin's version of an X-wing fighter, the DeLorean time machine car from *Back to the Future*, and sadly, a near perfect replica of his old house in Thunder Bay, complete with the backyard fence, vegetable garden, tree fort, and his father's blue Chevy pickup. Everything was impeccably detailed and accurate. "Wow, Dustin. You've really gotten good at this," she marveled. "It almost looks like you can bend the Lego the way you've got this stuff put together. It's more like I'm looking at a sculpture than a Lego piece."

Elise reached for what looked like palm-sized Iron Man helmet.

"Uh ... it's best to just look at them rather than picking them up," Dustin nervously reminded her while gently taking the ball of Lego from her hand.

"Sorry, Dusty. I guess some things about you haven't changed."

"What do you mean by that?" he asked.

"Well, it's actually a relief. I'm glad to see you're still you because ... you know sometimes when you don't see a person for a long time and then you finally see them again—they're different. Sometimes too different and it gets kind of weird. You're not, and that's good."

"Yep, I'm as weird as I've ever been. Don't worry, Elise, I have no plans to change."

She noticed that his shoulders had grown a bit wider, and his hair was now reaching below them. She hadn't seen him with hair that short since they were little. He was looking more Ojibwe again. She knew his mother would be proud, and she liked it too.

That night they stayed up late trying to set up the new computer. By 11:30 they had managed to get a dial-up internet connection.

4

The Wildest Ride

The peacocks woke Elise up at six the next morning. Dustin was still fast asleep, so Elise started down the stairs alone when she heard a voice in the kitchen.

"That's what they told me, Donny. She's in the I.C.U. again and she's going to be moved to hospice care tomorrow. I told Dave, and he's going to call the doctors again today."

Elise stopped on the landing, out of view. The voice was Aunt Myrtle's. She didn't move, knowing that this was a chance for more news about Dusty's mom that she was mostly not allowed to know.

"The cancer is moving faster, and they said she's now in stage four."

"So, what does stage four mean? Does that mean she's gonna ...?" Uncle Donny's voice trailed off into silence. The kitchen stayed silent for a long twelve seconds or so. Then Elise heard noises like the pans on the stove and drawers opening for cooking.

"It's a shame, though ..." Uncle Donny began.

"I know, I know ... but we need to respect what his father has decided about Dusty no matter how we feel about it," Aunt Myrtle interjected.

Elise sat on the stairs and waited until the smell of the coffee was good and strong before she entered the kitchen.

"G'morning, Aunt Mertie," she opened, enthusiastically.

"Good morning, Elise. Did you sleep well up there in the spare room?" Aunt Myrtle asked.

"Yeah, I slept fine, thanks. I'm not used to all the birds in the morning, though."

"Well, with all you and Dusty have planned, I'm sure you'll be sleeping right through them in a day or so," she answered. "In fact, between scrubbing down the Tin Goose trailer and trying out the rides before they pack them down, you'll both be plenty tired by sundown."

"Sounds like fun," Elise said, trying to look excited.

"That upstairs bedroom you picked for me to sleep in is so beautiful. Dusty didn't tell me you had a daughter," Elise complimented. She couldn't help but notice how the curtains matched the bedspread, the walls were painted dusty pink with white trim, several stuffed animals sat in a corner and there was even a brush, comb, and mirror set out on the top of a dressing table. It was apparent the room had been set up for a girl, but whom? The closet was empty, and so were most of the drawers.

Aunt Mertie cleared her throat, "Well, it's ready for the girl I haven't had yet, I suppose." She quickly changed the subject. "So, are you ready for a busy day? I see you're already dressed and ready to go."

Dustin's Great Aunt finally turned from her work at the stove to take a good look at her. She noticed Elise's radiant, crystal blue eyes and captivating smile in the morning sunlight... there was something about her smile that seemed to fill the whole room with optimism, and the feeling warmed her heart for a moment. The hope of having a daughter like her someday excitedly crossed her mind, but she stuffed away the thought and breathed a quiet sigh knowing she was getting too old to wish for such things in her life. "Dusty's daddy will give you two a ride over to the fairgrounds on his way to Grand Rapids."

Dustin came down a few minutes later. Elise stifled a giggle at seeing him with bed-head hair and puffy, squinting eyes. Aunt Myrtle set a plate in front of him and turned to get some pancakes off the griddle. A rooster crowed off in the distance.

"What time is Dad leaving for the fairgrounds, Aunt Mertie?" Dusty asked, yawning.

"In about five minutes," his dad answered from behind him before emptying his coffee cup and winking over at Elise. He was moving through the kitchen fast and had on a tweed sports jacket and jeans with a weatherworn, brown wide-brimmed field hat. Being tall and slim, and with his light-hearted sense of humor, he always reminded Elise of Indiana Jones combined with The Man with the Yellow Hat from *Curious George*. "Can you both be washed up and dressed in a hurry? We've got a big day ahead of us."

Within minutes, Dusty's father was out the door, and a low rumbling came from one of the smaller barns, rattling a stack of Aunt Myrtle's china. Elise already knew that sound and was excited to get another ride in the big blue Chevy pickup.

Back in Thunder Bay, the truck stood out as an oddity on the street. Neighbors would often politely comment on how noisy the muffler sounded in the morning or how the oversized tires seemed too big for a pickup in the suburbs. Dave and Uncle Donny had purchased identical trucks on the same day twenty years earlier, the day Donny landed a regular business account with a large traveling fair company. Dusty's dad took impeccable care of his rig over the years, replacing parts, repainting, adding custom details and such, while Uncle Donny just drove his twin truck into the ground. It now sat behind the barn, tires flat, peeling paint, rims sunk in the mud, rusting away. Weeds grew so high around it only the side mirrors and cab roof could be seen in the summer. Dave's truck, however, remained a beautifully maintained beast, respectably polished, and always ready for adventure.

"Hop in, you two," Dave hollered over the rumble of

the motor. Elise rather liked the idea of climbing up to get into a vehicle; she loved the feel of being up high, riding in a machine that vibrated with power. The engine roared, and she felt herself being thrown back into the seat as the truck sped down the long gravel drive.

The morning air smelled sweet as it blew through the open windows of the cab. Elise's hair kept flying in her face and Dustin's. After politely removing several blond hair assaults to his face, he rolled his eyes and reached down under his seat to produce an extra baseball cap for her to wear. The cap read: "Burlington Novelty Warehouse; a barn-load of fun!" She raised her eyebrows as she read the front of the cap.

Shrugging her shoulders, she put it on.

"You know ..." Dusty's father began, "last spring, this truck would not start, no matter what. I tried all kinds of things—even took it to a mechanic who replaced the battery, the starter, switches, and relays, but nothing worked. So, you know what I did?"

Dustin turned his head to look out the window as if he wasn't listening. He knew where this was going, and he didn't want to be caught blushing.

"I don't know. What did you do, Mr. Windworth?" Elise politely asked.

"I just gave it to Dusty. I handed him the keys and told him to see what he could do," Dave said with pride. "So of course, he studied the problem, read a few things, tinkered and poked, and lo-and-behold on the third day ... bingo! He fixed it. That boy seems to be able to fix anything around here these days and has come up with a few unique contraptions of his own."

"It was just a bad battery cable. I looked the problem up online at school one day, searched up a few discussion threads on it and looked for patterns other people tried that worked. Dad just missed it, I guess," Dustin humbly clarified.

The truck pulled into the fairground parking lot. "I'll pick you two up around five-thirty," Dave called from the rumbling truck. "Be careful around the rides they're taking down today, and Dusty, take Elise on the Ferris wheel this morning. They'll have it down by noon."

"Alright, Dad," Dustin called as they turned toward the gate.

"Your dad's a pretty cool guy," Elise mentioned as they walked among the vacant, breezy fairgrounds. Most of the fair workers were still waking up in their trailers.

"Yeah, well ..." Dustin's voice trailed off as he looked off toward the livestock buildings.

"What do you mean by, 'Yeah, well?'" Elise pressed.

"I mean, things aren't always what they seem," Dustin began. "I mean, he has a way of always looking cheerful on the outside, but I really don't think that's what's going on inside. He never talks to me about anything. Well, you know—anything that matters. I'm not sure he's even looking for jobs anymore because he's stopped talking about that too. Sometimes I can hear him crying at night in his bedroom, and it makes me feel weird to hear him cry."

"About your mom and all, right?"

"I think so. I haven't seen him talk to her on the phone since we moved here. He won't tell me anything, and sometimes I have no idea what's going on and why we can't go back. Actually, I do know why we are here, so Dad can make some money. And I know why Mom's in Canada, so she can get medical care because she is on Canadian health insurance. But I don't know why we can't go to see her, or why we hardly talk on the phone. You know, it's been *six weeks* now since I talked to her on the phone."

"Wow, Dusty. I had no idea." She decided to stop the conversation there. She wasn't ready to talk about what she knew, not ready at all.

As they approached Uncle Asa's concessions trailer, Elise noticed right away how it looked different than all the others in the row. It was old, like something from the 1950's, with polished silver sides and a rounded top. Perched on the roof was a large metal turkey wind vane that read, *Tin Goose Broasted Turkey Bar*. Two round spotlights on each end of the white roof aimed up at the sign. The serving window which folded out from the shiny aluminum wall was closed and partly shaded from the morning sun by a red and white striped awning which hadn't been completely rolled up yet. Dustin led his friend around the back. They were greeted by a large, mangy mutt panting and leaning its body against Elise's leg.

Dustin knelt down to greet the dog. "Hey there, Corn Dog," Dusty said as he scratched the mangy animal behind its ears. "Meet Bibbidy-Bob Corn Buns. He's my Uncle Asa's dog. He's a mess, but he's the nicest dog you'll ever meet."

"Say, "'Hi,'" Corn Dog!"

"Grrouff!" The animal promptly responded, wagging a filthy, ragged tail.

Dustin stepped up to the trailer and knocked on the curved metal door. After a few seconds, the door opened up a crack. A pair of brown eyes glared at them, peering through wire-rimmed glasses sitting on the bridge of a wide, amber nose. The eyes shot a quick glance at Dustin and Elise, and then back to Dustin again. A frightfully skinny boy with a 'fro of short, twisted curls spiraling in every direction swung open the door. "Hey Dust. He's talking with the fairground's manager or something. He'll be back in a few minutes."

"Okay, Morty. Hey, this is Elise ... you know, my neighbor from Thunder Bay," Dustin introduced.

Morty instinctively looked at the floor to avoid immediate eye contact, forgetting to invite them into the tiny workspace. Dusty just stood and waited a few extra seconds. Elise sensed that she needed to do likewise.

Morty glanced up briefly, “Hi Elise, it’s eh, nice to meet you.”

Elise smiled back politely and tried to think of something to say to move things along. “So, are you two cousins then?”

“Oh no, we’re not related at all,” Dustin explained. “Morty is actually my nearest neighbor to my Uncle Donny’s farm, a little over a half mile down. But Morty does live with *his* Uncle Asa. You see, I just call him Uncle Asa because Morty had always called him that, and I guess I just started doing it when I heard him do it. He *is* pretty much an uncle to me, even though he’s not.”

Elise was able to follow the whole crazy explanation. She wanted to know more. “So, how long have you known your Uncle Asa, who is not really your uncle?” she asked Dustin.

“Oh, well he’s totally cool. Ah, well you’d have to see it to believe it ... his farmhouse, I mean—barn-house ...”

“It’s not actually a real house, Dust,” Morty chimed in. It’s more like a big barn we live in,” he murmured looking up briefly, but avoiding more eye contact.

“It is a real house because you both live there, *and* it’s unbelievably cool,” Dustin continued. “Speaking of belief, he’s actually a preacher too ... Well, he stopped doing that a few years ago, I guess. But he does a lot of other stuff on the side. Not just regular stuff—amazingly awesome stuff like upcycling this old Airstream trailer into a rolling kitchen! He thinks a lot and says neat things. He doesn't just sell turkey legs at the fairgrounds."

Elise looked at him puzzled.

"Dust has known him all his life," Morty added while re-tying his shoelaces in the doorway, which were already tied. "Uncle Asa is kinda like a really smart kid in a grown-up's body." He stood and began looking around for things to do inside the trailer, for places to hide his gaze a bit longer.

Elise leaned into the doorway to get a look at all the stainless-steel cooking gadgets. "I guess I'll just have to meet this Uncle Asa, now won't I?" she said with a smile to Morty, who briefly glanced up to see it, then grinned himself.

"Morty, just tell Uncle Asa we'll be back to scrub down the trailer in an hour, eh? I want to take her on a few of the rides before they take them down. Do you know where Teddy is?"

"Yep," Morty replied, relaxing and gaining confidence. "I saw him heading over to the midway just before you came. He's probably tinkering with the Black Widow ride again."

"So, about this dog ..." Elise inquired as they left the trailer. "What's with the name Bibbidy-Bob Corn Buns?"

"Yeah ... The name sort of evolved over several incidents. We mostly just call him Corn Dog now," Dusty began. "He was a stray that Uncle Asa decided to keep after Morty found him. I think Asa did it to help Morty feel better about being taken away from his parents because they were really messed up. He had just moved in with Uncle Asa and seemed depressed and scared. He hardly spoke a word most of the time. You can see he still has a hard time around people, but when he found this dog and started taking care of it, Morty kind of relaxed. So, Uncle Asa let him keep it and started calling it Bob because it was the first name that popped into his head. The dog goes absolutely crazy for corn dogs. We found this out after we brought some back from the fair a few years back. I mean nuts! Jumps up and down and whines and cries until every last one is eaten, and the odor is finally gone. So, then we started calling him, Bob the Corn Dog. Then, one rainy fall, he kept going out to the cut corn fields to roll and sit in the mud. He would come back with dried mud and corn kernels all stuck to his fur, especially on his butt. So, the name changed to Bibbidy-Bob Corn Buns after that."

"Oh wow! That is just way beyond what I'd ever guess!" Elise replied with a giggle.

They headed over to the midway area, where most of the rides stood still. A few of them were flashing their lights in the morning sun, sitting empty. One ride was being dismantled and folded up by several fair workers. They found Teddy bending over a large electric motor. He had on coveralls, a grease-smudged baseball cap, was smoking, and smelled a bit like musty carpet.

"Good morning, Teddy. Can we get a ride on the Ferris wheel?" Dustin asked.

Teddy looked up. He had a thin, unshaven face and he seemed to keep his lips in a fish-like position as the cigarette hung out of his mouth, a line of smoke rising from it. He looked at Elise, then back at Dustin. He didn't smile. He just squatted by the motor with the wrench in his hands, contemplating the moment while the cigarette just hung there balanced on his lip.

"Lil' early for a date, isn't it, Dusty?" Teddy blurted out through the fish mouth.

"Ha-Ha, very funny. This is Elise. She's an old friend from Thunder Bay," Dustin defended.

"Well, if I were you, I'd be thinkin' 'bout ..."

"What do ya say, Teddy," Dustin interrupted, keeping off the topic of girlfriends, "can you fire it up for us?"

"Yeah, sure, sure, so long as you're not a payin' customer," Teddy's lips were looking more like a duck beak now. He glanced in both directions as a precaution; just to be extra sure the manager wasn't around.

Teddy technically wasn't allowed to run rides with real people on them since the mistake he had made four years back. He was only allowed to work on them. When the fairgrounds were open, he worked in the dunk tank machine dressed as a hobo clown. He had been assigned to taunt and heckle the crowds until somebody bought a ticket to throw a ball in hopes of hitting the release arm to drop him into the water and shut him up. Teddy's current job didn't bother him as much as the memory of the tragic accident, the one everyone in Burlington heard about and remembered. During the off season he worked odd jobs or cleared snow. He knew it was better to be dressed as a clown, that way no one recognized him.

Teddy placed a key into a round plug and flicked a few switches. The Ferris wheel suddenly came to life with blinking and spinning lights as the motor hummed, ready to be put into gear.

"You know, this is the biggest Ferris wheel in the entire state. You can see for miles from the top," Dustin informed Elise as they got into the gondola and pulled down the safety lever. It was his favorite ride. He didn't enjoy being flipped around on the wild rides anymore and was bored with the roller coasters.

"Wow, neat," Elise nervously replied as she felt the platform vibrate underneath her.

"It's sixty-eight feet. Not as high as my Uncle Donny's silos, but a lot easier than climbing an eighty-two-foot ladder!"

Elise was already beginning to feel dizzy just thinking about it. Her heart began beating faster. She felt a lump forming in her throat.

Teddy reached into the car and double checked the safety bar with his hand. His eye caught Dustin's for a moment. "That's for Casey," Teddy said through his fluttering cigarette before turning back to the controls.

"Don't worry, you'll like it," assured Dustin.

He watched Elise cringe and tense her back when the machine began to move. The ground shrank beneath them as they rose into the air, Elise stiff-armed the safety bar and closed her eyes briefly. Dustin noticed the panicked look in her eyes and knew exactly how she felt. It was the same reaction he felt when he found out Mom had cancer, and she started making trips to the hospital. Then the visits to the hospital got longer, and he was left alone with all those feelings while Dad worked, and then Dad stopped going to work. By the following summer, after several late-night shouting matches in the kitchen, Dad stopped going to see her at the hospital too.

Those feelings of spinning and twirling, of being jerked around and not knowing what was coming next started all over again when Dad asked him to pack up his things from his bedroom. They were leaving. They couldn't keep the house any longer because Dad lost his job and couldn't find a new one fast enough to pay for doctor bills and house bills. They were leaving without Mom to move to Minnesota. Uncle Donny's farm was a great place to visit, but it certainly wasn't home, and leaving Mom behind in the hospital was crazy! That puke-ready feeling in his gut had never really gone away since he closed his bedroom door for the last time ever.

When he was younger, as soon as he was tall enough, Dustin had gotten himself addicted to the spin-dizzy rides and roller coasters. He rode those rides on a free pass until closing time night after night on those late summer visits to Minnesota, but now he hated them all because they reminded him of everything that happened, that confusion and fear coming from somewhere inside his gut, and it wasn't fun to ride them anymore. He preferred the Ferris wheel now.

The giant wheel glided around, approaching the top for the third time. Dustin leaned over and whistled loudly to Teddy giving him the stop signal using his hands. The wheel stopped at the top. The gondola swung back and forth for a few moments. "Are you okay, Elise? Do you want to get off now?"

"No Dusty. I just want to sit up here for a few minutes and try to get used to it. I'm actually quite terrified of heights these days," she confessed through a polite smile. She tried to loosen her grip on the bar, but her hands refused to let go.

"Oh, I guess I had forgotten the tree climbing incident," Dustin recalled.

"Yeah, well, I haven't been to many high-up places since then, but I want to try to get over it ... Try to get used to it. Maybe I'll like heights like you do," she suggested.

"Well, I can't say I like them ..."

"Hey, listen," she interrupted. "While we're up here I've got something I need to tell you."

"Um, okay." Dustin nervously replied. He could see Elise was getting serious, and he began to wonder if Teddy had a point with the whole "date" thing.

"Dusty, what do you think is going to happen to your mom?" she carefully asked.

"Well, the last I heard they were giving her chemo treatments and that she won't be out of the hospital for a long time. Why?" he asked.

Elise looked off in another direction without looking down. This was going to be hard to do, but she knew she needed to do it. She needed to tell him. She owed it to him as a friend; he deserved to know the truth. "Do you know what stage four means in hospital language, Dusty?"

"No, I don't. Do you?" he replied, wide-eyed.

"Well, not really. But I heard your Aunt and Uncle talking. They were discussing your mom this morning, and they didn't know I was there. They said something about stage four and something else about moving your mother to hospice and, well ..." Her voice became shaky. Tears began to form in her eyes.

Dusty knew what she was getting at. She didn't have to finish. He stared straight ahead. He had dreaded this moment, the moment he would find out about the end. "Did they say she was going to die? Did they say it?" Dustin wiped his eyes and sniffled.

"They meant it, Dusty. It's happening. I'm so sorry!"

Tears began flowing down her cheeks, and she forced back the urge to sob as best she could.

Dustin blinked several times, holding it all in. They were on top of the world. The Ferris wheel was stopped for the moment, covered with a thousand blinking, spinning lights. He could see all the fairgrounds below, the barns, the empty rodeo grandstands, the circus tent, and the small village of campers that the workers were slowly emerging from in the morning sun. But it was getting hard to focus clearly. He looked up, far off into the distance, almost to Canada, it seemed. He wished he could just jump out and glide over the distant forest to see her and let her know he loved her one more time before she died. But he had no wings, and he sat in a metal box, with a safety bar, that would soon take him back down, down to the ground in Burlington, Minnesota, two hundred and fifty miles away from home. She had always been the one to take care of him, but now, in her final days, who was going to take care of her?

5

The Letter

Dustin was able to bury the feelings for the time being, and he and Elise came into the kitchen laughing and talking about the silly chicken dance Uncle Asa did every time he had a $500.00 day. Aunt Myrtle had dinner ready, and it smelled great. Elise told everyone about all the fascinating, bohemian fair workers that she met and how she braved the Ferris wheel. Dustin could do a perfect imitation of Teddy using a coffee straw as a pretend cigarette and talking with fish lips. For now, there was no shortage of laughter as the ice cream, peanuts, and chocolate were brought out for dessert.

Aunt Myrtle waited to give him the letter. She put it off until long after dinner, just in case it would ruin his appetite.

"Dusty, there's something for you over on the counter. It came in the mail today, and it's from your mother." Aunt Myrtle tried her best to sound positive and happy. She even smiled and winked, just to start things off at a high point. She hoped it wasn't a mistake to mention this in front of Elise and everyone else, but she knew he would need the support.

Dustin looked at Aunt Myrtle with an instinctive smile that quickly morphed into a look of concerned contemplation. He glanced over at the counter. The padded envelope was still sealed. It was thick looking, appearing stuffed with many pages of folded paper. He took a deep breath.

"Is it okay if I read this myself upstairs?" he politely asked.

"Sure," his father said with a surprisingly serious look. Dustin headed up to his room with the weighty envelope.

August 20

My Dearest Dusty,

I'm afraid that my time is coming shortly to go and meet my maker. Please know that my situation is not your fault and that I miss you very much. I want you to remember me smiling at you, and you smiling back at me like we used to do on our explorer picnics. Focus on the good memories we made together and place your hope on seeing me in another place someday, where there will be no more sadness, death, or tears, only joy.

Please trust in your dad's leadership. He is a good man. I know sometimes he doesn't talk about personal things. I want you to know that it was not his decision to leave me and go live with Aunt Mertie. It was my idea. I did this to protect you from more pain, but I owe you an explanation.

The truth is that your father and I weren't getting along before he lost his job in Thunder Bay, and we were going to lose the house. Things just weren't good between us for a lot of reasons and I said and did some things I shouldn't have. And then my having cancer and all its problems made things even worse. I had to stay in Canada since it is the only way to pay for most of my medical treatments. I insisted that Dad take you to Minnesota to provide a future for you and himself, and I hurt him by doing that.

However, I made a much bigger mistake. In the midst of all our troubles, I started a relationship with someone else to get me through instead of relying on your dad. He knows this.

I know your father still loves me; he tells me so, but he is angry and hurt because of what I did. He is also trying to keep his promise to stay in Minnesota. I still love him also. I always will. Sometimes in life we lose our way from the path when we get confused and scared, but I am back on the path now. Well, this man I thought I could count on has now pretty much left me to finish my life on my own. There is a nurse here who looks out for me now. She is kind and understanding.

I can't ask your father to come back after hurting him like this, but someday I hope he can forgive me. I am asking you, Dusty, to forgive me. I have been blessed to be your mother, and I know forgiving me will help you heal too.

For now, your Aunt Mertie will do for you what I would and be a mom to you. Just know that someday your dad may find another person to marry, and that's okay.

The gift I sent you of a computer is a powerful tool. It can be used for great good, or evil. It may help you become someone who helps many others in the world, or it may cause you to become amazingly selfish and self-absorbed. You can let it captivate and distract you from the real life to the point of being useless and petty, or you can use it to open up the world to you. Just remember, the decision is yours each time you flip it on. Time is your most valuable gift in life, how you choose to use it each day cultivates your future. I hope it's a great blessing to you, just as you have always been to everyone with all your creative ideas.

You can see that I have enclosed my eagle feather with this letter. I so dearly wanted a ceremony for you with the elders, but that is not to be. I am confident, however, that I am passing my feather to you because you will do something worthy of wearing it someday soon.

My story started in the Bear Clan, at the Osnaburgh First Nation Reserve. As my Ojibwe name, Shaniya, revealed, "I was a woman on her way," and I left the reserve to attend high school in Thunder Bay; hoping for a better future but always taking my past with me. I have been blessed with many good days, with your father, and especially raising you. Now as I go, I have asked Kitchi Manitou, whom you and I now know as our Creator God and Saving Warrior, to watch over you and keep you on his path of light, purity, and strength.

Here are my final words for you. Always do your best with what lays next to your hands, seek the truth, make room to give to others, and your hope will take up wings like an eagle and fly. I look forward to meeting you in a new place someday. Remember my smile. I will always remember yours.

Loving You Forever,
Mom
(Typed by Mrs. Allerton, RN.)

It was true. She was going to die.

The letter left his head swirling. Spin-dizzy, like the rides he hated now at the fair. As he lay on the bed staring at the ceiling and twirling the large feather in his hand, the picnic memories returned.

"T[illegible] the best secret spot yet! Don't you think, Mom[illegible]d while leaning on his elbows on a pic[illegible]hip cookie in his hand.

[illegible]lue lake surrounded by [illegible]es, backlit by late [illegible]s to find a new secre[illegible]heir adventures alway[illegible]music, food that wasn't [illegible]im until the sun went do[illegible]t Dusty's mom had invented [illegible]tion, which she was never able [illegible]n the neighborhood. His dad oft[illegible]s working, preferring the quiet ch[illegible]s own backyard to the unknown road[illegible]ake Nipigon Country, or the wilderness of Came[illegible]s.

"Well, I love the view, but this one took four hours of driving so if we come again on a sunny day, we'll have to leave the top up on the Mustang. Look at you, you're already turning pink," she said as she reached out a finger to touch-test Dustin's already red nose.

Dustin reached back to touch-test his mother's nose. "Yep, you're in trouble, Mom. It's a little harder to tell on you, but the finger press turns red pretty fast on you, too!"

Dustin did not come back downstairs the rest of the evening.

6

Jokes, Gags, and Resources

Aunt Mertie was right, Elise thought to herself as she walked down the stairs to the kitchen for breakfast. She had slept right through the crowing of the peacocks that morning, and now the sun was high in the sky. Boxes of cereal were left out on the table, and seeing no one was around, she poured herself a bowl full of Krispy Rice.

She opened the fridge door and began scanning for the milk jug, and as she looked up, there stood a disguised Dustin, grinning. He was sporting a pair of yellow plastic glasses with oversized, spiraling 3D eyes, a large plastic nose with an attached bushy mustache, and a rubber skull cap that made him look bald, except for a 12-inch rainbow mohawk of hair standing up along the middle. He promptly opened his mouth to reveal a long, retracting fake tongue resembling a lizard, then snapped it back into his mouth.

"Nice," was all Elise could think to say as she closed the fridge door, "Very nice, Dusty."

But he wasn't finished, because when she closed the door, she could see his hands had become ugly, clawed reptile feet. As she looked up at his bowtie with the red flashing LED lights, a squirt of water caught her in the face from the plastic flower clipped onto the pocket of his tee shirt.

"Not nice!" she screamed, thinking of a way to return the prank.

Next, he quickly produced a velociraptor puppet head from behind his back. He improvised his best reptile voice, "You know, Elise, you really gotta try coming out to the barn this morning. All my friends are there just waiting for you to give them a squeeze."

"I don't think so!" she yelled as she held up the gallon jug of milk to block the next spray of water directed at her face. "Are you hungry little raptor? Does Rappy want some Krispy Rice?"

She grabbed the first open box behind her and dumped it over the top of Dustin's head while he simultaneously made the raptor puppet squeal and chomp at the falling cereal as he emptied a plastic flower in her direction. He finished her off by hosing her down with a small can of silly-string.

"Okay, okay! Truce! I give up, you got me," Elise conceded sitting down and pulling the string from her head and arms.

Dustin yanked off the hat and glasses and sat down. He was still laughing. Elise was glad to see him happy, though it made no sense after getting the letter. She knew what was probably in it. Last night, while he was upstairs reading it, Dustin's dad and Uncle Donny had explained to her that his mother was getting closer to dying. She had to find out.

"Are you alright? I thought you'd be so sad this morning," she cautiously pitched to him.

"Yeah, I'm great. Hurry up and eat. I want to show you the barn." Dusty got up and grabbed the broom.

"Okay ... and why are you so great?" Elise probed as she poured the milk.

Dustin stopped sweeping for a moment and looked around to be sure no one was within listening distance. "Because he *has* to say 'yes' now."

Elise looked at him puzzled as she stuffed her mouth with cereal.

"You know, my dad *has* to let me go see her ... and if he doesn't let me go today or tomorrow, he won't have any excuse when your parents come to pick you up because they can drive me up for free," he said gleefully returning to his sweeping. "I even gave him the letter, so he could read it for himself. It's going to clear up a lot of problems they have. I slipped it under his door last night, so I plan to talk to him this afternoon when he comes home."

"Wow ... so do you want to tell me about the letter?" Elise asked realizing the awkwardness of the question too late.

"Nah, I'll tell you later. Let's go to the barn. It's the coolest collection of wacky, stupid stuff you'll ever see in your whole life!"

The barn fit Dustin's description perfectly and held out a few more secrets as well. It was a huge, old pole barn, the kind that was handmade with log beams and wooden pegs before cars were invented. It stood taller than the house, and perhaps three times its size. Although the outside was covered in peeling red paint, the inside of the first floor was not barn-like at all. Instead, it had tall, white walls, bright lights, and rows and rows of huge bins made of giant cardboard boxes sitting on wooden pallets. Each box was filled with assorted colorful plastic objects. Attached to the main barn was a long addition covered with a sheet metal roof.

As they approached the barn, Dustin explained how the addition used to be the milking parlor, where the cows were milked. Dustin's father and Uncle Donny had converted the barn into a supply warehouse. "The orders are packed in boxes, and the boxes are rolled down a long conveyor ramp, to be collected, sealed, and marked with postage at the other end. A mail truck comes on most days to pick up the boxes on a landing at the far end of the milking parlor, where the milk truck used to pick up the milk.

"The problem we have these days is that people aren't ordering from us. My dad said we're getting fewer orders every month, and something will have to change soon, or they'll have to close it up altogether," Dustin confessed.

"Are they getting worried, Dusty?"

"Well, they both have their own way of trying to play it cool. My dad buries his head in the papers or books, and my uncle just does more fishing. I can tell Aunt Mertie is getting nervous, especially since they had to let their part-time worker go last month."

"It smells peculiar in here ..." Elise observed as she slowly walked down the aisles, taking inventory of what she saw. "It's sort of a combination of cheap plastic and oldness."

The colossal cardboard bins around her were filled with every kind of plastic toy imaginable: giant sunglasses, rubber snakes, pirate swords, umbrellas that looked like animals, fake handcuffs, zombie-arm back scratchers, maracas, inflatable hammers, sombreros, a zoo of stuffed animals ... it went on and on. The containers filled the entire first floor of the barn and were set up in long rows with aisles between them like a giant-sized checkerboard with a box on each square.

Dustin pointed to a far corner with about ten tall cylinders, like torpedoes standing on end, lined up along the wall. There was a long bench next to it with a few simple tools and spools of ribbon. "That's where we do balloons for people in town. We just did an order for 350 last week. It was a wedding, so they were all white.

Boring—except when we filled up an entire semi-trailer with them. That was cool ... like walking inside a huge rubber cloud."

"What are all those bomb-looking thingies along the wall for?" Elise asked.

Dusty leaned over to a spout of one and turned the valve at the top just a little. He inhaled some helium and then spoke in a tiny, munchkin-like voice, "That's where we keep the helium, little girl. It's the helium that makes things float ... makes 'em go up, up, up and awaay!"

"So, ma'am, what'll it be?" he said in his regular voice, looking at her while standing with both hands on the counter. Above him were at least 100 different kinds of shiny Mylar balloons tacked to the wall with numbers on them for reference. "We've got bees, and birds, including the angry kind, kittens that say hello, owls, and little Spanish girls that love to explore. We've got trains, fish, toy astronauts, Winnie-the-Pooh, and little mice too! How about a round one with your age on it? We have one through sixty-five. After that, it's only by fives. Butterfly? Graduation? How about a ..."

"You just pick one for me, Dust." Elise could tell that he was coming dangerously close to pointing to all the "Get Well" balloons and wanted to end it. "Let's see what you come up with."

He picked up a three-foot-long, colorful butterfly with wings that each needed to be inflated separately. He quickly tied the string and handed it over.

"Wow! It's so beautiful. Definitely the best balloon I've ever gotten. Thanks!" Elise said, suddenly feeling a bit awkward again. "So, this barn is so huge, but what's upstairs? Do you keep more stuff up there?" she asked, quickly changing the subject of getting a gift from a boy.

"Yeah, it's totally huge up there. But we don't store product up in the haymow. It's not heated in the winter and there is no electricity, but it's full of cool junk, though. Want to see?"

"Absolutely!" she replied in relief.

"Hold out your hand," Dustin requested.

"Okay ..." she said and complied with her right hand. She was getting even more nervous now and couldn't believe he'd ever actually try to kiss it.

"This is what we do with the littlest buggers at the fair," he said as he tied the balloon string gently around her wrist. He knew just how to do it, so it stayed on without feeling tight. "We don't want to end up with a giant butterfly trapped in the haymow, now do we?"

They climbed a series of dirty boards nailed to the wall near the corner of the barn which led up to a trap door. Dusty pushed open the door from below and climbed through. Elise climbed up behind him. It took a few seconds to adjust to the light, which came through two dingy little square windows about twenty feet up on each end of the gabled roof. At first, she could only see all sorts of shapes, some small and others large. Then she began to recognize things: a dresser, a table, an old wooden rocker, a trunk, some old lawn chairs, and then larger objects, too. Everything was covered in dust, cobwebs, dusty tarps, or bird droppings.

Elise jumped and let out a yelp at the sudden flapping of wings along with a harried repeated cooing in the dark shadows overhead. “Don’t be bothered; they’re just mourning doves. They’ve lived up here for years. I think they’re more surprised than you are to see us,” Dusty reassured.

Soon the larger objects came into view. An entire pioneer-style wagon, with fancy painted wooden wheels stood before her, with the seat at the front ready for a passenger. But beyond the wagon was something huge. Its frame loomed over the entire back half of the barn loft and appeared to glow in the dim shafts of light. As she made her way toward the mysterious hulk, she could tell it had wings on it that spread from wall to wall, a round nose at the front and a majestic tail rising at the back. A slight glint of light reflected off the huge propeller which loomed just above their reach.

“Oh, my goodness! Dusty, is that an airplane?” Elise noticed the dirty blue and yellow plane appeared to be missing its top wings. The upper set leaned along the side wall of the loft. It had been a biplane, one of the kite-like planes made after World War One. It sat like a forgotten museum piece, a lost treasure, now discovered again.

"Yes, that's my great grandpa's plane. He used to deliver mail and drop stuff on top of the fields with it. I can't think of what they called him ..."

"A crop-duster," shouted a voice from somewhere in the darkness.

Elise was momentarily creeped-out, but then realized it was Dustin's dad.

"That's where *his* name came from," said a deep voice, coming from a tall silhouette.

"Whose name?" they both said to Dave at once.

"Dustin's name," Dave replied as he walked toward the plane. "He used to give me rides in this plane ... Your great-grandfather, Ash, used to take me up into the clouds with it after dusting farm fields."

"What was it like ... riding in an open plane, I mean?" questioned Elise.

"It was truly magical, like flying with the gods, up among the clouds ... The greatest thrill I ever had. I never wanted to forget Grandpa Ash. He was a very special man. He and his plane did a lot to help a lot of folks around here, so I decided to name my son something that would always remind me of him every time I heard the name," he said holding back some emotion.

"*Dustin* ..." his son said aloud in thoughtful realization. "Dad, why didn't you ever tell me where my English name came from? It's kind of cool, you know."

"I had planned to sometime, but that sometime hadn't

come until now. I guess this is a good place to find out, isn't it? I'll see you two later ... I've got some orders to fill, and I just wanted to make sure you were okay up here," Dave said as he began to descend the ladder down the hatchway.

"How in the world did your great-grandfather get all these things up here?" Elise asked.

"He didn't. My grandfather, and later my dad, and Uncle Donny hoisted it all up through the center of the barn." Dustin pointed up to a set of huge ropes and pulleys near the ceiling. Great Grandpa disappeared years ago in a cargo plane he was flying into wilderness of upper Ontario. Since they never found the plane, they decided to store his old one in case he somehow survived. The pulleys were originally used to get the hay up here in a hurry, but they came in handy later to pick up all his old stuff to store it. There used to be a huge opening in the center of the barn. Look at the floor. See, you're standing on the new wood section they put in when they made the barn into a warehouse. Now, these cool things are all just stuck up here with almost no way to ever get them out," Dustin ruminated aloud.

"Let's get in it," Elise suggested. "I want to see how it feels."

They both stepped onto the lower wing and climbed into the small, open-hole, single seats of the cockpit. Elise got up first and climbed into the seat in the back.

"What are these old dirty pads for on the seats?" inquired Elise.

"Parachutes—you sit on them while you're flying. But in old planes like this, if you really got into trouble, I guess it was kind of like flying a kite with a motor on the front. If the motor stopped, you just tried to coast down," Dustin suggested.

Elise looked ahead at Dustin. "Hey, why are the controls in the back?" she asked.

"I don't know. But I do know what all the gauges were for," he bragged. Dustin jumped out and walked back to her seat. "The gauge on your left is the tachometer. It tells you how fast the engine is spinning. The one on the right is for airspeed, so you can tell how fast you're going way up in the air. The big fancy one in the middle is a compass and an inclinometer. It tells the pilot if the plane is pointed up, down, east, or west. The big one in the lower middle is the altimeter that tells you how high you are off the ground, and the little one on the right tells you air pressure."

"Why do you need to know air pressure?" she inquired.

"I asked my Uncle Donny that same question once. That's so you know if the air is too thin. You see air gets thinner the farther up you go. You go too high, and you can pass out, or worse, the plane's engine could stall," he politely explained.

Dustin climbed back into the front seat. They were too old to pretend and make noises, so they just sat quietly for a few moments and imagined the same thing: no barn floor below them, only blue sky. No cares, no worries, just a rumbling engine, and wind in their hair. The shiny mylar butterfly floated silently above their heads, reflecting sparkles of moving light around the cavernous attic.

"It must have been totally awesome to fly this way," Elise thoughtfully said.

"I know a way we could fly today," Dustin suggested.

Within minutes, they were down the ladder, and Dustin had started up what sounded like a tractor. He came down the aisle driving a forklift. Spinning the machine sideways in one of the narrow aisles, he extended two long steel forks underneath a wooden pallet and gently lifted a giant box into the air. Once positioned in the aisle again, he lowered the box, drove it outside the barn through the center sliding doors, and dropped it behind the building along the wall, directly below a hayloft door on the second floor.

Dustin returned with the forklift and shut it down. "Follow me back up," he pointed, and they both ran back to the hayloft ladder. Once upstairs, he led her over to a sidewall, lifted a latch and slid open a huge door. Down below was the giant box, six feet across each way and four feet high, filled with rubber chickens. He turned around, faced her, and pinched his nose as if to dive. "It was nice knowin' ya'," he said through closed nostrils. Dustin jumped backward out of the window,

"Geronimo!" He landed smack in the center of the giant rubber-chicken mattress, his body squeezing out a huge chorus of squawking crows from the pile beneath him. After a bounce or two, every movement causing more squawking, he jumped out of the king-sized box and signaled for Elise to try.

Elise stood and looked over the edge. It was farther down than just one story. She thought about it, maybe up to fifteen feet even. It was a big barn.

"C'mon, Elise!" challenged Dustin. "Forget the tree incident. Forget the fear. Just jump. Oh, and be sure to aim for the rubber chickens!"

Elise wanted to just let go of her fear, but the movie of her falling from the tree and shattering her ankle kept replaying in her head, over and over. Then she thought of a reason to let go of it. It was Dustin. He needed her friendship. He needed to have some fun with her. She focused on that fact and decided to let go and jump no matter what at the end of her countdown. "3 ... 2 ... 1, Geronimo!" she shouted as she felt the thrill of free-falling and then bouncing into the huge box of noisy rubber chickens.

That first terrifying jump was exhilarating and was soon followed by at least an hour of doing all sorts of versions of jumping, pretend-diving, and fake accidents. At one point, Dustin emptied two pockets filled with little plastic army men tied to parachutes. They all floated down together, landing commando-style all over Elise while she lay on top of the rubber chicken mattress after finishing a perfect backward swan dive.

"Why the heck do people say 'Geronimo' whenever they jump?" Elise wondered aloud as they walked back to the house loose-legged.

"I have no idea," Dustin replied. "But I know a way to find out really quick. Let's look it up online."

7

Discoveries in Cyberspace

After finding out that "Geronimo," came from a movie about an Apache leader that jumped over a cliff, they decided to see if there was a name for those little plastic army men that came with parachutes. It didn't take them long to spot them online.

"Pooper troopers?" Dustin read aloud in disbelief. "They actually call those plastic parachute guys pooper troopers!"

Elise and Dustin looked at each other and both broke out laughing. They soon moved on to more important unusual words and facts about the world.

Before long, Dustin decided to call up Morty, next door, and have him come over to look up some of the odd words *he* had heard or read. Riding his bike, he arrived within several minutes, excited about the opportunity to uncover idiocy online.

They decided to see how fast they could find ten totally obscure things that no one else knew. It only took seconds to find out that exact word to describe the lazy people who sit around and brag about stuff: trombenicks. A spurtle is a wooden porridge spoon. Don't believe anything a snollygoster tells you, and you can never touch your acnestis because it's the part of your body you can't reach. Elise discovered Captain Crunch's real name was Captain Horatio Megellan Crunch. Dustin determined that Zane was a nihilarian: a person who deals in things that lack importance. Morty suggested using your spurtle to scratch your acnestis, and before long they were falling off their chairs onto the floor laughing. Dustin's favorite word was hippopotomonstrosesquipedalian, which means to be talking about extremely long words.

Later, after Morty went home and everyone was in bed, Dusty began some research of his own that *he* had been itching to do all day. He started with "hospice," which he found out was where they take you when you can no longer take care of yourself, usually your last stop before you die. Then he moved on to discover all about the stages of cancer and how stage four was the final stage which meant the cancer growth was very advanced and almost unstoppable. It was as bad as he thought.

He recalled a time when he was only six years old and had cut his finger trying out Dad's safety razor; the blood just kept coming, and he was so scared. It stung, and he knew he was in trouble in more ways than one.

"Dusty, tell me everything you know about cats,"

Mom said softly to him as she gently worked his finger under the cold-water faucet. It throbbed, and he wanted to scream and cry, but the question threw him off from his focus on the pain and panic.

“Kittens are fragile and fuzzy,” he started, “and when they get borned on Uncle Donny’s farm, their eyes aren’t opened yet.”

“What else, Dusty?” she coaxed.

“Well, some cats are tame, and some are wild. Sometimes you can tame a wildcat if you use food and hold it carefully. You have to get it to trust you by petting it a lot first.”

“Do you remember the kitten you tamed out at Uncle Donny’s farm?” she asked as she reached for the peroxide to pour into the wound.

“Yeah, we named him Sherbet because he had that green and orange stain on his white fur. We never knew where the colors came from, did we, Mom?”

“Nope, and it didn’t matter either. He was loveable just the way he was,” Mom shared as she finished wrapping the finger.

“I wonder what happened to Sherbet,” Dusty pondered aloud.

“Don’t know. That’s a good one to ask Aunt Myrtle next time we’re out there.”

Dustin looked down at his bandaged finger, but it wasn’t bandaged, it was much longer now, but still had the scar on it. He had to find out how much time she had left and how to get to her as soon as possible.

"Hello, Thunder Bay Provincial Hospital, this is Arnon speaking, how may I direct your call?"

There was a sniffle on the other end, along with a short pause.

"Yes, hi. My name is Dustin Windworth, and I am looking to speak with my mom. Can you connect me?"

"Sure. If you could tell me her name, I'll see what room she's in," the operator replied.

"Her name is Meredith Windworth, and they are treating her for cancer," Dustin said in a business-like tone.

"Okay, she is on the hospice floor, so I will need to transfer you over to the front desk first. Please hold."

"Click."

"You've reached the hospice desk, this is Abigail. How may I direct your call?" asked the on-call nurse.

"Yes, hi ... I'm trying to reach my mom in room 421. Can you please connect me?" Dustin politely requested.

"Oh, you must be Meredith's son, Dusty. She's talked about you so much, but I'm sorry to tell you, Dusty, that your mom isn't able to talk on the phone right now. Why don't you try again tomorrow, say, around eleven in the morning, and we can see if she is more lucid at that time. Okay?" she asked in a manner that begged for him to agree.

"Yes, alright ... I can call back then. Thank you," he said as he hung up the phone, tears streaming down his cheeks.

8

Conference with Dad

It was late, and he knew his dad had already gone to bed, but it couldn't wait. He knocked gently on the door. A few moments later, footsteps began creaking on the old wooden floor.

"Dad, can we talk about Mom?" Dustin asked.

There was a long pause. Dave put his hand up to his forehead and rubbed his eyebrows with indecision. "Yeah, Dusty, come on in."

Dustin knew this might be tricky. The last time they had talked about Mom for any length of time, Dad had lost his good humor and declared that they wouldn't be discussing her until he brought it up himself. He also knew much more about why his father was reacting the way he did. Dustin reasoned his dad probably knew by now that the "other guy" was out of the picture. But if Dad read the letter, he would learn how Mom felt about her mistake and especially about him. He would see how she had no time left to wait for things to work out and that the time for action was now. He would see it all and know what to do.

"Dad, you know Mom doesn't have much time. Can we go see her now?" Dustin began, looking hopeful at his father.

His father sat down on the bed and silently ran his fingers through his bed-head hair. Dustin stood in a long silence, awaiting his father's reply.

Dave leaned over, reached for the nightstand, opened the drawer, and pulled out the letter. Looking down at the floor, he said nothing, but silently shook his head, "No."

Dustin couldn't believe it. She was dying, and he couldn't go see her? This was crazy! Why would his father act this way? How was this at all useful or right?

"Dad, give a real reason why I can't go see Mom," Dustin protested.

"I didn't want to tell you this, but I guess we've reached a point where you need to know. She and I agreed this would be the best way to do things. I was not ready to drive to Thunder Bay to see her knowing she had someone else, but also, her condition has worsened, Dusty. She doesn't look like she used to and is now on a lot of heavy medication. Your mom wants you to remember her as she was when she was healthy. If we went back, it's likely she may become more stressed by us being there. It's true, Son, losing someone you love is very painful, but we don't want to make it worse than it already is. Your mother loves you. Just trust in that and cherish this letter from her. It says a lot of great things in it." Dustin's father handed the letter back to his son, the pages already showed signs that it was carefully studied.

Dave stopped, turned his head, and stared out the window for a long ten seconds. There was nearly a half moon that looked as if it were riding through clouds in the night sky. "Know too, that I still love her. It's just gotten a little too complicated for me at this point. You can try calling her if you wish, but ..."

"Dad, I've already tried that ..." Dustin interrupted. "They told me she wasn't able to speak on the phone at all. I just wish I could have at least been calling her more often before it got this bad. The point is, she's still alive, so we have to at least try!"

Dave turned from the window and reached out to hug his son. "I'm sorry, Dusty ..." he began, but Dustin was already turning for the door, slamming it shut behind him.

9

Thinking Two Feet Off the Ground

The last day of summer finally arrived. Traditionally, most people run around in a panic on the final day of summer trying to do last minute 'back to school' shopping. However, at the farm there was no such concern, partly because money was running dangerously low, and partly because everyone knew there was little going on the first few days at school besides rules and procedures.

They spent the morning sleeping in and laying around the farmhouse, but it didn't change how Dustin felt about his situation. He tried calling the hospital at eleven o'clock but got the same response: She was not able to take a call right now. After dinner, he decided it was time to move ahead with sorting things out.

"Let's go over to Uncle Asa's. I'm sure he'll have a few ideas," Dusty suggested to Elise.

They went out to a smaller barn which was full of old junk to pick out a few ancient bicycles to use to get over to Uncle Asa's house. Although it was considered "next door" in farm country terms, it meant riding about three-quarters of a mile each way on a dirt road, and bicycles were quicker than walking. Dustin had not been on a bike since his was stolen.

Dustin and Elise spent at least an hour getting the bikes into minimum condition to ride more than ten feet. Rusty chains needed to be freed and oiled, flat tires pumped up, and cobwebs fully removed before they were ready for test rides. By seven-thirty, they were on their way.

They rode down a skinny gravel lane, flanked on each side by yellowing cornstalks waving in the evening breeze. Upon turning the corner, Elise was immediately impressed by a line of huge, colorful metal sculptures, stretching almost half-a-mile down the next road. Each piece stood between six and twenty feet high and was constructed with heavy steel parts from farm machinery, old tools, and rakes, even metal car rims, in the shapes of people, plants, animals, and creatures with parts that moved or spun in the wind. It was a fantastic sight to behold. A few of them made noises, and they all had signs of some sort on them expressing a name of a person, idea, or famous politician. Some of the welded-steel masterpieces had political statements, others had words of wisdom or verses on them, and a few were just plain silly looking.

"Let me guess ..." Elise began. "These were made by your Uncle Asa, weren't they?"

"Bingo!" Dustin replied. "Except, remember, he's not really my uncle. He's been making and selling them for a living since his wife died about six years ago. He used to be the pastor at Aunt Myrtle and Uncle Donny's church, but he quit when his wife died, and now he does welding, fixing people's houses, and selling turkey legs from an old trailer. He still speaks at church sometimes, but only on special occasions."

As they approached the farm, Elise instinctively looked for a farmhouse. She spied the largest barn which had double-arched trim over the windows with a large cupola on the roof. What Elise found curious was how there was no house around, only a few smaller barns near the larger one and a huge garden with a circle of pine trees nestled around its perimeter. A silo was attached to the barn and had windows cut into it, making look like a turret on the side of a castle. The front of the barn and the silo-turret were neatly painted, but the sides were all peeling and weatherworn.

"Why doesn't he paint the sides of his barn?" Elise questioned as they walked up to the front door.

"Don't know. There's a lot of quirky stuff about him, but he always has reasons if you ask him," Dustin replied as he pulled on the fancy antique doorbell.

Elise was glad she had already met Uncle Asa at the Tin Goose concession trailer earlier at the fairgrounds. He had a unique look. He was a large man with kind eyes set in a solid, ebony complexion. Asa's fluffy hair and scruffy, curly beard looked as if he hadn't visited a barber in months, and although the glasses that magnified his eyes seemed a little too big, perhaps a bit out of date even, one could rarely find him without some form of smile on his face.

The door was opened by the familiar, friendly, hairy guy. "Hello, Elise, Dusty. Come on in. Elise, welcome to my home. I'm honored to be a host for you."

Elise thought this was a bit of a weird way of greeting someone, but after thinking a few seconds more, she kind of liked it. It was different. It was genuine and kind.

She noticed the inside of the barn was not at all barn-like. It was a huge open room with walls made of rustic pine and oak panels. In the center was a comfortable setting of couches and chairs arranged around a large coffee table made from a cross-cut of a huge tree trunk. The whole place was filled with many interesting and odd things to look at, everything from antiques on the wall, to a stuffed mountain lion. She decided it was a bit like a museum. Nothing appeared store-bought, and everywhere she looked, books sat lying around in little piles, even on the dining table. Many of them were open or had odd things, like a gum wrapper, or pieces of used aluminum foil sticking out of them for bookmarks. Her eyes followed an old carved spiral staircase that didn't belong in a barn. At the top was a large balcony that wrapped around three sides of the huge room they were standing in, all open to the ceiling maybe twenty-five feet up. An enormous chandelier that looked like it belonged in an old church hung from a long chain, lighting the room.

Morty appeared from an upstairs doorway and greeted them from the railing. “Hey, Elise, welcome to our barn. Sorry, we didn’t get to tidying up before you came.”

“Let’s meet out at the great oak,” Uncle Asa suggested, knowing where they were headed already.

“You gotta see his front yard. It’s totally unreal!” Dustin announced as he led Elise out the door.

She had to stop for a moment to take it all in. Instead of a farm field, a huge sunken garden lay before her with a sparkling rectangular-shaped reflecting pool at its center. The garden itself was probably twice the size of her backyard in Thunder Bay. A huge, circular steel ring serving as an open gateway marked the entrance and beckoned visitors to walk through and explore. Around the shallow pool were meandering brick walks leading in different directions with stairways and narrow crushed gravel paths leading upward and disappearing into mixtures of flowering plants, bushes, evergreens, and small ornamental trees. It was a vast Eden-like maze that seemed to hide mysteries.

Elise followed the winding paths down to the reflecting pool. An unusual ornate iron frame rose out of a grouping of flowering azalea bushes, gently bowing like a loaded fishing rod, coming to a point about five feet above the water. The sculpture appeared to have a leak. She stared a few moments to figure it out. Every thirty seconds or so a single drop of water would fall from the arch, breaking the glassy surface of the reflecting pool with concentric circles that would radiate outward to the edges.

Large old white pines flanked the background of the garden but in the center, beyond the rise on the far side, stood an immense oak tree. Its limbs stretched out from the huge trunk at least twenty feet in each direction. Although Elise wanted to discover all the garden's secrets, Dustin led her around the pool, up the terrace steps, and toward the tree.

As they crested the backside of the garden, a new surprise came into view: a large pond on the far side of the great oak. Fields of corn waved in the breeze beyond the pond. Elise immediately noticed the unusual set-up below the oak tree. There were seven striped hammocks mounted around the trunk of the tree, evenly spaced like the spokes around the hub of a wheel. On the outside end, they were each mounted to a six-foot pole, and each pole had a different colored triangular flag attached to it. Elise ran down the hill to pick out a hammock. Dusty ran behind her, followed by Morty. Uncle Asa brought up the rear since he saw a few weeds in the garden along the way he had to pull.

"It's our talking spot," Morty informed her as they lay face up, looking into the enormous branches above them while waiting for Asa. He had set up the circle of hammocks, so they were all facing the tree's massive trunk and each other as well. Sounds of the pond and birds chirping in the garden echoed under the ancient oak as it filtered the sunlight above while providing a breezy shade. It had an amazingly calming effect on them.

They could hear Uncle Asa crawling into a hammock but didn't bother looking over. They were all mesmerized by the flittering sunlit leaves above them as they rocked gently.

"So, what's going on?" Asa's words broke through the oration of nature around them. He already knew the problem Dusty was going to bring up, he just needed an opener.

"Dusty's got troubles with his dad again," began Morty.

"I got a letter from my mom," began Dustin. "She told me she was dying, and also said that she had hurt Dad big time. I showed the letter to my dad hoping he would finally let me go to see her, but it didn't work. I don't know what to do because she seems all alone in the hospital and I want to be there with her. I tried calling her at the hospital yesterday, but the nurse said that she wasn't awake or even able to talk on the phone."

"Things aren't always what they seem," Asa began. "For example, you may perceive yourselves as pretty much sitting still right now, but that is very far from the truth."

"What do you mean by that?" inquired Elise for everyone's benefit.

"Well ..." Asa began, "we are just laying here, dangling a few feet above the Earth and it feels as if we are not moving at all, but in reality we are on the surface of the globe spinning around about 750 miles-per-hour. However, when you look up, you only see a tree, mostly still, with a few leaves moving about. And what's more, spinning at 750 miles-per-hour is only one of the ways we are moving at this moment. There are actually at least four that we know of while lying in these hammocks."

"Wow, that's crazy, Uncle Asa!" Elise responded, using the "Uncle" part to fit in. "What are the other three?" she asked.

"Well, our Earth, the planet we live on, is hurtling through space at about four-hundred and fifty-thousand miles per hour, circling the Sun. Beyond that, our entire solar system is out on one arm of the Milky Way galaxy, circling its center at about a half-a-million miles-per-hour, and beyond all that, we know that each galaxy is hurtling through space, expanding away from other galaxies. I think I read ours is heading toward the Hydra constellation at somewhere around 1.5 million miles-per-hour. The point is we often have to function only knowing part of the truth in life, only a piece of a larger story. Dustin, you are part of a larger story, and I'm not so sure you've gotten the whole picture yet."

"I know I haven't been given the whole truth, but the question I have is, with all this bizarre space stuff you just told us, how can a person even know what truth is?" Dustin questioned. "I mean ... I think I know what's going on now, but I don't know what to do next."

Quiet reigned for few moments. A breeze gently rocked the hammocks, choruses of crickets were singing, a red-winged blackbird made its "Kaa-wee" call from the cattails in the pond.

Elise sensed how this worked. Everyone stayed silent; then someone would talk when they had something important to say. She thought this was way better than just chatting about empty, stupid things that most people filled the air with. It was a bit like a meeting with Native American chiefs and medicine men or a bunch of professors all sitting around a table in a big university working on some great idea together. It felt good. She stayed quiet.

"Dustin," Asa started again, "I think when it comes down to knowing what to do, the easiest way to find your direction is to begin with doing what you *know* is right. Yeah, there are plenty of people that will say you have to just 'follow your heart,' and I think there's some good to that statement, but we need to be aware that our hearts can deceive us sometimes into thinking wrong is right in order to get something quicker. The litmus test is whether a person is doing something only to benefit themselves (which often hurts others in the process), or whether they do something out of love, teamwork, or some higher ideal or virtue, which in the end, they will never regret."

"Uncle Asa," Morty piped up, "what exactly do you mean by that?"

"Sure, Morty. Let's say there are two neighbor kids living on the same street, and one neighbor has a dog but does not take very good care of it. The kid that owns it leaves it outside in the cold, does not feed it enough, and yells at it, even smacking it with a stick sometimes. He loves the dog but isn't a very good caretaker of it. Then let's say the dog starts wandering over to the other kid's house, the one who has no dog at all, and no way to get one. The 'dogless' kid decides to start giving the dog the table scraps because it's hungry. The dogless kid recognizes that the dog isn't treated well by its owner and decides to try to keep the dog inside his own house and adopt it as his own because he's always wanted a dog. In fact, he decides that this was 'meant to be' and when the dog's real owner comes by asking about it, the dogless kid finds himself lying to the owner and telling him he has not seen his dog."

"You tell me ..." Asa challenged in his warm but gravelly voice, "was the dogless kid justified in taking his neighbor's dog for himself, or not?"

"I think you gave away the answer inside of your question, Uncle Asa," Morty pointed out. "You used the phrase, 'taking his neighbor's dog,' which gives away the truth of what happened. You can't just take someone else's stuff just because you don't like the way they treat it and use that as an excuse to steal something from someone."

"Exactly!" confirmed Asa. "But we can also see how the dogless boy was following his heart without using his head first. In life, a lot of people end up miserable this way. There are authorities the dogless boy could call to help the dog, but he wasn't in a position to just take the pet."

Elise decided to break the next heavy silence with a lighter question. "I'm wondering, Uncle Asa, why did you choose to hang seven hammocks around this tree and not three, or five, or a dozen?"

"Uncle Asa, can I answer that one?" requested Morty. He already knew from all the other meeting times they had had before with friends, visitors, and groups from the church. "He did it because seven is the highest number of items for the human brain to remember without practice. That's why phone numbers are seven digits too. You see, if there are seven people here who have never met, they might all remember each other's names, plus they can associate each name with a color, using the flags. It's easy to remember that way, and people don't have to spend extra mental energy on remembering names."

A leaf began its fall from the top of the tree, making its way down, spinning and colliding with other leaves until finally landing on Asa's sweater. Asa picked up the russet colored oak leaf and spun it around in his hand. "Dusty, can you recall the story you heard at a tribal dance last year that you told me about?"

"Oh yeah, Running Bear, a clan elder, told the story of the sugar maple tree. In the spring, when the leaves are born, the breeze comes and makes the leaves whisper to each other. They learn they are giving and receiving life from a huge tree that has been growing for countless moons. The leaves cannot see the tree they are on, only nearby leaves, but they are told that every one of them is needed, both large and small. All the leaves bask in the sunlight and give life to the tree, but also storms come, diseases, and insects nip away at them. Some leaves get discouraged and stop believing in their story and leave the tree. After summer, when the sun begins to hide and frost comes to visit each morning, the leaves begin a celebration of their gifts of life by dressing up in colors of reds, yellows, and oranges. After the celebration, they each leave the tree to make a place for the spring buds to grow. Only then do they finally get to see the awesomeness of the great tree they shared life with all summer."

"…Part of a larger picture," Asa mumbled as he admired his oak leaf.

Elise was amazed and delighted at this odd, country sage she had discovered, and hoped that she would get more chances in the future to chat in this unique way. As usual, Dustin felt like he was walking away with something he didn't have when he arrived at Asa's. He wasn't exactly sure what it was he had yet, but he felt better about his circumstances somehow, as if there was something new in his heart that would make a difference. However, as they rode back home down the dirt road under the stars that night, a fresh source of anxiety hit him: school. The first day was tomorrow, and he could only hope things might be different. He relied on the comfort that he would get to start the week with Elise alongside him. Since Elise didn't start for another week, Aunt Myrtle had called the school, explained the circumstances, and secured permission for her to come as a temporary visitor. If nothing changed, at least she would know what it was like for him. They didn't say much while riding, just the sound of old rattling bicycle wheels on gravel, amongst a chorus of crickets.

-10-

Back to School

Dustin awoke to the sound of the ancient clock radio on a night stand cluttered with an empty glass, his pocket knife, a half-devoured Snickers bar, and a small pile of Roald Dahl books borrowed from Asa. Tucked in the corner was his mother's eagle feather resting at the base of her framed picture. He rolled over, pulled the sheets over his head and lay there listening, reminiscing about Elise's visit and the fun they'd had. She had made it so much better, and he could still hope to catch a ride up to Thunder Bay in a few days.

Regardless, it was time to return to the familiar tribulation again—school in Burlington. He knew how bad he was with academics and remembering boring facts he didn't need or care about. Anxiety about getting low grades, not knowing the answers when called upon, or choosing to say the stupidest things at all the wrong times began to creep under the sheets to join him. *So many ways to look like an idiot,* he thought to himself.

Then there were Zane and Harley's stunts, thoughtfully designed to make sure the idiot feelings got refreshed again and again. He hated it all, and he hated himself when he was there. He preferred staying invisible, but that plan rarely ever worked out.

He pushed the sick feeling in his stomach aside, said a quick prayer for his mother, sat up, and flung the sheets off in violent determination to leave the past behind. This year was going to be better than the last.

Dustin and Elise both stood at the end of the long gravel driveway in the morning breeze. Dustin did what he could to explain to Elise that things were not the same as when he went to school in Thunder Bay. Back there he had done things, said things, made friends, and felt some respect and acceptance. Back there he was not the only Ojibwe with a braid, but that was not the case here. At Wooddale Middle School, it seemed like everything he said was taken wrong, and along with his Canadian accent, his "musical" name, and indigenous looks, he might as well be walking around with a big target on his head.

The bus pulled to a stop along the gravel drive, its folding door entreating them to climb aboard. "Well, Dust, maybe this is the year things will change," Elise said while carefully managing her trick ankle up the steps; it was a little sore from jumping out of the barn loft. "I know it's hard, but you've got to stay one hundred percent positive."

Several kids flashed a confuse[illegible] stare as the new blond girl from Dustin's stop w[illegible] he sat down next to him on the aisle si[illegible] at him, then winked and grin[illegible] "I'm here to start yo[illegible]

[illegible] and hoped she [illegible]

In[illegible]'s right foot wh[illegible] Harley had care[illegible]ion to trip Morty[illegible] folders. Binder[illegible] forward out of h[illegible]. His chin hitting the grou[illegible] instinctively grabbed for his glasses[illegible] might get "accidentally" stepped on by Harle[illegible] adult-sized body which now towered over him, arms crossed and head shaking in disapproval.

"Get up, you little grub! I see you still haven't learned how to walk ..."

On his knees, Morty slowly started reaching for each book and folder, feeling the burning of embarrassment in his cheeks. He was starting over nearly the same way as last year. Morty didn't do well in these situations, and Harley knew that. Instead of saying something, or sticking up for himself, no useful words ever came to his mind. His emotions were now in charge, the same way they had been since he was too young to speak—panic, shame, and basic survival taking over. At times like these Morty found himself frozen, his thoughts laser-focused on the overpowering feelings commanding him to believe: *I am small, I am weak. I am not going to fight back, and everyone knows it.*

As Morty reached for his pencil box, a swift kick from Harley's shoe snapped it open, exploding pencils and pens into flight down the hall and underneath the many feet shuffling by.

"Sorry, little dude," Harley jeered. "I'd love to help, but I don't want to be late for class. Oh, and by the way, we all lost the pencil boxes back in the *fifth* grade."

Zane was looking on with calm satisfaction from several lockers over. A mastermind of hate and cruelty at Wooddale, he was too socially slick to make trouble in such an obvious way but was happy to put Harley up to it for a little entertainment. Smiling, he looked up from Morty's private nightmare to see Dustin staring straight at him in anger with the most stunningly pretty girl standing next to him, her hand over her mouth.

Dustin was livid. This was too much. The first day of school had barely started, and they were back at it already. He remembered the feeling of a fist hitting his own nose last year, of the pain that spread through his face, cheeks, and then into his eyes, making them water even if he wasn't crying. He recalled the shame of being "beat up on," as Aunt Myrtle called it when she finally found out. He hated the constant anxiety of worrying when the next time would come for him to get cornered again, and he was sick of the sick feelings. He had to do something, and with Elise at his side, he found his confidence did not disappear for once. Standing close enough to Zane to smell his cheap idea of cologne, he blurted out, "Really, Zane? Again? You can't think of any other way to be the big shot around here?"

Zane produced his best look of sterling innocence, "What? I'm just standing here, watching this tragedy in front of me, and you're fussin' up like some little girl. More Dust–in-the-Wind I guess ... Speaking of girls, I guess you found yourself a really cute one here, but is *this* the best you can do for friends: Morty Wimpo and Rapunzel?"

Confident and unmoved, he leaned against the lockers in his red and white sports hoodie with pushed up sleeves, waiting for Dustin to give in and walk away.

Dustin stepped up to Zane, his nose directly aligned with Zane's ski-jump. He stared into Zane's eyes for a moment, and everyone nearby froze. Then a waterfall of words began to flow out of Dustin. "You're a hatemonger, Zane, aren't you—a chain yanker who thinks it's cool to diminish smarter people like Morty. Well, you can keep up your nihilarian hobbies if you feel the need, but we're done with them! Yes, we are all quite confident your despotic, socially sadistic concoctions will only lead bully-boss wizards, like you to ..." Dusty paused for a moment. Looking left and right he noticed that at this point at least a dozen other kids were leaning in to hear what the long-haired, but now, apparently word-wise, Dustin Windworth had to say. He faced Zane to finish with enough anger left to jab a pointing finger in his direction, "...to nowhere land!"

Dustin turned away from a bewildered and speechless Zane, grabbed a handful of pens off the floor for Morty, and with the blonde-haired goddess at his side, departed down the hallway.

He rounded the corner and flashed a shocked look at Elise. She mirrored it back.

"Okay, I—am—in—so—much trouble now!" he declared aloud.

"Oh, you are not!" she protested. "You were totally awesome and those handy words we found really put him in his place, Dust."

"Yeah, *funtabulous* is all I can think of," chimed in Morty. "Man, I don't even care about what happened to me now. That was so cool! You must have found a few extra words online to use."

"Well, you know Zane isn't going to forget it," Dustin fretted.

"You got that right, Dawg!" Morty said, shocking himself with his own words. "Later, Dust, and thanks a lot!" He did a little touchdown dance and then headed left at the end of the hall on his way to science.

At each class he entered, Dustin would present a permission slip written by Aunt Myrtle and approved in the office, explaining the situation with Elise being in school. It didn't take long for the comments to begin circulating.

During fourth hour class, a note was passed down the row to him. Each kid who passed it along opened it briefly, took a quick read, and moved it to the next with a grin or muffled laugh. He unfolded it while Elise was distracted with sketching a portrait of his new biology teacher, Mr. Boda, who was sporting an impressive Bob Ross 'fro. After reading it, he knew that getting through lunch was going to be nearly impossible.

DUST IN THE WIND,
WHAT R U DOING WITH THE BLOND CHICK? IS SHE YER LONG LOST COUSIN OR SOMETHING CAUZ THERZ NO WAY YOUD END UP WIT A BABE LIKE HER IN A MILLEON YEARS DUDE! SO JUST ADMIT IT, SHES LIKE YER COUSIN OR WHAT? THAT'S THE WORD DUDE! XOXOXHAHA!

Dustin didn't show the note to Elise. He crumpled it up and tossed in the trash as soon as possible. During lunch, they sat as far away from Harley and Zane as possible, but it seemed like droves of kids were sweeping by, staring, doing double takes and surveillance for other cliques from across the room. Morty joined them late due to the long lines and getting cut in front of by bigger, older kids. He picked up on what was going on right away. He knew they would be in for trouble if they tried to keep it up for three whole school days, but he kept this opinion to himself.

"So which bike is actually yours?" Elise inquired as they walked out the front door at the end of the day. "Wait, let me guess, it's the one with the lousy spray-paint job, so I'd guess the ..."

"... Hunter's orange one," Dustin finished for her. "Yes, that's it. And yes, it's so ugly now Harley doesn't even need a lock for it."

"Boy, don't you just want to hop on it and take it back right now? It doesn't belong to him! It's not right!"

"Yeah, I know. But it's in the past now." Dustin paused and turned to face her. "Elise, why do you want to keep being friends with a stupid, lost-cause loser like me? You seem more like the type to hang out with cool guys like Zane."

"Dusty, I don't want to hang with people like him. He's all about himself. Do you remember how we got to be friends?" questioned Elise.

"Yeah, yeah, I remember. You had frogs, so all the other girls on the street were grossed out, and since I didn't play baseball and we both loved going to the pond, we ended up a couple of odd BFFs, didn't we?" Dusty recalled with a grin on his face.

"But as usual, Dusty, your silly, non-stop imagination had us taking frog catching to a higher level. Remember the 'Phantasmal Frog Frolicking Park' you built?"

"Sort of ..."

"Yeah, so you combined my Barbie poolside fun set with one of your Uncle Donny's old snake aquariums to create the ultimate frog playground. Remember how you had Barbie and Ken inside doing a scientific study of giant frogs and you backlit it with your mom's old desk light? Then you begged her to take you to the pet store to get a fishbowl pump so you could circulate water down the slide for the frogs. You even created an automatic insect feeder that released flies and bugs every few hours. It was so cool, and I loved that you let me keep it at my house!

Dusty, the point is that I had no other friends on the block, but you still cared even though kids made fun of you for having a friend that was a girl. Do you know what that's worth?" quizzed Elise.

"Not really," he replied.

She turned and got in Dustin's face. "It means that I can trust you as a real friend, and I haven't found many other friends that I can really trust since you moved, and that's worth a lot to me! Why do you think I came all the way out here to Minnesota? It wasn't to climb a giant silo or eat some cotton candy! It was because you are a *true* friend of mine, and I'm hoping it will stay that way, even though you have to live here." She turned her back to him, defiantly crossing her arms.

"Wow, okay. I get it."

There was a long pause while Dustin stared at the ground, searching for more. He looked up to talk to the long, golden hair hanging down her back. "Well, in case you're wondering, I happen to feel the same way too ... About you, I mean. I guess I'm just not as good at putting it into words like you just did," he admitted.

Elise spun around and gave him an "I knew it was true" smirk.

11

The Fallout

By the time they got off the bus at the end of the driveway, Dustin knew the idea of Elise going to school with him would not work. Besides, her parents had called in the afternoon to let Aunt Myrtle know they were coming back to pick her up a few days earlier. That left only one more day for Elise to stay.

They both sat on the front porch steps after dinner with Morty. He had brought over Corndog and was throwing sticks for him to chase in the best way he could for a kid who was not into athletics.

"So, what are you guys going to do about tomorrow?" Morty asked. He could see how rough today was for them and was curious about whether they were planning to go through with it again.

"Oh, well ... I guess Elise's parents are coming to pick her up early, probably tomorrow, so she's only going to be here one more day," Dustin informed to keep the conversation from going back to the school topic. It didn't work.

"Yes, Morty," Elise chimed in. "So, we've got only one more day to weather, and I've already got a few ideas on what to say if Zane or Harley try to pull something new on us."

"Actually, Elise, I think I'll have to go alone tomorrow."

She found herself blinking a few times at what she just heard. Dusty didn't want her to come to school with him? She was shocked, and suddenly awkward feelings stampeded into the conversation. It took a few seconds for her to think of what to say. She decided to hide her hurt feelings for the moment and reason with him.

"You sure you want to do that, Dusty? Two brains are better than one in your situation, and besides, maybe they'll just get used to it and accept the fact that we're friends."

Morty was already shaking his head. He bit his lip, looked down at the grass and raised his eyebrows. He didn't want to get in the middle of things.

Dustin took a breath. "Elise, I really don't think one day will change anybody's mind. If anything, it may make matters worse. If they see you again, it'll just give them another reason to get started on me again, and that means it will be that much longer I'll be catching heck for bringing a girl to school with me."

"What do you mean by a girl?" She began to forget about hiding her feelings. "Am I your friend, Dusty, or just a 'girl' to you? Obviously, everybody else just sees me as some girl you brought to school, but is that how *you* see me now? I kind of thought you had more sense than to just fall for how everybody else thinks. You never used to be that way, and I liked it. You're letting them get to you, Dusty. You don't have to change, you know," she protested.

"I'm not changing, nothing is changing. It's just that I've got to live here after you've gone home—every day with those jerks! Give me a break! Can't I just want to fit in?"

"Fit into what, Dusty? Do you really want to *fit in*? That means you have to start thinking like them—being like them. Is that what you want? You don't like the way they treat you, remember? So how is it that you now think you need to think or act as they want you to? Why? I'll tell you why. It's because you think you're a victim; just a plaything for their entertainment, like the stick in Corndog's mouth! You're starting to let them train *you*."

"Look, Elise," Dusty blurted out. "You have *no* idea what I have to deal with right now! My mom could die any day, and I can't do a thing about it, most of the kids at school think I'm a Canadian freak who plays with balloons all day, and you saw where my bike is parked ... You know—the bright hunter's orange one that I don't ride anymore? Can you just cut me a little slack here?"

"You're *not* a victim, Dusty! Stop thinking the way they want you to! You're letting them make you forget who you really are."

"Well, if I'm not an idiot, a dork, a geek, or a wimp, then what am I?" Dustin yelled back as he got up, stomping across the front porch and slamming the door behind him.

When Morty got the courage to look up at Elise, she was staring off into the fields across the road, still sitting on the steps, resting her chin in her hands. Tears were finding their way down her cheeks, forming delicate shimmering streams reflecting the orange glow of the sunset over the fields. "Maybe it is time for me to go," she whispered. "Time to go ..." After wiping her eyes and looking up, she found herself alone. She resolved that this was the way of things right now, and she had to make the best of it and try to offer what she could with whatever time she had left.

The next morning, Dustin stepped onto the school bus alone. Aunt Myrtle had gone out to shop for the dinner she had planned to make for Elise's parents. Dave and Donny were in the house discussing something, so Elise found herself wandering around the barnyard, thinking of what she could do. Walking past the silos and looking up, Elise thought about seeing him up there waving to her and tried to imagine what it would feel like to be up there too. She sat down at the base of a nearby tree, leaned back on the trunk and gazed up at the tower before her that she could never climb. *Impossible! It's impossibly high*, she thought. She looked at it for a long time and then decided to look at it from a different perspective.

She walked up to the colossal cylinder and touched it. It felt solid, like cement behind heavy smooth steel. She lay down in the gravel, with her head directly below the ladder and gazed up the tube-shaped steel safety cage that surrounded it, like a tunnel of metal framing, leading up to the sky.

A thought popped into her head ... *What if I tried it? And if I did, I wonder how far up I'd get?*

Dave was walking by the kitchen window and saw her lying at the base of the silo with her hands tucked under her head. He felt a pang of panic at first, wondering if she had fallen, but then saw her cross her legs. "Hey Don," he called to his brother. "You want to see something? Look outside."

Uncle Donny looked out to see her lying on her back, her arms now above her head, gazing through clasped hands. It appeared as if she were creating her own, personal spy-glass to peer up the silo railing. "That's a unique young gal your son's got for a friend there, Dave. A smart little thing ... Looks like she's thinking up a storm lying there. I hope she'll be okay."

"She'll be fine. I spoke with her this morning. She understands," Dave explained. "She's got wisdom ahead of her years."

Elise had begun to sketch what she saw on a small pad she had with her. The next time they glanced out the window, she was nowhere to be found.

It took Elise only five minutes to get halfway up the silo because she decided just to keep focused on climbing the ladder and not to stop. But her arms ached, and she was getting out of breath, and the fear was beginning to creep back into her. She paused to do battle with it. She had gotten this far up by only looking at the ladder in front of her and never looking up or down. Frozen to the side, she thought she ought to try looking down, knowing that it would be a lot scarier up top.

Suddenly, she found herself back in the top of the apple tree, eight years old, hearing a younger voice of Dustin calling up to her.

"Climb higher, Elise! You can do it. I swear you can see the buildings of downtown Thunder Bay from the top! You just shimmy up that big limb all the way up as far as you can, then pull apart the leaves above you and step up on that little, crooked branch. If you get that far, you can stick your head right out of the tree."

She saw herself reaching out for that top branch, balancing and stretching her arm as far as she could to grab it—but her arm was shorter than Dustin's. She replayed the horror of losing her grip, slipping, and knowing she was falling too far—that jarring pain shooting up her leg, the cracking sound, the blood, the shock and regret that followed. Like a monster slowly creeping into her nerve endings, she began trembling as pieces of old nightmares came crashing back into her head full force, stabbing at her.

She glanced down, and a wave of dizziness broke over her. Dave's blue pickup looked like a toy from this height, and she was twenty or so feet higher than the electric service pole. She took a deep breath, shook her head, and refused to relent to the fear. Defiantly, she stared down at the ground while hanging onto the ladder, blonde strands blowing around in her face. She took one more deep breath and looked up this time.

Though fixed to the ladder, white-knuckled and shaking, her body felt as if it were moving sideways. The slowly moving clouds above only created more vertigo. She looked back at her hands gripping the steel rung and the dark blue silo wall in front of her. She held on and waited for her head to clear. It didn't happen right away. She had to wait and breathe for several minutes, but eventually, she found herself ready to take ten or twenty steps more before having to stop and practice getting her clarity all over again. As she found her rhythm, calm and confidence began to return to her body, and the dizziness subsided. When Elise reached 78 feet she peeked over the top of the ladder onto the rooftop catwalk. She began mentally preparing herself to crawl up the catwalk to the hatchway—waiting and breathing ...

Dusty was right. The view was amazing! The late summer fields of corn and soybeans below her resembled a golden ocean as they waved and danced in the breeze. Looking down from the railing, she saw a small flock of sparrows flying in a uniform, zigzag formation. The birds skimmed a treetop below, and then came sailing upward toward her on a breeze, zooming right over her head so close she could hear their wings beating, and the tiny, personal chirps between them. Sunshine warmed her head as the wind tickled and played with her hair in celebration of her victory. She had done it! A major battle now won. She looked off to the west, down the gravel road lined with colorful moving sculptures and recognized the farm that belonged to Uncle Asa. She could make out a tiny figure walking among the buildings and knew it was him. She decided to go and see him later. She wasn't done exploring that garden.

Elise kept her secret from Dusty's family when she returned to the house. Aunt Myrtle had come home, and all three were getting ready to go into town on an errand and didn't want to leave her at the farm alone.

"Elise, we're heading into Burlington to pick out one of them new cell phones for Dusty's dad and me. We figure it's time to get into the future a little bit since everybody's always expecting me to have one on me. You want to come with?" Uncle Donny playfully asked. "Dusty told us you've already got one and we could use some advice from a young person on this. By the way, lunch is on us, as well," he threw in with a grin.

She proved to be an invaluable resource for helping them pick out a new smartphone. She explained that when Uncle Donny was on the road, he could use it to get directions, and even see his own dot on the map, showing him where he was, and where to go. Elise requested that they drop her off at Uncle Asa's house on the way back.

12

Revelations

Elise found Asa in his shop barn, an ancient radio up on a corner shelf blaring a rhythmic blues tune she didn't recognize. He was bending over a metal creation with his welding mask, apron, and gloves on, his body eclipsing the blinding light flashing and filling the barn, a flurry of hot, glowing sparks flying in every direction from his focus of creative energy.

She watched him contently from the corner of the doorway, observing the way he cut and shaped an old rusty steel plow blade into a new piece of art. She got out her pad and began to make a sketch. The steel was thick and heavy-looking, and the smell of the cutting plasma assaulted her nostrils in a surprising manner.

Corndog found her standing next to the open double doors and sat down beside her leaning his weight on the side of her leg, hoping for a little love. Elise crouched down to pet the mutt and surveyed the workshop. It was full of antique, forgotten, rusty junk. Pieces of plows, metal rims, old road signs, hubcaps, and piles of copper plumbing pipe; items that had become worthless to others were Asa's canvas for art. Well-worn tools were strung across tables and on the dirt floor. She watched him labor for a long time, not wanting to startle him with a welding torch in his hands. He was so focused on the piece. It resembled a giant spiraling snail shell with burned metal sunflower shapes sprouting from its back on old springs. She suspected he would paint it with some bright colors when he was done building it. Sweat dripped from his arms, and the shirt on his back was soaking wet, but he remained unconcerned about comfort. Every so often, he stepped back to get a better look at the direction his creation was going in.

She wondered about him. Why did he live in the barn and where was the house? Why did he spend all his time making crazy sculptures and gardens when he was trained to be a minister? The real reason she came, however, was to find out how to help Dustin before she had to go.

When his music ran out, Asa turned the valve on his torch, snuffing out the supply for the loud, angry flame he had been using to cut metal. All was suddenly quiet, except for the sparrows up in the barn loft.

"Hey there, Uncle Asa," Elise said, trying not to sound uncomfortable.

Asa turned around and lifted his welding mask to see who was speaking to him. "Elise! What a nice surprise to see you! Well, what do you think of my latest?" He tilted his head a little toward the still-smoldering spiral of scorched metal. “I’ve got to confess, a lot of my best projects come from workshopping ideas with Dusty. That’s where this one came from. I need a title for it ... You know, a name. You want to help me out?”

“Hmm ...” Elise thought out loud as she walked up to it.

“It’s okay to touch it. The metal cools off fast, and I was only working on that lower corner.”

She felt the smooth, solid panels of the shell, large enough for someone to climb onto. The sculpture looked playful, but without paint on it, possibly terrifying to a little kid. She noticed each flower was mounted on a long metal spring, and with a gentle touch, it would bob back and forth. Making a mental connection, she commented, “You designed them to move with the blowing wind. Right?”

“You’ve got it, precisely! Now, how about that title? I never allow myself to think about it too much. So, what just jumps out at you?” he asked.

“Patience.”

Asa looked up and raised his brow as if the idea itself flew from Elise’s voice into his head. “I love your choice, Elise! May I use it?”

“Of course,” she replied with a satisfied grin. She loved how courteous he could be in conversation.

“Uncle Asa, I wanted to talk to you about Dusty. I’m getting worried about him.”

As he looked at her in contemplative thought, she noticed how big and bushy his eyebrows were, like two friendly, fuzzy caterpillars hanging above his eyes. Then she observed his eyes. He hadn't been wearing his glasses underneath his welding mask. They were big and caring, glassy and wet, but also hiding a deep sadness beneath. Regardless, there was still a spark in him, a sort of playful optimism remained there that could never be taken away. He looked at her a moment, then glanced off into the fields. She could see he was just as concerned, maybe more, as a parent or a father might be, not just a neighbor.

"Yes, me too. Morty told me about your talk last night, and I must say that I admire your brave attempt to help him see that he isn't to blame for the problems or situations he finds himself in."

"But what can we do?" she asked. She was confident he had an answer she could take away with her.

"Elise, at times like these I find praying the most useful." He paused as if a half-finished thought was still making its way out of a cocoon in his mind.

"Elise, there's a tree in my orchard you ought to see. Two years ago, there was an awful ice storm. It snapped the branches off many trees. I went out to shake the ice off the smaller limbs to keep them from breaking, but one of the larger limbs on this particular tree was just too big and too high to reach. I had to watch it get so weighed down, and with the wind, it finally broke off, destroying a large part of the tree. Then after the storm, I stepped in, trimmed it and helped it heal. The tree never looked pretty after that, but it's a stronger tree now, fuller and covered with blossoms in the spring. It's the tree in my orchard that produces the most apples."

Hands on his hips, still wearing his heavy welding gloves, he turned and looked squarely at her, his welding helmet still on his head with the face shield open. "Elise, you can't always stop a heart from breaking, and it's hard to watch it happen, but you can do things to nurse it back to health when the storm is over; and when you do it right, the results can amaze you."

They both looked down at the uncut grass below their feet, searching for more thoughts. Elise didn't know what else to ask about it. It was too big for her—too heavy, like the big snail made of spiraling steel plates.

"Asa, do you think I could just spend a little time hanging out in your garden for now? I'd love to do a few sketches of it this afternoon."

"Certainly, Elise ... that place was made for times like these and, if you don't mind, I'd love to see your drawings when you're finished."

He politely turned, pulled down his welding mask, and snapped something that made his fire stick come back to life with a loud hiss. Checking back once more, he saluted her off, assuring her that it was okay she was leaving.

After school, Dustin found Elise in Asa's garden sitting on a little bench made from metal tractor seats with plow disks for backrests, staring into the pool. It was incredibly comfortable for a rusty, metal sculpture chair, and had been made to seat two. Corndog was lying against her feet.

"Can I sit down with you?" he quietly asked.

"Sure."

Dustin wasn't ready to talk about what had happened last night or about what he had said to her. "Do you know we are sitting in what was once Uncle Asa's basement?"

Elise furrowed her brow at the sudden odd opener. She expected an apology.

"That sculpture over there that drips really slowly ... The one that leaves circles in the pool ... That marks the spot where she died in the house fire."

"Where who died?" she asked, confused.

"His wife."

Suddenly it all became clear to her: his barn house, the garden, the paths, the reflecting pool with the concentric circles made by the slow-motion dripping, and the sadness she saw in Asa's eyes. She began to look around the garden for more hidden clues.

"You know, he told me once about this drip sculpture. He said that it represents every act a person decides to do or word a person speaks in their lives, both good and bad."

"What do you mean?" she asked.

"He told me that he made a bad decision one day. He worked at the church late a lot, and one night when his wife called him home for dinner, he told her he had to work late again. I guess she had lit candles for him and forgot to blow them out. When he got home, the house was on fire, and he found her on the floor at that very spot—you know, dead from the smoke, I guess."

They both sat in silence for a few moments, waiting for the next drop to fall into the pond.

"He told me that all our words and deeds are like drops of water in a still pond, and even though we don't see it, the effects of what we do or say go out in all directions, changing things in ways we mostly never know. That's his way of saying that we are all affecting the world somehow. I'm not sure if it's true, but at the funeral, I heard people were whispering that his wife was pregnant at the time she died."

"That is so incredibly sad, Dusty. That's why he built this garden, isn't it? For her. It's so awful but this place is so beautiful and amazing. I just feel like I want to stay here all the time if I could. Do you think he is over it yet? Does he blame himself for her death?"

"I don't think he will ever be totally over it. It happened about six years ago now. He seems better. He helps people out a lot, but he doesn't work at church anymore. He just makes these bizarre sculptures and sells most of them.

"Elise—I'm sorry for yelling at you yesterday," he finally blurted out. "You don't deserve to be treated like that, and I was a real jerk."

"Yeah, I *know* you were, but I forgive you," she said with a chuckle. "Can I try to explain something without you getting all mad again?"

"Try me. I promise I'll just stare at the water and listen."

"You are not the problem, Dusty. You're in a whirlwind of troubles right now, but it won't be forever. Please don't let what kids at school say shape what you think of yourself. They don't know you; they really don't. When they do, they'll change. You've got to just hang on to who you truly are right now and just, like, be okay with that."

Dustin's eyes began to tear up. He wiped them off before more could get started. He hugged her, not knowing how else to thank her, knowing time was running short.

Corndog stood and ran up one of the paths after something he saw.

"I'm really hoping that's just one of those friend-type make-up hugs and not the *other* kind," warned Morty as he made his way down a path toward them with the dog now at his side. "Dusty, your Aunt Myrtle called and said that Elise's parents were going to be coming in too late for dinner, so she invited Uncle Asa and me to come over and eat your food."

"Morty, can you get Uncle Asa to give us a ride over in

the Power Wagon?" Dustin requested as they headed up a gravel walk toward the barn.

"Absolutely! There's no better way to travel than that!"

Elise likec [illegible] vy, but this truck [illegible] It sat in a tiny [illegible] d even start. It wa [illegible] ch sat on dented [illegible] s. The red paint [illegible] heavy steel-rimm [illegible] n the front, was h [illegible] s, the rounded cab [illegible] ning board and p [illegible] side, she could see the dirt floor of the barn peeking through rust holes below the front seat.

Morty walked past her and began unchaining the tailgate to open it. "Dust and I always ride in the back. Trust me; it's way better in the open air."

"You mean in the back of the pickup?" she asked incredulously. "Isn't that, like, dangerous or against the law or something?"

"I don't know, but out here in the country, no one cares, and we're just heading down the road to Dusty's place. Climb in."

They all found a place in the empty wooden truck bed. Elise sat between the boys, directly under an oval-shaped window behind the cab.

"All aboard the rusty-but-trusty express," Asa yelled as he opened the squeaky door and jumped onto the torn, filthy seat. A few seconds went by, but nothing happened. Elise could hear him move a lever inside the cab releasing something, then the sound of the gas pedal slamming on the floor two or three times. Finally, the whine of a starter motor came out from under the hood followed by a broken rumbling, shaking the entire vehicle while it was still parked. She shot Dusty an unsure look as she smelled an oily kind of exhaust. With a clunk and a roar, the primitive, giant machine lurched forward, moving out into the weakening afternoon sunrays, springs creaking along the dirt path that led out to the road.

"It's a 1955 Dodge Power Wagon," Dusty said without much emotion. "I guess it was used as a logging truck or something when it was new. Uncle Asa uses it to move around a lot of his sculptures, but it won't go very fast down the road. He says he likes it that way."

"Way too many people in a hurry. I'm all done with being in a hurry," both boys said in unison, imitating Asa's voice.

The rumbling and creaking weren't at all annoying to Elise, rather unique, making her feel as if she were riding in an old rocker, or some piece of history, except it was alive and breathing—moving, even though it should no longer exist. It was taking them somewhere as an old friend would. She loved the smell of the fields filling up her nose and the tingling coolness of evening falling from the sky on her arms. As the truck slowly rocked its way down the road, she drank it in knowing that by tomorrow it would all be gone, and she would be back in Thunder Bay, smelling urban air, going to school, and doing busy city things.

"It's kind of a pain on the paved roads," Morty chimed in. "People don't like it and are always beeping and zooming around us when he drives it, except folks that know us. They beep too, but in a friendly way and wave instead of just using one finger."

"Yeah, it's kind of like this truck was *truly* made to go down dirt roads and paths real slow. That's what it's best at. It seems wrong to try to speed down a road with it, like making your grandpa try to run a marathon race or something," Dusty thoughtfully added.

Elise suddenly sat up, her face aglow. "Okay, I've got some news for you two. Something incredible happened to me today. Are you ready?" she asked, about to explode.

"What is it?" Dustin asked. They both turned to face her.

Elise got a sudden look of victory on her face, crossed her arms and announced, "I climbed the silo ... all the way to the top!"

"No—way!" Dustin said, stunned. "Morty won't even do it. How did you ..."

"Sheer determination. I got started and just didn't want to go back down until I made it to the top. It was hard. It took a lot of thought—you know, convincing myself that I could do it, that I wouldn't die," she proudly revealed as she displayed her blistered hands as evidence of her unbelievable feat.

"I got dizzy a few times," she confessed. "I was scared I might pass out or something, but then I just kept breathing and thinking really hard that I wanted to get to the top. Dusty, it's totally awesome up there! Birds flew inches over my head, and you can see forever."

Dustin felt proud of her accomplishment. Then his thoughts flashed back to his mom, like they often did at happy moments, reminding him of his reality. This feat of hers got him thinking about his sad situation in a new way. Elise did something really big, really hard, something nearly impossible for her. Then he thought about his plan to ride back to Thunder Bay with her parents. Deep down he knew it wouldn't work. In his gut, for some reason he knew they would tell him "no." His dad would tell him "no," and his Aunt Myrtle would remind him to follow his dad's advice. He could picture it all, hear it all—he could feel it. He would ask, but he needed a backup plan because, just like Elise, he was not going to stop until he made it. Now was the time to float *his* idea on his friends.

"Alright, you guys," Dustin began soberly, "in case

Elise's parents can't drive me up to Thunder Bay, I've got a backup plan."

Both friends glanced at each other nervously.

"Can you keep it an absolute secret?"

They both nodded.

"The bus line. There's a bus that will take me all the way up to Thunder Bay from Nashwauk. I just have to get to it from the bus that runs between Burlington and there."

"Where are you getting the cash, Dust?" Morty asked.

"My bike money ... I've got enough to cover the bus fare with twenty bucks to spare. He pursed his lips in determination and stared at the sunset. I'll ride one of the old junker bikes to school, then ride from there to town and get a ticket at the bus station."

"Do you think they'll sell you a ticket?" Elise asked, hoping he would realize it probably wouldn't work.

"Yeah, they might think you look like one of those milk-carton runaway kids," Morty advised.

"I know. If I could just grow a mustache or something overnight, it sure would help."

"Maybe you could use some leftover Halloween makeup to make yourself look a little older, without it looking too fake," Elise blurted out before realizing she was helping now.

Dustin looked down at the cracks in the wood bed of the pickup. "It's all I've got right now, guys."

"Dusty, just know I'll do everything I can to convince my mom and dad to take you," Elise tried to reassure him. "I'm sure they'll let you go with us. Let's just hope your dad will change his mind."

The truck turned into the long gravel drive up to Uncle Donny's farm.

"Well, I just can't believe all the things this little gadget can do," Uncle Donny explained to everyone over dinner. He was especially impressed with the flashlight button and spent way too much time demonstrating it for everyone with the lights off. "A flashlight on a phone ... What will they think of next?" Dustin rolled his eyes at his uncle's newfound fascination. "She helped us get a good deal, too. Sixty days free!"

Dustin knew what Uncle Donny meant by that. He was actually talking about the fact that they were nearly out of cash right now. He knew Uncle Donny and his dad were both going to use the phones to try to get new jobs somewhere because the business was finally going broke. There had been only one small commercial order in an entire week, and it was nearly fall when most fairs and circuses were closed for the season.

Dinner was over way too quickly, and before long,

Uncle Asa and Morty were on their way out the door. It was all happening too fast for Dustin. How and when was he going to ask for the ride to Thunder Bay? Now he'd lost the extra bargaining power of having Uncle Asa nearby when he got the guts to approach his father. The right moment just wasn't coming.

He looked out the window. It was getting dark, and he could see a pair of headlights heading up the driveway. It was Elise's parents coming to pick her up and take her away to Thunder Bay. This was all ending too soon to come up with a carefully worded request. It was just going to have to happen now; a do or die moment.

Dustin walked over to his dad sitting on the couch reading the paper with a pen in hand. "Dad, can we talk out on the porch for a minute?"

Dave was smart. He had already anticipated the request to go with Elise Thunder Bay, and Dustin knew it.

"Dad, you know what I'm going to ask, don't you?"

"Yeah, Dusty, I think I do."

"Dad, I'd only miss a few days of school, and listen, I can use my own money to take a bus back here. So, you don't have to worry about a thing. Please, Dad—please, can you let me go?"

Dave didn't want to get this started. He knew it might end in a fight. He didn't want to make Dustin angry, and he knew Dustin wouldn't understand either. There was no way he was ever going back there again while she was still alive. Dave didn't know how to handle seeing her, and he knew it would probably be even more complicated for Dustin.

"I know this is hard, Son. It's hard for me too, impossibly difficult and scary. Now, I want to give you what you're hoping for, I do, but it's not just my decision, It's your mother's too. We both agreed."

Dustin knew this was a long wordy, "no."

"I'll tell you what, Dusty. I know this has been hard on all of us, so tomorrow, I'll let you stay home and spend some time trying to contact her. You can try writing her too, you know. You haven't done that in a few weeks now."

"Dad, she'll never get any letter I write in time."

"Dusty, you don't ..."

"Dad, it's okay," he surrendered. "I get it. It's okay. We can stop talking now. I'll try calling her tomorrow, I guess."

The car doors slammed shut, and Elise's parents were walking up to the porch. It was too late now. *Time to put on the polite host face for now,* Dustin thought. He wanted to make sure her parents still trusted him in case he got the chance to go up to visit Elise sometime in the future.

They found each other on the porch. She had her butterfly balloon in one hand and her sketchpad in the other. She passed the pad to him. "I did some drawings of stuff I liked around here. Keep it for the next time I come, okay?" she said pulling out her best smile and brightest eyes. She sensed the winning smile wasn't working on him this time. It would take more than that. She leaned forward and whispered, "Don't forget to email me whenever you want, alright?"

This time he didn't hesitate to give her a real hug, from the heart, as a true friend saying goodbye, and he didn't care at all what the others thought, or what he even thought. He only knew he was saying goodbye to the best person in his life right now, and within moments, the minivan, along with his friend, disappeared into the darkness.

He had missed the ride. It was time for plan B.

13

The First Escape

Dustin sat up awake in bed. He didn't take advantage of Dad's offer of a day off from school because he had a plan to go see her. Determined to get through to his mom, he began the process of calling, even though it was late. He was careful to ask for Nurse Abigail, knowing his chances were much better with her. He was shocked to finally hear those words from Abigail he had only hoped to hear so many other days.

"Dusty, I'm so glad you never give up calling. She is awake and can take your call, but you may find it hard to understand her sometimes, so if you want me to, I'll sit nearby her bed in case she needs me to clarify something for you."

"Sure. Thank you, Abigail," Dustin said, feeling confused, but grateful.

There was a long pause on the line.

A weak but recognizable voice filled the silence. "Dusthy? Is this my Dusthy?"

Dustin had to take a moment to comprehend what was going on. It was his mother's voice he was hearing, but she sounded like an elderly lady with a bad lisp.

"Mom, yes, it's me. It's so good to talk to you. I miss you so much!"

"I mniss hew too, son. You thalk, I lithen, okay?"

Dusty took a second to think of some things to talk about that weren't depressing, things that his mother would like to hear.

"Mom, bet you can't guess who I just spent the last five days with?" he opened.

"Who?"

"Elise came down. Her parents dropped her off on the way to Chicago ..."

He told her all about the surprise, working at the fairgrounds, jumping out of the hayloft in the barn with her, hanging out with Uncle Asa, climbing the silo, and all the happy moments in between he could recall.

"Thcool okay, Dusthy?" she asked him during a quiet moment.

"Oh, it's okay. Elise came to school with me on the first day. I'm sure I'll like it more when I make more friends," Dustin reasoned. He purposefully left out all the latest issues with Zane and tried to keep the mostly one-sided conversation going. He could tell his mom was as interested as she could be, but something didn't seem right. After a few more minutes, Nurse Abigail came back on the line.

"Dusty, I think your mom is starting to have a bit of trouble staying awake right now. It's not your fault. It's her medications. They're very strong."

"Abigail, can you tell me what kind of cancer my mom has? I don't even know."

"Dusty, your mother is suffering from head and neck cancer. That's the reason why she is having difficulty speaking. She has had several surgeries which make it difficult for her to speak or eat now."

"Abigail, could you just put her on the phone one more time? I didn't get to thank her for the computer she sent me," Dusty politely requested.

There was a pause for a few moments with a few professional sounding people talking in the background before the phone receiver was picked up again.

"Dusty, she's asleep now and will not be waking up for a while. Can you try again in the next day or so at around the same time?" she asked in the kindest voice possible.

"Okay, I will. Abigail, just one more question. How much time do you think my mom has left to live?" Dustin croaked out, trying to keep his shaking voice as even as possible, hoping for a real answer.

"Oh, Dusty ... I just can't say. That's in God's hands, I suppose. Just keep trying to contact her, and I'll do all I can on this end to take care of her," Abigail assured.

"Abigail, I want to come see her!" he blurted out.

"I know you do, Dusty ... I know you do. Call back again soon, okay?"

"Yes, I will."

"Nurse Abigail?"

"Yes," she replied, trying to remain patient.

"Thank you, Ma'am," Dusty said and promptly hung up the phone.

On the other end, Nurse Abigail slowly put the phone down. She thought about how polite the desperate boy on the other end sounded and felt his pain. She decided to go on break. She knew she was due for a good cry and this situation had done it for her.

Although grateful to finally talk to his mother, the conversation felt incomplete, like sitting down to a Thanksgiving dinner and never getting to the turkey or dessert. He knew he wasn't finished talking with her, and decided it was time to carry out plan B.

Dustin left the house the next morning an hour early and in high spirits. He told Aunt Myrtle that he was in the mood to bike the four miles to school today and that he needed to borrow her old bike. She noticed his backpack seemed a little full, but assumed it was just additional stuff he needed as he got settled into his first week.

Regardless of having to ride a 1972 vintage women's one-speed with a Toto basket in front, to Dustin, the crisp morning ride felt wonderful. Tractors were out harvesting in the fields, and the trees were already showing some vibrant fall color. Happy visions of the fun he had with Elise still rattled around in his head, and he was confident that he might even see her again soon if everything went as planned:

1. Get through most of the school day so no one would count him absent or call home.
2. Leave school right after fifth-hour class, and skip out of last hour study hall to allow time to get to the bus station and buy the ticket.
3. Get on the bus and assume a low profile, as if he were on a ride to Grandma's.
4. Transfer in Nashwauk and get off the bus in downtown Thunder Bay. Then call Aunt Myrtle to let her know he was okay. They would be worried for less than two hours before his call.
5. Get a cab to drive him over to the hospital, or just walk the mile and a half.
6. Surprise Mother at the hospital. Stay as long as possible, then call Elise or worry about how to get back later. Maybe Dad would actually come, see Mom, and pick him up.

As his feet spun the pedals round and round, the pavement rushing by below, he ruminated in the rising sun. Dustin knew it was against his father's wishes to go, maybe even his mother's, but their wishes weren't ones that showed love right now or brought the family together. What was right? What did he *know* was right?

To go and see his mother one last time; how could anyone argue it was wrong?

Dustin's school day was pleasantly absent from strife or heckling, and although Morty suspected something when he didn't see him on the bus, Dustin distracted him with the idea of needing the exercise for when the new bike worked out. He suspected Morty didn't really buy into his story, but it answered the question for now.

Fifth-hour seemed to take forever to come, but the weather was holding out perfectly as he exited the building and headed for the bikes. He pulled his aunt's ancient, crusty bicycle from the rack and glanced down at the metal basket strapped between the handlebars, perfect for placing his heavy pack into, but as the backpack slammed into the basket the metal rim of the front wheel smacked onto the pavement.

Dustin looked down to find the old rotten tire, which held up all the way to the school, had finally sprung a leak and gone flat. It was well over a mile to the bus station, and walking meant missing the last bus out that afternoon.

The orange glare of Dusty's stolen bike was always easy to spot in any bike rack, but on this particular afternoon, at this moment in time, it positively glowed. He only had time to pause and think for a few moments. It *was* actually his bike, he reasoned, and it also happened to be the only other bike on the rack without a lock besides the rust heap he rode to school that day. Then he thought of his mother and threw any other reasoning out of his head, grabbed the orange thing with two wheels, threw the pack over his back, and took off.

Dustin's bike felt like an old friend as he pedaled away. He recalled what it looked like on the day he got it as a gift from his parents three years earlier: the black powder coated rims gleaming, perfectly clean, with a bright red birthday bow on the handlebars. It was sitting out by the picnic table in the backyard of the house they once lived in. That was all gone now, including the bike, but here he was still riding it. He chuckled to himself at the thought while breathing in a bit more air than usual, the free kind of air.

He wished he had taken the time to leave a note for Harley of where to find this orange bike that Harley's mother claimed was his. That would have been prudent. But he had forgotten that detail, and it was too late now. Dustin rode on, switching back through alleys in town in case school authorities got word of what might be going on and went searching for him.

Purchasing the ticket was a lot easier than he thought. Nobody asked any questions. As he waited in the bus station, trying to keep a low profile among a few odd people, he nervously waited for it all to end, for his dad, or the principal, or some policemen to come through the door and grab him, but nothing happened. No one came for him.

He got onto the bus, about the fourth seat back, and looked out the window at his vandalized bicycle sitting in the rack outside the station. He looked down at his hand, holding what remained of the bike money he had saved all summer for. Life didn't seem fair right now, but it was fair enough if he could make it to see her in Thunder Bay.

Then he heard the whistle, and chills ran down his spine.

It was a whistle Dustin had heard many, many times before, so many times, in fact, that he could still hear it when he went to sleep after a long summer day at the fairgrounds. It sounded like a rock-n-roll cardinal on steroids, and he knew it was aimed directly at him. It was Teddy, the Bozo Clown who worked the fairgrounds dunk tank, calling to him from the back of the bus. Using a cheap microphone and an amp, Teddy had perfected the obnoxious whistle sound over the years to attract and annoy nearby crowds into purchasing dunk balls to throw at his target. Dustin took a deep breath and slowly turned around.

Teddy, looking even more unshaven than usual leaned out from one of the seats near the rear of the bus, tipped his dirty ball cap, made his trademark fish-lip face, and pointed directly at Dustin with a goofy smile. Now if there was anyone that might allow him to run away from home, even if just temporarily, it would be Teddy. He was one of the craziest, roughest workers at the fair every year, driving visitors nuts by day in the dunk tank with his loud whistles, jeers, and taunts at the crowds, and then drinking and smoking away most of his pay at night. Dustin had been discovered, but he doubted Teddy would blow his cover, so he relaxed as he watched the haggard man walk up the aisle to join him.

"Well, well, what do we have here?" Teddy began. His clothes smelled like smoke. "Ya goin' somewhere, Dust? Shouldn't you be on one of them yellow-colored busses? I thought school started for ya already this year."

The bus driver released the air brake with a hiss, closed the doors and pulled away from the curb.

"Yeah ... Teddy, you know about my mom, right?"

"Oh, yeah ... eh, is she out of the hospital yet, Dust?"

"Not really. She has cancer, and I'm going to Thunder Bay to see her," Dustin said flatly, trying to hide his emotions.

There was a long silence while the bus drove on. Teddy had been around awhile and had met and known hundreds of people over the years. He figured it out right away.

"You going to say goodbye, aren't you?"

"Yep, I don't think she has a lot more time," Dustin divulged as he looked out the window.

"Where's your Dad?"

"He's, uh ... He's staying back in town. He's not coming." Dustin was looking straight forward now, avoiding eye contact. "So where are you headed, Teddy?" he asked, changing the subject.

Teddy, making his deep-in-thought fish lip look now, nodded his head slowly. He knew Dustin was doing this in secret, but the reason he was running a[illegible] pecting. It was li[illegible] somewhere in th[illegible] thinking and he[illegible] ation, as if he co[illegible] afely, and this wa[illegible]

[illegible] e the accident, an[illegible] said. "I guess you[illegible] ple life here in Bu[illegible]

[illegible] o face Teddy. "W[illegible]

"[illegible] tired of being the brunt of the jokes, the reason for bad stuff happening, the jerk that everybody knows is never goin' nowhere. It means I'm through with fighting with Laura about when I can see

Andi. I guess it means I'm buggin' outa' here for good," Teddy boldly revealed.

"You going to Thunder Bay too?"

"Nah, I'm still staying state-side. Getting on the west line at Nashwauk. Just searching for a new direction, I guess."

"Did you get a new job or something, Teddy?"

"Yeah, don't I wish? Everybody wants to hire a dunk tank clown, right? Or worse, a dunk tank clown that killed a kid 'cause he was too stupid to latch a ride the right way. Or better yet, how 'bout a dunk tank clown that gets a kid killed, gets addicted to booze and smokes, gets in fight after fight with his wife and never spends any time with his own kid," Teddy spit it all out, sarcasm and contempt flashing in his eyes. "Dust, after years of wakin' up every day with that feelin' of guilt, trying to drink it off, joke it off, deny it, and nothin' workin', I've finally decided that I'm a lost cause at this point. So ya know what I'm gonna do with what I've got left? I'm getting *myself* lost and seeing where that takes me. Crazy, huh?"

Dustin thought about Teddy's life deeply for a few moments. Flashes of memory replayed in his mind. He had known Teddy ever since he started coming to the fair when he was little and never thought of him this way. He remembered when Teddy would help him into the kiddy rides, always joking and smiling. Then he started doing the clown act. Dustin thought the clown act was a promotion until he found out the truth.

"You know, Teddy, I thought it wasn't your fault about that girl. My Uncle Donny told me that the latch on the safety bar went bad or something, and that's why the girl fell out."

"Casey. That was her name, Dust. I still remember her smiling when she got on. Cute kid—and every day I also see her lying on the grass and that look on her lifeless face… Yeah, they all decided it was the ride, and not me, that's why I still had a job with the fair company, just not runnin' rides no more." Teddy sighed deeply, his eyes growing shiny without tearing up. "But *we* both know what I do for a livin', right? Fix the rides. I should have seen it when I was checkin' that day. Look, Dust, seeing I got nothing to lose here, I'm gonna make a confession to you no one's ever heard. I had a nip or two of the sauce that morning, so I can't exactly say how clear I was when it all happened. Now I don't even know if that's what made the difference, but I got a lifetime of wondering about it from now on. She's gone, and I can't bring her back, Dust. It's wrecked my marriage, too."

"Teddy," Dustin pondered aloud, "you're still alive, though, aren't you?"

"Yeah, well, being dead might be a lot more restful than being tortured alive every day."

"I don't know," Dustin argued. "You can't do much when you're dead, you know. Except maybe …"

"Fertilize dandelions. I know, Dusty. But I don't know any other way to go but *out* right now."

"Doesn't Andi need you? I'm sure she loves her daddy like any little girl would," Dustin suggested. "Someone told me once that things aren't always what they seem in life. He said that sometimes we're a part of a bigger picture we can't always see until later."

Teddy sat back in the cushy seat, folded his arms, and searched his heart, tightening his fish-lip look to maximum level. "Interesting point, Dust," Teddy admitted. "That kind of thinking sorta' makes me start to feel better, but it doesn't take away the gorilla of guilt that rides on my back every day."

The bus rode on as they talked, remembered, and reasoned about things in their lives. They arrived in Nashwauk a lot sooner than they expected.

"Give my best to your mom, Dust," Teddy called as Dustin exited the bus. "It was good talking with you. I'll be thinkin' 'bout some of what you said back there on the road."

Dustin made his bus transfer without a hitch and found a new seat. He leaned back, pulled his hat over his head and decided to take a nap. Waking up in Thunder Bay was going to be a great feeling.

The gentle rocking of the bus put him quickly into a deep, satisfying sleep. He found himself waking up where he sat as the bus rolled along the road so smoothly. The ride was so smooth in fact, that he couldn't feel any road movement or engine vibration at all. He felt that he was becoming weightless. After mild concentration, he felt his body lift off the seat and start rising above the aisle. None of the other passengers seemed a bit alarmed that a 13-year-old kid was floating inside the bus traveling at 70 miles-per-hour. It was a wonderful feeling, looking down at the seats and passengers, nothing holding him down. As he concentrated more, he found he could float higher, defying gravity, buoyant upon the air, all the way to the ceiling, which after rolling over, he could propel himself along with a gentle flick of his toe. He floated his way to the back of the bus, did a silent summersault in the air, and pushed off the back window to glide back toward his seat near the middle.

Midway through his grand, weightless glide, he began hearing a hissing sound. At first, it seemed like the hiss of air out of a balloon, but just as the hiss ended, Dustin found himself waking up in his seat. Glancing out the window, he realized they were at the Canadian border checkpoint. Dustin knew the routine of how his dad would quickly tell the guard where they were going and what they were up to, and he would pass them along.

He assumed the bus driver would simply do something similar, and they would all just move on, so he could get back to his napping, but the driver shut off the engine. The door opened, and an officer got on.

"Passports, please," the man said, and Dustin suddenly realized what was going on. He recalled that in the last few years his dad would pass something to the guard, and he would pass it back, but Dustin never paid any attention. His heart began racing faster as the man worked his way up the aisle getting closer to him. He tried to think of what to do. He wished Teddy were still there to maybe cover for him or pretend to be his dad or something. There was no plan. There was no time. There was no passport.

"Young man, your passport, please."

It came at him so fast all he could do was start going through his backpack searching for something he only wished was there. He swallowed hard and felt the border security guard watching him. He attempted to give the guard a puzzled look. It wasn't his way to lie so directly, so he sat silent.

"Young man, I'm going to ask you to step off the bus until we sort this out," the uniformed man said to him.

Dustin's thoughts accused him as he walked off the bus. *I should have known this wouldn't be so easy. Why didn't I do more research? I should have known this.* He knew he was in more trouble than he could deal with and there was no way out.

"Son, without any real identity you can't cross this border into Canada. How about we keep this real simple? Do you want to tell me who I need to call to come pick you up?" the officer gently asked.

Dustin knew it was over. Plan B had failed.

His father had little to say to him all the way home. Dave knew what this was about and figured this was punishment enough. However, he did ground Dustin for the weekend for taking the bike without asking.

Dustin asked him to pick up his previously stolen bicycle, which he later stole himself to get to the bus station, and return it to the bike rack at the school.

-14-

The Gift

On Monday, halfway through first-hour social studies class, Dustin got the call he was expecting.

"Dustin Windworth, please go down to the principal's office," Ms. Callahan announced for all to hear.

"Ooh, Dustin! You better put a book in your pants, boy," someone shouted.

"That kid is busted, crusted, and getting re-adjusted! You know he cut class yesterday and stole a kid's bike," came a loud whisper from across the row.

When Dustin opened the office door marked, D. Henderson, Harley was already sitting there, but looking a little nervous himself. Dustin knew why.

"Dustin," Principal Henderson began, "it has come to my attention that you skipped out of sixth-hour yesterday and that you also took Harley's bike. Is that true?"

"Well, sir. It depends on how you view truth in this case," Dustin began.

Shocked disapproval sketched itself across Principal Henderson's face.

Dustin realized his "truth" comment was a bad idea but saw the futility in trying to fix it. "Yes, I used the bike," Dustin started, "but the bike is actually ..."

"Where's the bike now?" Principal Henderson interrupted.

Dustin pointed out the window to the hunter's orange bike in the rack out front.

"Which bike?" Principal Henderson questioned.

"The orange one and it's mine," both boys said in unison and looked at each other.

"Dustin, just because you use or "borrow" something doesn't make it yours. I'd think you'd understand that by now at your age," Principal Henderson counseled.

Dustin looked down at the carpet. He couldn't tell what color it was. It looked like barf until you took apart the colors of browns, oranges, greens, and tans. *They probably chose that color out of convenience,* he thought to himself. *If someone did puke on it and the stain didn't come out, it would probably just blend in, and no one would even notice.* He knew that trying to win this wasn't worth the fight. He knew there was an additional sentence for skipping a class coming to him. He already looked like a guilty idiot, no matter what angle he might try on someone. He was the stain on the barf-colored carpet, just like Teddy. It was time to blend in.

"So, Dustin, what do you have to say about your actions?" Principal Henderson pressed.

Dustin looked up at Harley and produced a smile, "Harley, I'm sorry for taking the bike you say is yours. I hope it didn't cause you too much inconvenience."

"It's alright, Dust. I'm good with it now," Harley complied, knowing this got him out of the office and off the topic of his theft of Dustin's bike last spring or any other recent issues.

Dustin left the office with four days of after-school detention, which meant someone had to pick him up from school. He couldn't stop thinking about Teddy, but instead of a gorilla of guilt, it was more like a mad chimpanzee on his back trying to steal his last banana.

An hour after school was over, he sat outside waiting on the concrete steps, feeling trapped more than ever now. He tried to accept the fact that he might never see his mother again. The thought was a bitter pill he just couldn't swallow yet.

I've made enough trouble, lost enough chances for friends, how can I just blend in?

Then he thought of Elise. *Am I supposed to blend in?*

He looked up to see Asa's old red Dodge Power Wagon pull up to the front of the school. Morty was leaning out the passenger window.

"Your dad said we could pick you up all week from your detention, Dust. Climb in."

The old red truck with its odor of unburned fuel and oil was a welcome relief. So was an invitation for dinner at Uncle Asa's.

The late summer evenings of Burlington, Minnesota welcomed the cooler air of fall early. Uncle Asa suggested a fire in the woodstove after dinner, so Dustin began loading up the firebox and noticed Morty walking up with a small crate of dynamite.

"Fire starters ..." Morty mumbled as he fumbled to grab a red colored paper stick out of the box and pull the wick straight on it.

"Yeah, right," replied a slightly unnerved Dustin. "Have you and Uncle Asa gone insane? You'll start a lot more than just a fire with one of those! Get those things out of here! Not a safe joke, Morty!"

"No, really," Morty said holding one up close to Dustin's face. "They're not real. They actually are for starting fires."

"He's right, Dustin. Cool. Eh?" shouted Asa from the kitchen area of the conver[illegible] can order almost [illegible] your face made th[illegible]

Mort[illegible] into the stove, lit [illegible] ning up the stove [illegible] box in mismatch[illegible] started a game of [illegible] stuffed chair plow[illegible] table.

The game didn't help take away all of Dustin's disturbing thoughts about school at all, so when Uncle Asa casually looked up and asked him about how things went with Principal Henderson, he was more than ready to get it all out in the open.

"I keep hoping that this is the worst it will get and that things have to start getting better soon, but each day more stuff happens, and life keeps getting worse. So now I'm worried about what new bad thing is going to happen to me next. It feels awful, and even if I wanted to escape it all, I can't."

"What would it look like if you did?" Uncle Asa challenged.

"What do you mean?" asked a puzzled Dustin.

"If it could all change into the way *you* want it to go, what would that look like? Describe it for me."

"Well, I know I can't save her but, I suppose I'd get to see my mom to say goodbye."

"That's a start," Asa coached as he put down his book.

"And I guess if I have to stay here in Burlington, that my teachers and other kids wouldn't think I'm such a loser."

"You mean that they would know who you truly are—see the value in you?"

"Yeah, and it would be nice if my dad and Uncle Donny listened to my ideas more instead of just shooting them down all the time," Dustin finished.

Dustin hadn't completely finished. The part about being able to see Elise more often in the future was purposefully left out, due to it sounding a little too much like a romantic longing, because he rather enjoyed her company.

"So Dusty, if those are the things you want to see happen in your life, what are you doing, or plan to do, to see those things come about? And how do those things you've already tried connect to others around you?"

Dustin looked thoughtfully into the firelight flickering behind the glass window in the wood stove. Popping noises from the inside of the stove echoed in the room. He realized that he had been trying to improve his life, but only from a self centered perspective.

"Well, I have to admit that I hadn't given much thought to what others are feeling, other than how it affects me." Dustin kept his gaze locked onto the woodstove flames. "I guess that's kind of selfish, isn't it?"

"Perhaps you're onto something here, Dusty. Think of the person in your life that you sense is the absolute happiest, most content person you know. What do you sense that person cares the most about?" Asa quizzed.

"People," Morty announced with confidence. He already knew this about Uncle Asa himself, how he reached out to him, had adopted him, regardless of his fears and quirkiness. He saw Asa as a person who possessed happiness and contentment.

"So ... What you're saying is to be happy, you just need to forget yourself a little and care about others just because you do," Dustin added.

"You care, just because it's within you to do so, and you forget about what *you* want for a while. Better yet, you can trust a higher power in your life to provide you with those things you feel you're missing instead of worrying," Uncle Asa preached. "That's the faith part."

When Dustin put his head on his pillow that night, he thought with an open mind about helping others as a way to get through his own problems. He thought about who to help first. He thought about how Uncle Asa found the fake dynamite on the internet and ordered it online. He thought about his Dad and Uncle, trying desperately to keep their business alive, and he remembered his suggestions to them to get a website, and it all clicked in his mind. He knew who he would help, and how. He would work and figure out how to do it, and it would be a great gift.

15

Redefining Business and Self

Aunt Myrtle was pleased to send Dustin off to school in a good mood. She didn't know why or how things changed for him, although she suspected Uncle Asa had something to do with it. She only hoped the positive outlook would take hold more permanently this time.

Dustin had gotten up early and had been researching on his computer for several hours before breakfast. He had asked her if he could use his dad's credit card number to set up a gift for someone online. It would cost $39.95. He handed her most of the rest of his bike money to cover it and asked her to give it to Dad when he came down to breakfast later. She didn't bother to pry into what the gift was or who it was for. It was nice enough to see him thinking of others, and she assumed it was for his mother in the hospital.

Later, during third-hour English, Dustin got special permission from Mr. Wolcott to use the computer lab during his detentions for the rest of the week to work on

a project. He had explained to Mr. Wolcott what he was
doing, ar … about it the
rest of th … t would
work out … student
before ir

It's gc … got to be
as fun fo … colorful.
There sh … e noises,
music, o … en on the
website. … y enough
for my U

"Aur … ords of all
the pro … I want to
write th … t school."

At home, Dustin was trying to keep a low profile about the gift in case it didn't work out. There was so much work to be done. He also needed a camera to take digital pictures of each product he couldn't find a picture of online. The picture problem worked itself out when Uncle Donny came to him on Wednesday evening asking for help with something on his screen requesting "updates."

"Sure, Uncle Donny. I can help you complete your updates, but I'll need to borrow the phone for a few hours, okay?" Dustin negotiated.

"Sure, sure, Dustin. You do whatever you young people do with this modern stuff to make it all work," Uncle Donny obliged. "You know Mertie, the guys down at the Earlybird

Cafe told me that whenever they get new 'technology,' they give it to their kids to play on for a while, and they figure it all out and make it all work right. Ya know, I think they've got a good point. Just take a look at Dusty, there!"

Dustin had already completed the updates before Uncle Donny was finished gabbing about it, but he had a lot more work to do with the phone. "Uncle Donny, if I can take a few pictures of your products in the barn to see how the camera works, then I'll show you and Aunt Myrtle how to use it, okay?"

"That's a great idea, Dusty," Aunt Myrtle agreed. "You just get to know that phone as well as you need to. Take all the time you want!" She knew most of the other ladies at church were already taking digital pictures of kids, pets, grandkids, and huge garden vegetables that they were sharing online and she was excited to get that all figured out for herself.

Thursday flew by at school. He'd mastered a few new algebra tricks, managed to avoid trouble since Monday, and was getting excited that his online project was nearly done.

"Yo, Dustin-the-Wind," came a whisper from across the row in study hall class. Dustin was thankful Zane and

Harley weren't in many of his classes this fall, but study hall at the end of the day was one of them. Harley had been a lot more reserved since the bike incident, not wanting to be found out about the real identity of the orange bike's owner. Dustin decided to attempt to ignore Zane.

"I said, Yo—Dust—in—the—Winnnd!" Zane continued in a loud whisper, making everyone else in the row stop and look up at Dustin for a response. Dustin slowly looked down the row to the now, chocolate-free nose tip demanding his attention.

"What is it, Zane?" Dustin reluctantly responded.

"I just wanted you to know that I'm looking forward to all the new geek words you're lookin' up after school in the lab, and I wanted to offer some advice that will help you make more friends," Zane quietly enticed.

Dustin hesitated for a moment. "What's your great advice, Zane?" he replied rolling his eyes and bracing his emotions.

"Yeah, Dustin-the-Wind, you should know that if you get enough big words to use on me someday, you might, just maybe, do absolutely *nothing* to change me, because when it comes down to it, you're Dustin–the–Wind, right? So, *'dust'* is like, a tiny speck—like nearly nothing—like, pretty much *zero.* It does nothing, except get caught in your eye. So that's the way I see it from my desk in the universe, Dude, and I'm thinkin' it's pretty much time to accept facts now that we're off the reservation."

Dustin just sat in his seat, not even knowing how to respond.

"Oh, yeah. One more thing, Dustin-the-Wind. Thanks for listening. It was a smart thing to do," Zane ended with a grin as he went back to pretending to solve an algebra problem.

Dustin took a deep breath and tried to focus on the next thing he was working on, his gift of a website for his dad and Uncle Donny. He was finding that the joy of doing something for someone else easily washed away the pain and disappointment of his issues at school, at least for the time being.

It all started during after-school detention in the computer lab. Dustin was researching different, new types of balloons his dad and uncle could sell from their website. He had learned that some of the items never even needed to come to the warehouse barn, they could just be shipped right from the factory to the customer, and they could get paid. He was looking up oversized balloons when a URL title caught his eye, **"Lawn Chair Balloonist Completes First Successful Flight Using Balloons Tied to Lawn Chair."** His name was Larry Walters, and he was a truck driver.

At first, it was general fascination. Could a regular guy really fly using ordinary helium-filled party balloons tied to a lawn chair? The idea of trying this briefly came to mind, but he dismissed it immediately knowing the great distance to his mother, the fact that he didn't "own" any balloons or have a chase party to help him when he came down. The whole brainchild that suddenly flashed into his head seemed ludicrous, so he re-attempted to focus on the gift for his family instead.

However, the more Dustin read, the more he could see how possible it might be, and part of his mind couldn't help but continue toying with the idea and taking notes.

- The pilot used ordinary weather balloons.
- The pilot rode the wind currents and predicted where he would go.
- The pilot controlled his height using a pellet gun to shoot out extra balloons.
- The pilot made his dream become a reality.
- More than one guy had tried this, and to some degree they were successful.

Larry, the Lawn Chair Balloonist, had made several mistakes. He cut himself free before he was ready and rocketed three miles up into the atmosphere. Passenger jets saw him floating among the clouds as he flew over an airport. Then he dropped his pellet gun, causing his balloon to nearly become snagged on power lines, and his flight to finally end in a rooftop crash. He ended up getting fined $1500.00 by the FAA (Federal Aviation Administration) for flying in an airport area but also became famous for a few weeks for looking incredibly stupid. Although looking incredibly stupid was something Dustin felt like he was already used to, he decided to forget the whole crazy idea a second time and went back to business.

But he couldn't.

He soon found another guy called Kent Couch. He had to chuckle that this guy was really named Couch. "He sure got off the couch," Dustin mumbled as he read. Couch was a bit more successful, but not on his first flight. He had to ditch early using a parachute to reach the ground. On his second flight, he managed to reach 16,625 feet and flew 193 miles tied to 105 oversized helium balloons. He used 5 gallons of water for ballast and a GPS to know where he was.

"Wow ... over 16,000 feet! What's ballast?" he whispered to himself as he typed it into the search box. He quickly learned it was extra weight for controlling how fast you go up or down.

Then he found more lawn chair balloonists; a couple of guys, Mike Howard and Steve Davis who made it into the Guinness Book of World Records for the greatest altitude ever reached using ordinary helium-filled party balloons. *Ordinary party balloons,* he thought. *Yes, it was possible!* They reached 18,300 feet and used 1,400 party balloons.

Just knowing it was possible was enough for now. He let it go and went back to the website project: Burlington Novelty Warehouse Online, *A barn-load of fun!*

Later in the evening at Uncle Asa's, Dustin couldn't help but continue the conversation about his situation at school.

Morty got it started. "So, I guess the word's out around school about your tutoring session with Zane, Dust. Sorry he's so rude. I hope you don't listen to anything he said, because it's all useless."

"If you don't mind me asking," Uncle Asa chimed in, "what things were said that were so useless?"

"Well, basically he called me a meaningless speck of dust. Let's see ..." Dustin started, dramatically acting as if he couldn't remember. "He said I'm nearly nothing, pretty much *zero*,'" Dustin said, staring down at the barn-wood plank floor.

"So, some people are trying to make you feel small, like nothing ... zero?"

"Yep, that's the new story for today's edition of the Dustin News," he sarcastically replied.

Uncle Asa thought for a few moments silently, then looked up at Dustin: "You know, Dustin, maybe he's got a point. Maybe zero is the best way to define you."

"Wow really, Uncle Asa? Don't you think siding up with a guy like Zane is a bad idea?" Morty questioned.

"It's true," Asa said. "Some people are just hard to define, and most people are more comfortable with a simple way to identify a person. For example, someone might say to himself, 'That dude's a gardener, or that guy's a preacher, or an artist,' but what if someone is called in their heart to be all three at once? That might not make sense to some people. Most folks have been conditioned to define people according to the most obvious thing that they do."

"Like at school, some kids are jocks, or gearheads, or tech geeks!" Morty chimed in.

"Yes, Morty, and when someone comes along that doesn't fit a predictable mold, it can be a little threatening or unsettling to others. It's like when people try to divide by zero; they don't know what to do with it, so they just call it undefined."

Uncle Asa jumped got up and ran over to a cluttered corner to pull out a whiteboard and an easel. He set up the whiteboard and grabbed a marker from a drawer, yanking the top off and writing furiously on the board. First, he wrote out $1 \div 0.1 = 10$. Next, he wrote $1 \div 0.01 = 100$, followed by $1 \div 0.000001 = 1{,}000{,}000$.

"What in the world are you doing math problems for, Uncle Asa?" Morty asked looking confused.

"If that's the way some of the kids at school want to define you, then let them, and let's see why that's really great!" Asa laughed.

"Look at anything divided up by a zero! As you divide even a '1' by smaller numbers (close to zero), you get larger and larger outcomes. The closer to zero as your divisor, the bigger the number you get coming out on the other end, and it's that big quotient that comes out at the end that matters to me. So, who cares if they call you a zero! Maybe that means you're open to *infinity*!"

Asa froze in thought in a moment of realization, then slowly looked over and met eyes with Dustin. "It means you're the kind of person that might accomplish anything!

You see, Dusty, the beauty of being undefined is you can't become too proud or arrogant about it—it's a low place with a high honor. In God's economy, it's the smallest bits that end up doing the most powerful things. What can a giant tree falling do compared to when one tiny atom splits apart?"

Asa drew a big sideways figure 8 at the bottom of the board.

"What is that, Uncle Asa?" Dustin inquired.

"It's you, my friend. It is the mathematical symbol of infinity—for the undefined. It means your friends and enemies are trying to define you as one who is most apparently limitless. They just don't realize it!" Asa revealed with a huge grin.

"To be defined is to have limits, and to have limits is to be contained—and to be contained is to, in essence, be imprisoned, especially if one wishes for more." Asa put the cap on his marker and placed it firmly in the tray, grinning with triumph.

Morty and Dustin sat back a little stunned, looking at each other in disbelief.

Asa bent low toward the boys, his hands on his knees, his huge eyebrows set low and serious, "Your friends see it, your parents see it, I see it, and your enemies even confess it. Now the final question is—will you embrace it yourself, and will you embrace it in others?"

Asa continued, "Do keep in mind, however, that for this math problem to work it assumes a division of sorts, meaning ..."

"...Meaning, that for it to work, you must divide yourself up among many people somehow," Morty proudly finished.

Asa stuck his pointer finger into the air, "Hang on a minute, I've got a quote you need to hear, but I've got to find it. You'd both benefit." He scurried over to a pile of books and began inspecting for bookmarks. "I just read it the other day. Now what was I doing just before?"

"He's asking because whatever pieces of paper or

wrappers he has on him tend to become bookmarks," Morty informed.

"Coffee shop!" Asa declared. "I read it at the Earlybird Café a few days ago."

"Look for a receipt, Uncle Asa."

"Aha! Here it is. From a book of quotes I was reading from. What's so fascinatingly perfect is the fact that this quote was written by someone the same age as you, but stuck in the worst of circumstances, hiding in an attic, unable to see the sky or go outdoors for two years during the German Holocaust of World War II.

"Anne Frank?" Morty guessed.

"Exactly, and she says, 'Everyone has inside of him a piece of good news. The good news is that you don't know how great you can be. How much you can love! What you can accomplish! And what your potential is!'"

"Now, even more ironic is another quote on a page nearby that I found was written by a U.S. Army Air Corps bombardier who flew in a B-24 Liberator plane on over 30 bombing missions over Germany, the very country that was hunting down Anne and her people. Og Mandino's missions couldn't free her in time before her capture, and he never met her, but oddly, he penned these words: 'I am here for a purpose, and that purpose is to grow into a mountain, not to shrink into a grain of sand. Henceforth, I will apply all of my efforts to become the highest mountain of all, and I will strain my potential until it cries for mercy.'"

Dustin could only shrug his shoulders in confusion.

"It means, just be you and stop holding back. 'You' is amazing enough, and if you can't find the amazing inside of you then keep looking because it's in there! It's in all of us. Don't spend a single moment worrying about what ya don't have. Figure out what you *do* have and use it with gusto!"

Just as Asa was about to announce to his small, two-person congregation that they just received his greatest sermon in several years, the phone rang. It was Dustin's father. Uncle Asa needed to take him home right away. There was news about Mom he needed to hear.

16

The Winds of Change

"Asa, it might be a good idea for you and Morty to stay for the news," Dustin's father said without his usual smiling, optimistic disposition as they all came through the side door.

Uncle Donny and Aunt Myrtle were in the kitchen too, eyes wide open with worry. Donny was busy working his way through a bag of chips with a half-finished can of peach soda in the other hand.

"The nurse from the hospital called a little while ago," Dave began, struggling to keep his voice firm and confident. Turning to Dustin, he announced, "She told me your mother has not been awake for several days now and it appears she is slipping into a coma from which it's likely she won't wake up. We need to be prepared to make the plans and the trip to take care of things after she passes. We could get called to come up there soon. Now is the time to stay strong."

Why don't we just leave now! Dustin thought, nearly

aloud. *Why must we wait until she is gone to go see her? What's the point of that?* Dustin was careful to keep his mouth shut.

"Dave, you think I ought to get some bags packed by tomorrow, just in case?" Aunt Myrtle asked attempting to be supportive.

"Yes, Aunt Mertie, that would be a good idea," Dave barely got out before tears began to rush down his cheeks. The tall man hung his head and walked out of the room.

Dustin couldn't sleep. He could only think of getting to his mother in case she woke up one more time. By midnight he was back on the computer researching all he could find out about lawn chair balloonists and cluster balloon flight. He decided to begin calculating to see if it was even remotely feasible.

There were so many pieces already at his disposal, beginning with a massive amount of helium and balloons sitting in the barn twenty yards away from his bedroom. How many balloons would it take? What direction does the wind actually blow? How much did he weigh right now?

A stream of ideas exploded in his mind. *Morty has a small bb gun—there's a lightweight, reclining lawn chair in the barn loft—there's an altimeter and an old parachute in Great Grandpa's plane.*

He did a quick search of prevailing wind patterns in

the upper Midwest of the United States and nearly fell off his chair. The regular wind patterns swooped up in a slight arc from Burlington, Minnesota right toward Thunder Bay, Canada. He printed them up.

"Wow, it's like I've got the wind of the gods at my back! Everything I need to make this trip is right here," he whispered. *The lawn chair balloonist had flown over 200 miles at speeds of up to 45 miles per hour. I only need to travel 250, and I'm lighter than any of those adults.*

Dustin typed *Balloons and Helium FAQ* into a search box and studied questions others had posted on blog sites about balloons.

Q. How long will a balloon stay in the air?
A. It depends on balloon types

- Latex 12": 9-10 hours tested indoors
- Latex 12" with Hi-Float coating: 48hrs tested indoors
- Foils/Mylar 18": 3-4 days indoors, XL (extra life) 3 weeks

Q. How long will my balloons last in very hot tropical sun?
A. Latex balloons with helium will only last 3-4 hours in the hot sun. This is because the higher temperature seems to increase the rate of escape of the helium. Foil balloons

are not designed to last in the hot sun. This is because foil balloons have a fixed volume—they will NOT stretch like latex when heated directly by the sun. The gases in them will expand and cause a sizable tear in the foil material.

Dustin started to realize just how dangerous this could become if he just missed one important detail. Having all his balloons burst while riding thousands of feet in the air? *Not good! Then again, I'm not in Panama, I'm in the cool air over Minnesota,* he thought. He typed a more specific question into his search box: *How many balloons would it take to lift a person off the ground?* Like a sharpshooter hitting a bullseye, he found his mark on another site.

Q. How many balloons will it take to lift a person off the ground?

A. Here's how you could figure it out:

Helium has a lifting force of **1 gram per liter**. So if you have a balloon that contains 5 liters of helium, the balloon can lift 5 grams.

A standard party balloon might be 30 centimeters (about 1 foot) in diameter. To determine how many liters of helium a sphere can hold, the equation is:

4/3 x r r r. The radius of a 30-centimeter-diameter balloon is 15 centimeters. Therefore:

4/3 x ϖ x 15 x 15 x 15 = 14,137 cubic centimeters = 14 liters.

So a normal amusement park balloon can lift about 14 grams, assuming the weight of the balloon itself and the string is small.

If you weigh 50 kilograms (about 110 pounds), then you would also weigh 50,000 grams. Divide your 50,000 grams by the 14 grams per balloon, and you find that you need 3,571.42 balloons to lift your weight. You might want to add 500 more if you actually would like to rise at a reasonable rate. So you need roughly 4,000 balloons to lift yourself if you weigh 50 kilograms, and you can adjust that number according to your weight.

"4,000 balloons! How long will that take?" Dustin said loud enough to be heard down the hall. He pictured himself taking off with 4,000 balloons lifting him. He carefully studied the picture in his mind: the lawn chair, gear, water, ballast, parachute, helmet, and a bag of bologna sandwiches. His head slowly dropped onto the desk as he realized that to make the journey he may need a lot more than 4,000 balloons. He pictured a single bologna sandwich tied to a cluster of balloons rising in the air ... *How many would it take to lift just one bologna sandwich?* Nevertheless, somehow it was going to happen. He could feel it.

Dustin realized he had a new problem on his hands to solve: timing. The only way to get away with this kind of stunt would be to do it in secret, over one night. It would all have to happen in one night. He would need a partner, someone who could *keep* the secret, someone who would understand what it was to lose a parent and feel alone. He knew exactly who to ask.

"So, class," Mr. Wolcott droned on, "when we talk about what a protagonist or an antagonist is in a story, what are we talking about? Dustin, can you tell us?"

Dustin had been busy doing something at his desk most of the hour and had not looked up once during the lesson, his right hand busily moving a pencil back and forth, with an occasional violent erasure. Mr. Wolcott had noticed, and it was beginning to annoy him. He wanted to find out what was going on and try to get Dustin re-engaged. Dustin did not look up. He did not hear his name. It blended in with the background drone of Mr. Wolcott's voice. He only saw the contraption appearing underneath his pencil, a picture of what he had been constructing in his mind for the past eight hours.

Melanie Welks leaned over to get a good peek at what it was he was creating. "He's drawing pictures of balloons, Mr. Wolcott."

At that announcement, Dustin looked up, realizing he'd been found out, just in time to hear a slight, nasal snickering that quickly avalanched into a roar of laughter, including someone cackling, and another student dramatically falling off his chair and grabbing his stomach on the floor.

Normally, Dustin would have turned three shades of red and embraced the shame he felt forced to accept so often, that haunting feeling of being superfluous, unconnected—alone. But this time it was different. He didn't care, except that he may have offended Mr. Wolcott. There was something in him now, something very small, but solid and real that stabilized him. Perhaps it was all that zero talk at Asa's; maybe it was that he was focusing more on others than himself now, or just maybe it was because he was on a mission now. He really couldn't be sure of anything except that he was moving now—going somewhere. To him, the adventure was already happening, and it felt like throwing a dry log into a starving, smoldering fire.

He chuckled along with the class a little, shook his head and apologized to Mr. Wolcott, who was now leaning on the corner of his desk, waiting out the wild, adolescent tirade. Their eyes met briefly with a look of understanding. Dustin was careful to tuck Elise's sketch pad away inside a folder for the rest of class.

"I have something huge to tell you, and I need you to take me seriously," Dustin began as he sipped chocolate milk from a striped straw across the lunchroom table from Morty. It took most of lunch hour to explain the research, his list of materials, and his sketch, so Dustin skipped eating.

Morty didn't question anything; he just listened in fascination, understanding both the possibility and the grave danger of what Dustin was suggesting. But knowing what he knew already about losing parents and family, he was ready to jump into Dustin's insane proposition, just as Dustin sensed he would.

"You've got some serious logistical problems to solve to pull this off, Dust," Morty began as they walked out of the cafeteria.

"Yeah, I know. One of my biggest problems is going to be figuring out how to get that many balloons blown up and tied on in just a few hours."

"I'd say your biggest issues are going to be how you're going to control the thing and what to do if you end up landing somewhere in the middle of a forest, or worse, Lake Superior!" Morty warned. "You'll have to be able to get it down fast, but not too fast, just in case."

The two got permission from Mr. Wolcott to work together in the lab on the "project" during Dustin's last day of detention. Dustin showed Morty the business website he designed off of a template from the internet, but he had just as many bookmarked pages referencing the art of cluster balloon construction and engineering, news reports, and weather patterns.

"Wow, Dust, you certainly give a new meaning to detention projects," Morty said.

"Yeah, well I guess I feel my whole life is in detention right now anyway ..." Dustin started.

"...and you plan to fly your way out of it!" Morty finished with an admiring smile. Then the corners of his mouth went flat. "Just keep in mind what you might face when you get back down."

"I plan to cross that bridge when I get to it," Dustin replied.

"Or swim, just don't sink!" Morty followed.

It was the last night to eat and chat at Uncle Asa's, and Dustin had one last question to wrestle with. He needed some help from the unkempt, bespectacled sage of Burlington.

"Asa," he began as they all stuffed their mouths with popcorn while sitting around a game table, "do you remember the conversation we had about a week ago when Elise was here about knowing right from wrong?"

"Ah, how fun. We get to discuss the finer points of

modern morality today," he said as he pushed his pieces aside to focus on the two boys.

Morty stayed quiet. He did not want to be the one to blow their cover by accident and thought that would best be left for Dustin to do.

"My question is, when is it best to use something that might or might not actually belong to you?" he said.

"Can you offer an example where we might start on this one?" Asa inquired.

Dustin was caught slightly off guard by Asa's question. He should have anticipated it, but his mind had been all over the place with all the excitement. "Ah, well, for starters, do you think it was right or wrong of me to use my own stolen bike to ride to the bus station last Friday?"

"That's a fantastic place to start," Asa excitedly began. "Let's see; the bike was stolen from you originally. You tried at one time and couldn't prove it as such. So, the common authorities, being the police, parents, principals, or what have you, all decided that bike belonged to Harley."

"Except your family, Dustin," Morty reminded them.

"Right, and us of course," Asa continued. "Common sense and religion say we need to comply with the authorities and their decisions, even when we might not agree with their decisions. However, sometimes people might make a decision or law which opposes something we know to be right. In those cases, we do need to follow what we know in our conscience to be right and do our best to convince whatever authorities to change bad laws. However, in this situation, they made a decision, and you made a reactive decision based partly on your rejection of their judgment."

"Okay, Uncle Asa, you totally lost me there," Dustin admitted.

"Hey, Uncle Asa," Morty piped in, "this may be a good time to ask one of those 'clarifying type questions' for Dustin. You know, the ones that I almost always figure out while everyone else is still thinking. I don't know what it might be, but maybe you can think of one."

"Great suggestion," Asa started. "Here's my question. When you took the bike from the rack, what thought permitted you in your conscience to take it then and there? Was it just convenience (it had no lock), vengeance (a chance to get Harley back), or a reaction to what everyone else was telling you was right, which you knew was wrong?"

"I guess it was all three, plus the fact that I'd already decided to return it to him even though it wasn't his to begin with."

"I suspect there was one among the three that really pushed you to do it. What was that motive?" Asa pressed. "Which one gave you permission in your mind?"

"That they were wrong. That letting Harley keep the bike was wrong, and that I had every right to take what was actually mine to begin with."

Suhaib.

Bushra Phuppi.

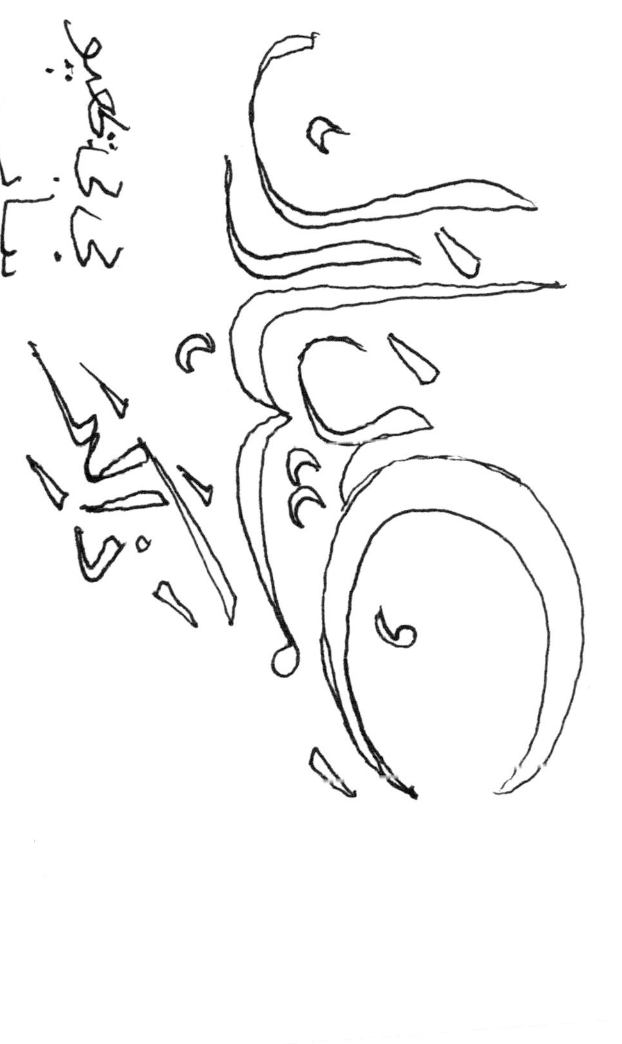

"Who legally possessed the bike, Dustin?"

"Legally?"

"Yes, in the eyes of the law and of Principal Henderson?"

"The "legal" decision was that it is Harley's bike now. So, I guess what I did was legally wrong, even though my decision was based on everything else being wrong too," Dustin pondered aloud.

Morty suddenly grinned and snickered, "I guess this is one time when a guy *can* say two wrongs *do* make a right."

"In a situation where true justice is not found, and unfair decisions are being made, things get pretty confusing fast. That's why justice is so important in society," stated Asa.

Looking down at the game board, Dustin posited, "Asa, what about when you're in a situation that appears obviously unjust or wrong, and the 'authorities' don't agree with your way of solving it?"

"Deep down, you'll know what's right, and if it's important enough to you, you may take action. But if you do, you have to decide how to do it in a way that is truly fair in not just your mind, but in the minds of the authorities and others around you. As we discussed last week, following your heart is what everyone says to do these days, but hearts *can* be deceiving. We don't want to fool ourselves into doing what's wrong, just because we want to believe it's right. That's a slippery slope that a common criminal may wander into as they rationalize their wrongs into rights so many times that they can tell us why they actually deserved the car they just stole.

"One other thing to seriously consider when we are faced with knowing what's right is our conscience; that tiny voice inside us we either choose to listen to or ignore. The laws and our conscience call us to a higher place: to be gentlemen of honor, to keep promises, to tell the truth, to defend the innocent, and to make our wrongs right whenever we can. Deep down inside, a part of us is always rooting for the hero in every story that does these things. And when we do cheer for that person, it's like looking into a still pond and seeing a clear reflection, not of ourselves, but of the true designer who intended for us to be this way. It's what young people call *awesomeness* and what old people call *glory*."

Dustin sat in silence and weighed what Asa said against his plan. He was considering taking a large amount of what remained of his dad and uncle's merchandise stock at a time when they were nearly broke, and the business was failing. He was about to take a huge risk flying in a way only a handful of people on the planet have ever flown. He had also designed a website that he was confident would save their business, but still, he couldn't be sure. His mom was dying, and he knew she wanted to see him again, as he did her. *What if ... What should I ... Who's at fault will it be ... I need to see her again,* he thought in silence.

Morty sat with his head on his hands, gazing across the table. He knew what was going on inside his friend's mind and waited for absolution from him.

"Dusty, are you okay?" Asa asked, a look of concern coming from behind his big glasses. "We either need to move on with the conversation, or you need to take your next move because it's your turn now."

17

Race to Freedom

Dustin was quiet the rest of the evening and on the way home. He didn't even try to hide the way he was feeling. Asa and Morty both saw the struggle on the outside, but Morty knew about the battle going on inside Dustin. The idea of telling his uncle about Dustin's plans crossed his mind once, and when it did, he had to wrestle with his own conscience. For about an hour, Morty sat up in bed making a list of reasons why to tell and why not to tell. In the end, exhaustion won, and he fell asleep with his glasses slipping down his nose, the list and pen on his lap, the decision not being made yet.

Dustin, however, had made his decision. This was it. Every second, every detail, every idea, and word counted because in the next 48 hours he planned to build a cluster balloon craft and launch skyward. He was racing two things now: his mother's death and the weather. A quick check online revealed he had about three more days of what they called "Indian summer," that extended time of warm, calm weather that sometimes hangs on as fall approaches. He knew in three days a cold front with rain, and in northern Minnesota, possibly snow, was approaching. Winter came lightning fast in Minnesota. He recalled several years back when he and his father drove back home to Thunder Bay in September in a snowstorm. If he missed this weather window, he would probably miss saying goodbye to his mother altogether, and frankly, winter in Minnesota was never something he felt was worth sticking around for anyway.

He slept well that night, knowing he had a plan and that he might not sleep much, if at all, until he was in the air. Waking at 5 a.m., thankful that it was the start of the weekend, he began a list of everything he might need and more. He needed food, water, warm clothes, a lifejacket, ballast, a lawn chair, a seatbelt, rope, fishing line, balloon choices that wouldn't fail on him, a whole lot of helium, and a parachute. Amazingly, he knew practically all of these things were right there on the farm. While everyone else busied themselves figuring out how to pay the bills without money, Dustin began quietly gathering up the things on his list.

Sunday morning, Dustin woke up with a terrific headache. "No," he whispered. *Is this really my fate ... to be too sick to do this?* He thought about how his mom might be doing, said a prayer for her, and crawled out of bed. Then it hit him. *Sick, that's exactly what I need today, just not tomorrow!* Sunday meant half the day at church, and as much as he needed help from above, he also recognized his schedule had already been set by the One in charge of the weather. Dustin headed downstairs to tell Aunt Myrtle about his terrible headache.

Aunt Myrtle saw that she may have a sick grandnephew and offered to stay back and watch over his situation. She wanted to take him to the doctor, but Dustin easily talked her out of it knowing that a doctor bill was the last thing she wanted added to her list of expenses. Staying back at the house, Dustin sent Myrtle out for meds. Everyone else headed out to church early to help set up, leaving the farm empty for him to move ahead with creating a design that only existed on a sketchpad.

Next, he needed to contact Elise and get her on board with the plan, so he carefully crafted an email:

Elise,
Big news for you, but you must promise to keep it a secret.

What's up? Getting ready for mass right now.
I'm coming to Turkey Day tomorrow. I plan on arriving sometime between 1 and 5 p.m.

That's awesome news, Dusty! How r you coming? Do u need a ride?
Flying. Will need to be picked up.

Sure. Where at? I will ask m&d.
Somewhere west of T.B. Not sure yet where. Don't ask your m&d!

So we meet at airport on west side of town, right?
Not at airport. West of airport. South of Kiministiquia River. That's where secret part comes in. Just you come. Put pegs back on your bike so we can ride back together.

Did u get a helicopter or something? What's up?
No, but when you see me coming in for landing, you'll know it's me.

But where exactly do I meet you?
Can't be sure yet. Hoping to land near Fort William Country Club or somewhere along Mountain Road. I will call or text you on my dad's cell phone to update you later.

But what if you come when I'm still in class?
I'll wait, unless you can get out of class. Keep your phone charged. I will see you tomorrow. Thanks!!! ☺

Wait, Dusty, what do you mean by hope to land?

Dustin was careful to end the conversation at that point. He did not want to tell her what he was up to yet. He knew she might try to stop him if she knew. He also knew that the airport was on the same side of town he needed to land on, and he needed to somehow avoid getting spotted or worse, ending up in the air traffic around the landing strip. His plan was to follow the winds as he saw them on the map and hope for the best. He knew he could possibly end up miles north or south of Thunder Bay but was willing to add that into the mix of chances that he was dropping into the uncertain brew of his fate.

Dustin's dad and uncle would be staying late at the church to help set up a potluck dinner. The farm was empty for now, and headache or not, it was time to begin gathering materials into a location for assembly. He chose the small, vacant tractor barn out behind the silos to work. Although it was unheated, had a dirt floor and was poorly lit, he was confident no one would be coming in the old building for anything in the next few days.

He lowered the aluminum folding lawn chair with its original mouse-nibbled padding from the barn loft. The parachute came out of the plane seat quickly, but the altimeter took a lot longer. He worked as furiously as a squirrel locked out of his hole on the first day of winter, penlight in his mouth, carefully unscrewing the gauge from the plane's control panel. His hand bumped up against a heavy yellowed envelope, causing it to drop onto his face. The title, *Final Destination Flight Plan,* was hastily scrawled onto it. Annoyed, he stuffed it back behind the dash and looked at the gauge, wondering if it still worked.

After looking over the fine condition the rest of the old plane was in, he decided on placing confidence in it. He thought about his great-grandfather flying the old crop duster and glancing at the same altimeter gauge while zooming through the air above fields, trees, and farms. "Well, Grandpa, I hope you don't mind me borrowing your altimeter. I never flew in this plane of yours, but I'm hoping in a few hours I'll know how it felt for you. I promise to do all I can to put it back where I found it when I'm finished," Dustin spoke in prayer-like tones.

Back in the tractor barn, Dustin began drilling and bolting together a lightweight frame to make the reclining lawn chair more rigid and create mounting points to tie ropes onto. While wrenching away, he attempted to visualize what the craft might do coming in for landing. He noticed a single ski leaning in the corner where he had left it when building the ski-bike and thought about how that plan didn't work out because he forgot one simple thing in the design. He imagined the landing again trying to see what he might be missing. This time he saw the leg of the chair catching on the ground as it drifted down with the wind, toppling him over and dragging him along the ground like a rag doll. He thoughtfully picked up the filthy, lonely ski, laid it next to the chair frame and grinned. He ran outside to fetch the other ski off the failed bike invention.

"You two skis are being reassigned to a much more important mission," Dustin declared into the silence of the barn as he drilled and bolted. Waving a chrome rachet in his hand above the chair he announced, “Shazam! The skis have become landing skids!” He grabbed five empty plastic milk jugs to use for water and ballast but realized that he would need more weight to dump when needed; another one of many questions he could not yet answer. He only knew that with the time he had left, he had to make every waking second count. By late morning, Aunt Myrtle was home, but he knew she had a ladies’ group to attend in the afternoon, which would give him at least four more hours to work.

Indoors, after taking the pain medication Myrtle dropped off, he continued to plan, sketch, list, and pack for the voyage.

- Water-resistant jacket and pants
- Long underwear
- Morty’s BB gun
- Scout knife
- Binoculars
- Jar of peanut butter
- Insulated boots
- Uncle Donny’s old motorcycle helmet
- Gloves
- Sunglasses and sunscreen
- Money
- Rope (in case of tree crash)

- Fishing vest life preserver (in case of water crash)
- Permanent marker
- Matches (in case of survival or signal fire)
- Small tarp (emergency shelter)
- Great Grandpa's old flying goggles
- Change of clothes and duffle bag
- Elise's sketch pad
- Dad or Uncle Donny's smartphone

The last tool on the list was one of the most important ones, but the most unsettling part. How was he going to get it without permission? It was another one of those unanswered questions. He figured the weight of his equipment, ballast, and the chair to be about the same as his own weight, 115 pounds. So, he had to lift maybe 230 pounds. He began doing the math on the number of balloons, and it was staggering.

In the barn, he timed himself inflating ten balloons from the helium tanks as fast as he could. It took about sixty seconds. That was about six hundred balloons in about an hour, and he needed about four to six thousand. Dustin pondered, *That could be up to nine hours of non-stop balloon filling, assuming none of them popped and they could all be sealed quickly.* It didn't count for the time to tie them to the metal lifting ring either. Another question he did not yet have the answer to. He put his head down on the desk and sighed. There was a knock on his bedroom door.

Morty poked his head in the doorway.

"Hey Dust, I was thinking a lot about your balloon timing problem, so I made a little gift for you yesterday in Asa's welding shop." He held up a strange looking pipe, about four feet long with seven nozzles attached to it and an air hose coming off one end. "See, you can attach it right to the helium tank with the hose," he pointed to a threaded hole on the bottom. "Then just spin the tank valve to inflate seven balloons at once. I didn't do seven for good luck—just because that's all the parts I could find. Do you think it will help?"

"Morty, you're a lifesaver! Yes, yes, it's exactly what I need! But I still need more time to launch by morning. There are still too many balloons to fill and not enough time."

Morty suggested they go out to the barn and look at the balloons to see what they had to work with.

"How about some of those oversized Mylar ones, Dust? How many have you got of those?"

"I don't know, Morty. My research said Mylar won't stretch in the sunlight and might burst," Dustin cautioned, "so I didn't plan to use any."

Morty, being adept at solving problems, relished the opportunity to try solving this one as well. "What if you surrounded the big mylar ones with the smaller latex ones so they would be protected from sunlight? Kind of like the yolk in the middle of an egg?"

"That might be possible," Dustin said. "Now that you mention it, we also have a lot of the oversized latex balloons left over because they were colors no one wanted. If we used the oversized balloons along with some Mylar in the center, we would cut our inflating time way down. It just might work!"

"We should also underinflate them, Dusty."

"Why? Don't you think we need all the helium we can get?"

"Yeah, Dust, but the higher you go into the upper atmosphere the lower the air density. So *logically* this will cause the higher pressure gas inside each balloon to expand out and would burst the mylar ones for sure."

"Yikes! Thanks for the life-saving pro tip, Spock. I've also got a ballast problem, Morty. I have only five gallons of water I can pour out or drink to keep the craft stable and dump in case I need to fly higher just before landing. I still need more weight that I can control in larger amounts. It's got to be something that I can drop anywhere in case I need to go up quickly to get over something."

They both began scanning all the bins of toys and trinkets. "How about these fake rubber arms, Dust?" Morty asked. "They have weight but still bounce off things."

"Morty, do you remember when Harley got caught lobbing water balloons at passing cars last spring?"

"Oh yeah ... Yikes! You're right. One of his water balloons smashed in the windshield of a moving car. Velocity times mass equals a big mess! I get it." Then Morty paused next to the rubber chicken bin. He grabbed one, held it up and gave it a quick squeeze causing its squeaker to wheeze out a dying chicken noise. "What about a toy that's rubber but hollow inside?"

"That's it!" Dustin declared. "We just need some sort of bags to hold them in so I can grab them one by one or let them all go at once."

"Right over there," Morty pointed to a dirty pile of old mail bags in the corner. The canvas sacks, which hadn't been used in years, were made with heavy brass grommets and drawstring cords. "And those drawstrings will work great to keep the bags closed in the air until you need them," he added.

"Morty, can you use the big shipping scale down by the delivery door to stuff about twenty pounds of rubber chickens into two different bags for me? In the meantime, I'll try hooking up your awesome Seven Balloon Ultra-Inflator 2000 manifold thingy to a helium tank for a test run."

"That's a go, Captain Dust," Morty said with a standing salute.

After hooking up an air hose between the manifold and the helium tank, Dustin opened the valve to see seven balloons inflate to full size in seconds. He then grabbed a bag of special plastic balloon clips that sealed each balloon closed in less than two seconds each.

Dustin walked back to where Morty was filling bags with rubber chickens. "Morty, I've figured the math: with one guy inflating and sealing and the other tying on strings we may be up to about 21 balloons a minute, but the string tying slows down the process. That means we could do ..."

"We could do maybe 1,260 balloons per hour and have over 6,300 balloons in the air within five hours of work," Morty announced while adjusting his glasses. "However, I'm thinking our hands will be bleeding with blisters and cramping up by that time."

"So, do you think we actually need four to eight thousand balloons?" Dustin asked with hope in his eyes. "How about I get you my research data along with the spec chart on how much helium each kind holds, and you can choose which balloons to pick and figure how much lift each one has to get me off the ground?"

"Well, I'd say you might be pushing my mathematical and pi skills to their limit today, but sure, I'll give it a go. Just be sure to sign my contract that I can't be held responsible for anything you decide to do once you get in that chair and cut the rope for take-off," Morty facetiously warned.

"Great! And thank you, Morty. I'm getting back to the assembly in the barn. Meet me there after you get my notes off my desk upstairs."

When Morty arrived at the tractor barn, he was shocked to see how far Dustin had gotten. The reclining lawn chair, now covered with hooks, gauges, a seatbelt, and a framework bolted under it looked a lot like a beach chair for a moon landing. A rope was tied to the top of each leg and led up to a large round metal ring six feet above, which was hanging from a ceiling rafter by a bent coat-hanger. "Nice set-up, Dusty. So, we plan to tie all the balloon strings to that five-inch diameter ring?"

"Yep." Dustin had carefully laid out all the materials from his launch list on the barn floor, including clothing, helmet, boots, lifejacket and more.

Morty picked up the parachute pack and began studying it. "You ought to know some mice have visited this parachute pack before you got to it, Dust."

"I guess that's to be expected after sitting about fifty years or more."

"You're going to put your faith in a fifty-year-old parachute that mice have been feeding on?" Morty challenged.

"It's not that I want to, it's just that I don't have the time to run to the grocery store to pick up another parachute today. I'm sort of in a hurry here, Morty, and I'm not planning to use it unless I find myself falling, and if that's the case, and it works, what a bargain it will be for me!"

"Yeah okay, Dust. So, I'll just get back to the barn and tighten up those numbers on the balloons because you really don't want to have use the parachute tomorrow," Morty said with a worried grin.

The boys parted ways for dinner but planned to meet up as soon as they could slip back out of their houses. For Dustin, it came earlier than expected since most of the adults in his house were a bit depressed and had a habit of going to bed with the chickens. Dustin found his dad's phone plugged into the kitchen and paused a moment to reconsider the whole crazy plot. Could it be done or was it just a desperate pipe dream? It was wrong to take a phone that wasn't his, but it was so much more right to tell his mom he loved her in person before she died. He unplugged it and slipped out the door to begin six hours of balloon filling.

18

SKYWARD

"We're getting close to zero-time, Dust," Morty reminded as he lay on the grass under the floating chair in the light of a kerosene lantern. He was scribbling something underneath with a marker, squinting through dirty, sweat-coated lenses.

Dustin was off in a corner polishing the old flying goggles and trying on the motorcycle helmet. It only covered the upper part of his head. They had worked through the night after Dustin had snuck out with the last of his gear as soon as he knew the adults were asleep. Morty had done the math and figured out that they only needed 3,242 balloons because they used so many oversized ones. They didn't know the exact number at this point. They just kept filling and tying over and over until the balloon cluster craft began to float with force enough for Dustin to sit in the chair and hover. Their fingertips were sore and had begun to blister. Above the reclining chair with the parachute pad, an enormous, dark, lumpy cloud tied to glistening fishing line hovered in the star-splattered sky. The cluster seemed nearly the same size as the big barn and would be visible from long distances the moment the first rays of sunlight peaked from over the horizon.

"May we have a status report of how you're feeling, Captain?" Morty inquired.

"Status report ..." Dustin spoke from the shadows, "my body feels a little weird from no sleep but psyched for the adventure. My fingertips are stinging but not bleeding, cell phone is fully charged, boots are double knotted, gear is ready and dry. I'm fully hydrated and just peed behind the barn. All systems go, Counselor."

The pre-dawn sky, a black, twinkling ceiling, shrouded their big secret in its darkest shades, and without wind, the cluster-balloon craft eerily hovered above the grass, held fast by three ropes looped around three large tent stakes pounded deep into the earth.

"I added two new communications features which I think you may like, Captain."

"Go ahead, Counselor, please inform," Dusty requested.

"The low-tech one is called the Pooper-Trooper Guided Drop Messaging System, sir. It works in any weather, requires no electronics or tethering, and can be initialized at any level of flight. All you do is write your message on the yellow plastic parachute of a glow-in-the-dark toy soldier, hold the chute open and away from the flight chair, and release. Somebody will get it, especially anyone seeing it floating down from the sky. You can also use it to mark a search trail before crash landing. Its only weak points are large trees or power lines."

"...An excellent addition, counselor! I will be sure to use it. Powerlines and trees are not my friends either; however, the world would look pretty bare and dark without them. What is the other comm system?"

"Well, sir, it's actually just a pair of headsets with a mic to connect to your smartphone so you can hear and speak hands-free. You should keep it plugged in at all times."

Dustin approached the chair with the helmet on, goggles strapped on top while slipping on his leather gloves. His eagle feather was tightly tied into his hair and fell over his shoulder. "It's time to fly, isn't it?" Dusty stated with resolve.

"Yes, it is. 5:04 a.m." Morty reached out to adjust the flexible arm of the mic in front of Dustin's face. "You're four minutes off launch schedule already, but according to the weather reports, your tailwind speed has been raised by one mph, so that puts you ahead of schedule, sir. You'll have to mark your launch time at 0505 hours. It doesn't sound as cool as 0500, but you're still the first 13-year-old kid to try this."

Dustin got in and snapped together the seat belt from Uncle Donny's junked pickup. "Morty, if anything happens to me, I want you to tell my family, Elise, and Asa that I love them very much and that they've all done their best for me, okay?"

"Dust, you're going to make it. I double checked your data earlier, and it looks good: a six-to-ten-hour flight. You'll be there in time for dinner. You just have to land before they see you. Got it? And besides, if you don't make it, they'll probably put me in jail, but don't worry, I've had worse. Communicate when you can and tell me how it feels to fly; I want to know."

"You got it, my friend." Dustin raised his gloved hand in the air and waited for Morty's hand to smash against his for an upright high-five.

"Captain, prepare for launch! If you find yourself rising too fast, hold on until you approach your cruising height of eight to ten thousand feet and start shooting out balloons. The gun is loaded and tied onto guide-rope number four on your armrest console. Don't let yourself become dizzy or confused. Shoot out more balloons if you feel light-headed and lower your altitude. If you pop too many balloons and start to sink, just release some of your ballast, but save some for landing, especially if you see power lines coming at you." Morty instructed. "I am now releasing your mooring ropes, so hold on tightly."

Morty slowly turned a T-shaped spike that had a long leather belt wound about it. With each turn, all three tent spikes spun slowly to a point at which upon the third turn, the ropes all slipped off of them simultaneously, and without a sound, the chair, with its dangling gear, began rising.

"Morty!" Dustin shouted from an already surprising height, "Tell Uncle Asa to pray I'll make it safely…" his voice was already shrinking in the darkness.

Morty's walk quickly turned to running to keep up with the mammoth moving shadow in the sky.

The peacocks began crowing at the giant, rising specter.

"I will, my friend. You can count on it," Morty shouted between cupped hands.

In what seemed like seconds, Dustin disappeared among the darkness and stars.

It was like lying in a hammock inside the smoothest elevator in the world! Dustin felt himself separate from all his troubles on the ground below as he lunged effortlessly upward into the twinkling heavens. Feelings of butterflies melting into light filled his being; floating, rising, and yet rising more. At one point he could no longer contain his laughing, knowing he was going home to see his mother one more time, maybe to stay. He might see his old scout buddies he grew up camping and conquering the wilderness with; what stories he would tell. And Elise, he could picture her face as she saw him landing his craft and the two of them riding back to town together, outsmarting and out-flying every effort to hold him back. He imagined an amazed look on her face, and it got him laughing again. He wanted only to think the best of thoughts about everyone, even his enemies, including the ones hiding inside. In this glorious moment, he finally felt better than okay. The satisfaction of thinking it up, every little detail, and making it happen, rose up inside as his body effortlessly ascended upward. He was on his way to solving an unsolvable problem. How wonderful it felt to fly!

The land below him, barely visible in the starlight, shrunk in a way he had never seen with his eyes. He could see Morty, a tiny shadow running home across a soybean field. The porch light was a speck, and the big light on Uncle Asa's barn cast shadows over his long line of crazy metal sculptures lining the road. The silos, which seemed of colossal height from the ground, looked like golf tees below his feet. Soon the roads became a grid of ribbons, and he observed that he was moving toward the northeast as planned.

Within minutes, the first whisper of a cloud appeared below his feet, flying by like a phantom in the starlit night. Higher he climbed, and before long, he could see the glint of peach-colored light on the horizon.

Flight time: 0520 hours. Dustin checked his armrest-mounted altimeter and saw the needle moving inside the seventy-year-old gauge, ever so slowly. Now approaching 8,000 feet, he was still feeling euphoria. Unable to stop the giggling, he reached for rope number four, the BB gun, like a drunken sailor.

As Morty's pounding feet approached the barn that he called home, he could hear the dog barking from behind the upstairs window and knew he'd been ratted out, not by a person, but by a loyal dog whose keen hearing picked up on the warning crows of Donny Windworth's rooftop peacocks.

Meanwhile, Asa stood outside in his garden, seeing it, understanding it, but having trouble believing it. He knew that the giant lumpy shadow he observed rising from the Windworth farm was no UFO, but the makings of two bright, creative, desperate young men. But where would this lead? And what role did he play, now that he knew? He paced in the garden, stars twinkling in his pond.

Morty came inside out of breath, expecting Uncle Asa to be waiting, but the barn was empty. He calmed down Corndog and slipped back into his bedroom, exhausted but hopeful for Dustin, yet in a panic about his own fate.

He began to wonder if his relationship with Uncle Asa would be ruined over this. Maybe Asa would decide to disown him. Maybe give him back because he was too much trouble. *Can an adult end an adoption with a kid?*

Morty's heart raced as old memories began flooding into his head: long yelling matches between his birth parents, his father's temporary girlfriends who ignored him, nights of being alone in the old, dirty trailer not knowing where his dad had gone, and worrying that he may never come home. That day finally came. That worry was real. He recalled the hours spent watching anything on television in the sweltering trailer for days, alone day and night. Waiting. The first time he felt panic was after he finally ate everything he could find until all he could do was drink water to keep away the hunger.

Waiting.

Nobody came for him. Hopelessness and abandonment revisited Morty, a stealthy, menacing demon of the night: cold emptiness creeping into him; a door left open in the dead of winter.

Forgotten. It was an awful feeling that he had been pushing down ever since the police came and took his nearly lifeless body away. It seemed like so long ago now, but the memory was still something he owned, and he knew it wasn't a dream. That's why he lived here.

Dustin's mom and dad were nothing like that, he thought. They had their problems, but they still cared and tried their best every day. *Yes,* he thought. *Yes, I did the right thing, and it will be worth it.* Deep down, he knew even Asa would understand why he helped his friend.

The truth. *What was the truth?* The truth was that Asa would forgive him even if he didn't agree because that's just what Asa was like. Asa was not his first father. Asa would never abandon him or ignore him. Morty didn't know what would happen to him tomorrow, but he decided then and there never to allow that ghost into his room again. It was okay to let it go. He wasn't required to accept the demon's presence any longer.

19

Wake-Up Call

Flight time: 0625 hours. Uncle Donny rolled over in bed and shouted across the hall. "Mertic, you wanna go check on Dusty? I don't think he woke up. I can hear his alarm clock again."

"Yep, I was getting up anyway," Aunt Myrtle croaked from her bedroom.

Dustin's bedroom door was already open, and the ancient clock radio squawked away as she approached. "...the object was caught on Coast Guard radar early this morning, and at this point they've visually confirmed it's a young man, maybe in his early teens, flying under a huge cluster of party balloons in a lawn chair ..."

Aunt Myrtle leaned over the stair railing, "Dusty—you up and around down there? The school bus will be here in just a few minutes."

The clock radio on Dustin's bedside table droned on, "Sources say the balloon cluster and pilot are headed northeast towards the Superior National Forest, further complicating chase efforts."

At that moment, Great Aunt Myrtle began adding things up in her head and it all summed up to a possibility that put her heart into overdrive.

"Dave!" she hollered sharply. "Have you seen your son this morning?" She began knocking urgently on Dave's bedroom door. "Dave, you up? I can't find Dustin and somethings going on that may involve him ... Dave!"

The house phone began ringing downstairs, so Myrtle headed down and answered it. "Myrtle, it's Asa. I've got some strange news for you, are you sitting down?"

"Myrtle, where's my phone?" Dave called from upstairs. "I thought it was on my dresser, and now it's gone."

Uncle Donny popped his head out his bedroom door, "If you're looking for your phone, Elise told me just to call your phone from another phone to find your own cell phone when it's lost. Great trick, huh? That girl's so smart. I'm dialin' you right now, Dave."

Dave shouted from Dusty's room, "Sorry, Donny. What'd you just say?"

"...sources on the ground continue to call into the station with reports and sightings about the lawn chair balloonist in the sky ..."

"Oh, no ... Asa, what do we do?" Myrtle screamed. "Dave!" she yelled back up the stairs, "That boy in the sky is your ..."

"Dave!" Uncle Donny called from his bedroom again. "I found your phone. Dusty's got it! He's on the other end and wants to talk to you."

"Lord in heaven, help us now!" Myrtle called out as she hung up downstairs.

"Dad, it's Dustin. I need you to listen to me for a minute and try to understand, okay?"

Dave was a trained accountant and used to doing math to sort out mysteries no one else wanted to recognize. By now he had pretty much figured out what was happening. His head began to feel like it was spinning as he tried to focus on the voice on the other end.

"Dad, I had to borrow your phone without asking, and I know that gets me in a lot of trouble, so I wanted to ..."

"Dustin," Dave interrupted, "Are you really in a lawn chair floating around in the sky right now?"

"Yeah, how'd you know about it? It's barely sunrise."

"Son, the entire county already knows! It's all over the morning news!"

"What? How could they know so quickly?"

"Listen, Dusty, is there a way for you to come down? You need to get to the ground before you hit the national forest. Do you hear me?" Dave pleaded.

"Dad, I'm on my way to Thunder Bay, and I'm not coming down. I'm going to see Mom once more before she dies, and I guess this time you and everyone else can't stop me."

"Don't do this, Dusty. I don't want to lose you too. If you *can* come down, I'm giving you an order as your father to bring that contraption down now!"

"No, Dad. Why should I keep listening to a man who doesn't care? We were a family and now Mom has neither of us! Well, I'm not going to stand in one spot, like you tell me to, and just wait for her to die alone. I'm going because I love her and it's what I have to do, and I'm sorry you don't get this love thing, but I do!"

"Dustin, I *do* get it, more than you know, but love and honor sometimes don't make sense when you have promises to keep."

"Well, to hell with your promises, Dad. They're not helping anyone anymore. You do what you want, but I'm on a bigger mission now!"

Dave scratched his head, not sure how to answer.

"Look, Dad, I did something else for you and Uncle Donny that you didn't want. It might help make up for me using up so much of your inventory. Click on my mouse on the computer in my room. There are already some orders on your new company website. Don't ignore them."

"Dusty, I don't care about the gag business! I just want you back safe."

"Da ... can't ... of range n ..."

The call was lost.

20

The Chase

Dusty's father didn't know how fast his truck could go. He had never tested it for that. He had always been the law-abiding type who tried to follow the speed limits. He was more into taking his time getting places. All he knew is that his son was a faraway speck, lost somewhere in the eastern sky, floating slowly away from him into the unknown. So even though the speedometer needle was pegged at 120 miles per hour as he raced eastward into the glare of the rising sun, he suspected he was sometimes traveling even faster.

Dave knew he wouldn't have the fuel to make it to Canada. He knew he might have to venture into the Superior National Forest, a vast maze of hundreds of square miles of trees, lakes, and rough fire trails reaching to the border. He swerved into a Gas-It-Up station, braked to a hard stop, jumped out, and started filling. He ran in to pay while the pump was still running. He had two twenty-dollar bills, one left in his wallet, and the one Dusty had left with him when he tried taking a bus to Canada.

"Here you go and keep the change," Dave said as he practically threw the money at the cashier.

A small TV hanging from the ceiling caught his attention for a moment. "A strange object is being seen flying over the south end of Tower Township, and we have live footage of it this morning ..." A reporter had started another broadcast.

"Mister, they seen a UFO. They got it live this mornin' on the news," the cashier informed. "I been tellin' folks them UFOs were for real. Yep, I always sensed them grays and reptilians watchin' us all from ..."

"That's my son up there!" was all Dave had time to blurt out before running out, yanking the pump handle from the truck, slamming the door, and leaving a line of smoking rubber on the cement drive.

He slowed down through Hibbing, just enough not to smash into anyone who happened to be driving at 6:17 in the morning before turning onto highway 169. The A.M. news channel was repeating the flying boy story every ten minutes now. He passed Chrisholm and kept driving up 169, sensing that if Dustin had planned this trip, then he knew the wind would be taking him toward Thunder Bay. If he followed the direction of the wind, he was bound to find his son. Dave screeched onto 83 North at Virginia, then switched back to 169 again. He passed Tower and Soudan and finally made it to Ely, a final outpost town on the edge of the National

Forest. Barely a mile out of town on Highway 169, he could finally make out a tiny floating speck in the sky he suspected was his boy. The truck was back up to full speed now, engine roaring, barreling down a lonely two-lane road like a blue bullet. The lines on the empty country road whizzed by under the truck. He had lost all track of time. Dave looked up again at the sky. He could now make out the form of a boy in a lawn chair, dangling below what looked to be a massive bubbling cloud made of millions of colored gumdrops. He completely missed the maroon colored Minnesota State Trooper patrol car sitting along the highway.

Officer Harding, sipping away at his open cup of steaming coffee, looked up and jerked his head trying to follow the speeding blue streak flying by. Coffee running down his chin and into his lap, he flipped on the lights and slammed the accelerator pedal to the floor. He had orders to monitor the object in the sky as it passed, and he did not know why the blue pickup was going faster than any vehicle he had ever seen in his sixteen-year career.

"Officer Harding here, I'm in pursuit of a 10-10 heading eastbound now onto Fernberg Road approaching Garden Lake Bridge. Suspect is driving a blue, early model Chevy pickup and traveling at a high rate of speed. Requesting immediate backup and intercepting location, over ..."

Dave saw the lights in the mirror and knew the stakes were getting higher now. However, there was no way he could stop. He lost his job, he lost his home, and he was losing his wife. He wasn't going to lose Dusty if he could help it. His mind began figuring the cost of his driving. He would probably get his license taken away, owe fines—maybe even go to jail. He continued to calculate. If he hit another vehicle, it would be awful. He needed to be very careful, and if it came down to it, he would be willing to swerve and hit an object to save any oncoming car. He resolved what he would do. He was not letting his boy out of his sight. He was not going to stop.

He flipped to an FM station to get away from the constant newscasts. He cranked the volume to drown out the siren coming up from behind. Tears began to fill his eyes, tears of regret, and tears of missing Meredith, and wondering how she must be feeling right now. *I should have just let him see her. I shouldn't have given in to my anger, (anger that no one else needed to see). I should have listened and talked to him more. I've just let him suffer alone, without me—let her suffer alone.* He wiped away tears on his sleeve, one hand at a time, keeping the other on the wheel. He wondered what Dusty was thinking about up there, whether he was scared or being his usual calculated self when it came to machines. Dave comforted himself trusting that if Dusty got this far already, he had spent enough time planning to know what he was doing, at least somewhat. *But who really knows what they're doing sitting in a lawn chair, thousands of feet in the air, tied to party balloons?*

Now he could see it; what he still had with Dusty. He had a wonderful, creative son that had been mostly alone for the past three years, and mostly raised by his mother, who had been missing from his life for over six months now. He had a relationship. It had all been squandered and left neglected for so long, and now he knew he needed him, he knew they needed each other, and most of all, Dusty needed his father to forgive his mother. Dusty had already forgiven her. Dustin was on his way to her, flying through the sky, all alone.

Dave decided he was willing to do it, all of it, to make things right, if he could only get Dusty back on the ground, safe.

He slammed down the brake pedal, locking up the back wheels and leaving long black streaks of smoking rubber on the pavement. He did this in order to make his turn quickly and keep as much space as possible between him and the squad car closing in on him.

Dave knew he had to go northeast, for now, to keep Dusty in view, but 169 was taking him further away from his son. He remembered Moose Lake Road headed directly northeast into the national forest area. It was perfect. He knew that by now he was somewhere near the national forest border. If he could make it in, the police would not be able to continue chasing him once he got onto the rough fire trails. It would be a long, brutal ride, but he could make it all the way to Canada if needed.

As hard as he drove, the patrol car was able to keep up with him. *Wow, this guy must be an ex-racecar driver or something,* Dave mused as he continued working the truck through the sweeping curves and ridgelines of Moose Lake Road. The trees were beginning to get closer to the road now as he ventured farther from civilization. It was becoming more difficult to see Dustin.

Dave knew how Moose Lake Road ended; in an abrupt hairpin turn leading down to the lake. It was one of Donny's favorite fishing spots. Dave and his brother had spent many hours there once they were old enough to drive. He could see the hairpin approaching. Slamming on his brakes again and swerving off to his right, he aimed the front of the truck straight for a barbed wire fence, broke through, and began heading across a field of ruts and dips, slamming the tires up into the wheel wells and bouncing the truck around violently.

Officer Harding could barely keep control of his car and hold his radio at the same time. "Suspect is now heading off-road in an easterly direction. Pursuit will be attempted across the field, over."

"Roger, Harding. A pursuit helicopter is en-route to you now. Backup is heading north on Canadian Border Road. One squad car will be barricading 169 two-and-a-half miles from you in case he backtracks, over."

"Copy that ..."

By now Officer Harding's coffee was all over the front of the car. His cup was on the floor rolling around along with his notes, clipboard, and an extra radio. The car kept bottoming out on the mounds of dirt as he struggled to see in the cloud of dust created by the pickup, now far ahead of him.

"Suspect just turned onto an unmarked fire trail leading northeast into the national forest. Will continue pursuit."

The forest fire trails were not designed for high-speed chases. In fact, they were often difficult to pass with a four-wheel drive truck going the speed of a bicycle. Dave had to invent a new way of driving, slowing down to a crawl before hitting potholes, sand pits, rocks, or tight turns, then hitting the gas again to move the truck as fast as possible down the narrow, straight sections of the path. Rocks and sticks pelted the truck from the sides and bottom as he made some headway away from the flashing lights behind him.

Harding was doing his best to take a road vehicle off-road. He found his body bouncing around in the seat, nearly hitting the roof at times, as he carefully focused on avoiding obstacles and a million ways to get stuck.

Bam! Bitta, bitta, bitta ...

"Harding here, I just blew a tire, and my vehicle is immobile. Please send assistance when available, over ..."

Officer Harding's pursuit ended in the woods.

With his left eye, Dave noticed the car in his mirror had come to a stop. He let out a brief sigh of relief. He had to find an opening in the trees to get a bearing on Dustin's position in the sky. He glanced up at the treetops repeatedly, hoping for a spotting. He could not see the sky beyond the row of trees. He could not see Dusty. A movement near the ground caught his attention. Something huge jumped from the woods in front of his truck. He only had time to recognize it as a moose before instinctively swerving, slamming headlong into a towering white pine.

"Harding here, suspect just hit a tree and appears to have stopped, over." Officer Harding was running as fast as he could toward the truck down the trail, his bulky bulletproof vest out in front of him, arms swinging. "Repeat, suspect has hit a tree! 10-53! I am pursuing on foot to the suspect's vehicle now. Do you copy me? Over."

"Copy that, Harding. We are requesting Canadian EMS to your location now, as well as back up, over."

Harding reached the truck, gasping for air. He stopped at the back bumper and pulled his gun out of its holster, hands shaking, then squatted down low for cover behind it. The horn on the truck was stuck on and blaring in his ear. Jagged metal stuck out near the front wheels, and the hood was crumpled back toward a shattered windshield. Steam was hissing from the front. The cab of the pickup looked empty. He quickly scanned in all directions for the suspect. Approaching the front door of the truck, he peered into the cracked side window. A tall man was inside, slumped over, his bleeding head resting on the steering wheel. He was not conscious.

21

Gaining Altitude

Elise was sitting in her second-hour Algebra when she felt her phone buzz in her back pocket. She glanced around carefully and pulled it out to see if it was him. Sure enough, it was Dusty. She asked to go to the bathroom and opened the text.

Elise, I am flying at about 10,000 feet and have reached the S N Forest area.

The text was followed by a picture of his view: tiny trees, ribbon roads, and a few Monopoly houses; much sharper than a Google satellite shot. He didn't realize that his foot and a corner of the lawn chair had gotten into the picture.

Elise texted back:

Why are a boot and a lawn chair in the pic? What's going on?

Dustin replied:

This is ...
A picture followed, but this time he took it above his head showing thousands of shiny strands like spider webs reaching up to a cloud of countless colored balloons.

Search up lawn chair balloonists, and u know how I travel. Don't worry, all is going well, but media know so they will try to follow. I plan to lose them in forest over the Boundary Waters. Wind will take me to you. Must land before I get seen west of A-port. Need u to find me and help me get to hospital. Will get back to u as I get closer. Cell service sketchy now. Can't tell anyone! Please say you'll help me!

Elise stood in the bathroom staring at the picture in shock, her heart racing inside her chest. Of course she had to help her childhood friend!

Okay. I will do all I can to help. Stay safe! Have to go, TTYL
Dustin followed:

TY, ELISE!

Flight time: 0827 hours. Dustin hadn't noticed just how numb his fingers had gotten during the short period of texting on his dad's phone. The glass of the phone felt like a cold knife cutting in his tingling hands, and he had to carefully watch what he was doing with his eyes as he slipped it back into his pocket. It took a real effort to close his fingers on the zipper to zip up the fishing vest he wore over his jacket. Rechecking his altimeter, it now read 11,500 feet. He could see it was time to slow down his ascent and level off. The patchwork view of farm fields and small groups of trees below was now becoming larger masses of forest, and he could see in the distant horizon what looked like endless fields of fall-colored broccoli and shiny puddles: the Superior National Forest and beyond that, Boundary Waters, a wilderness so remote, most of it could only be reached by canoe.

He bent over the side of the armrest to pull up on rope number four, "Time for some target practice." He was surprised again by the difficulty his fingers were having grabbing at the rope and pulling up the BB gun.

He clumsily got hold of the gun and placed it onto his lap. Morty had already loaded the first set of rounds to save time. Dustin stopped to put his gloves on to warm his fingers up a bit, but after waiting a few minutes, it wasn't helping. He took them off again and blew hot breaths into each one slowly to pre-warm the empty finger holes. Suddenly he felt a wave of dizziness come over him as if his eyes were snapping left to right in his skull for a few seconds.

Dustin shook his head and did some deep breathing. He knew this might happen but did not expect it to be a problem yet. He needed to warm his fingers first, and grabbing the cold gloves, he placed them on his hands and rubbed them together until they felt better.

He picked up the gun and aimed it at a balloon the same way he had when he and Morty had practiced in the barn, just below center. But as he moved to curl his finger around the trigger, he found it wouldn't fit through the trigger guard hole with the glove on it. He set the gun back onto his lap.

"Okay, so we will see how many we can shoot with numb fingers!" he protested as he ripped off his gloves.

He took careful aim again.

Pop!

The sound startled him. Dustin had not realized just how completely silent the world of the sky was. He re-aimed and shot a few more out.

A cloud began to envelop him. It started out as a fog, flying by thick and thin, like big bumbling ghosts passing. Soon it turned into an outright white mist filled with moisture which instantly covered everything, including his chilled fingers.

He waited for another opportunity to aim but was unable to see the balloons only twelve feet above him, so he pulled the trigger and shot into the mist—pop, pop, poppity-pop. A few of his shots managed to knock out several balloons at once, but soon it was time to reload. Dustin knew he might need to shoot out a lot of balloons, possibly several hundred to get the colorful cluster to stop rising. He had a job in front of him and was now wishing he had started a bit sooner.

When he reached for the box of BB's a new challenge presented itself. Not only were his fingers remaining numb, but now everything on him was coated in a fine wet slippery mist. It took a concentrated effort to pour the ammo into the tiny hole in the gun. He heard the little metal balls roll into the chamber a few at a time and thought about what to do with his freezing fingers next. He could only manage to place the box next to his body for now as he picked up the gun again. This time he was having a hard time just finding the trigger. "Okay, I need another quick warm up."

The cloud began thinning, and soon he felt the warmth of sunlight breaking through it. He placed his hands in his armpits. He then tried smacking them together in the gloves for a bit, bringing on more stinging pain. The sunlight felt good but was not warming the fingers enough without the gloves on. He thought about how he could be shooting away just fine with his gloves on if the rope tied through the trigger hole was removed. However, tied to any other part of the gun it may not hold. He weighed the risk in his mind carefully. If he removed the knot around the trigger hole, and carefully held the gun until he was finished, he could tie on the rope afterward. On the other hand, if he went back to bare hands, he may end up not getting the job done in time, or worse, unable to warm his hands back up.

Another wave of dizziness rolled through his head.

"Getting too late to invent something new here," he mumbled as he began to untie the tether from around the trigger guard. He had to think, to watch, and try to tell his numb fingers what to do to loosen Morty's knot.

He glanced at the altimeter. The needle continued to climb and was getting closer to 12,000-foot mark now.

Flight time: 0937 hours. Off in the distance, the silence of the sky began to break with the chopping sound of helicopter blades. It was coming from somewhere in the clouds below him, and it made his adrenaline start to kick in at a new level. *The last thing I want,* Dustin thought, *is to be caught by news cameras or shot out of the sky!*

Soon the chopping of one helicopter blade combined with the sound of another and at this point, he suspected they weren't just sightseers. He looked down and saw he was clearly over the forest now. They wouldn't be able to follow him too long once spotted.

Dustin went back to his untying work, and with a final jerk, managed to pull open the knot and slide out the rope. He put on his gloves again and carefully raised the slick, moisture-covered gun. As he began to fire, the popping sounds of the balloons made him forget about the muffled helicopter motors wandering about the clouds. Bang, bang, pop, bang sang the balloons that held him aloft.

Suddenly, from a cloud below him, a massive, Blackhawk helicopter emerged. Dustin could hear the whipping sounds of the propeller cutting the air, the engine whining as if it were next to his ear. As it rose towards him, a mass of suction began to tug his craft downward. *Too close,* Dustin thought as he pictured himself being hacked to pieces in the sky. Instinctively, he gripped the armrests and leaned to one side, looking down to see whether he was on a collision course with the massive, whirling blades, angling the chair just enough to allow the damp gun to slip off his lap. He could see it tumbling down, shrinking into a speck below him and then disappearing. His heart dropped.

Nurse Abigail was watching the morning news in the breakroom of the hospital. A news helicopter had gotten the first shot of a boy rocking in the cradle of a giant balloon cluster 10,000 feet in the sky. In her heart, she suspected it was Dustin, the boy that kept calling his dying mother in the hospice ward, but she had to be sure, so she sipped her morning tea slowly.

"That's right, Darla. We have confirmation now of the balloon boy's identity. His aunt and uncle called the authorities, and he's been identified as 13-year-old Dustin Tecumseh Windworth."

It was all she needed to hear. She headed down the hall to Meredith's room leaving her steaming cup behind on the breakroom table. The TV was already on with a fully alert Meredith Windworth sitting up, fear and excitement in her eyes. Abigail sat on the bed, put her arms around Meredith and just held onto her. It was going to be the wildest ride of their lives.

Teddy was sitting in a diner outside of Fargo, South Dakota, finishing his breakfast with a cigarette when he saw the broadcast on the wall-mounted TV. He found himself staring, dumbfounded at first. He walked up to the screen, speaking to it as if Dustin could hear him.

"Dusty, ya gotta know that's a one-way trip," the waitress overheard him say to the TV. She saw him standing there, talking with a cigarette just hanging onto his lower lip as if it were about to take a swimmer's dive into the coffee cup he was holding beneath it. Next, she spotted the scruffy looking man holding up his mug in a salute to the flying boy on the TV, muttering something about *going* someplace.

The waitress behind the counter decided she ought to move things along, so she walked up to him with his bill. "Ah, sir, here's your check. I'll just be over behind the counter when you're ready to pay."

He turned to face her, eyebrows raised in realization. "Yes, Margret." He read her name pin and looked into her eyes with a confident, relaxed smile that he hadn't shown anyone for a long time. He found himself suddenly lucid, clear, and wide awake in a way he hadn't felt in years. "I'm ready to pay now. It's okay. I'm finally ready now."

Teddy found himself on a bus again, but this time headed back to Burlington. It seemed that all he could think about was getting as close to his family and friends as fast as possible.

He walked up to the front. "Bus driver, you got a good news radio channel we can listen to on board here? I got a hot story I can guarantee all the folks on board'll appreciate listen'n to this morning."

Flight time: 0944 hours. Morty sat in his second row seat in Ms. Sandford's third hour U.S. History class. The Civil

War lesson had come to a halt after the announcement on the P.A. about teachers using their own discretion regarding urgent student requests to watch a Wooddale classmate on the news. Of course, every teacher had decided to follow the story.

Morty began feeling queasy in his stomach. Having Dustin offer an on-air class presentation on the finer points of balloon-cluster flight was not part of their plan. Shifting his eyes left and right, he took a few slow breaths to calm himself and take in the new information.

“This is Darla Darling, and we are continuing our exclusive coverage of the drama unfolding in the sky today. We have been able to get the phone number of the actual sky pilot and are awaiting our cue for an exclusive live, on air, in the air, interview ... Yes, okay, I am being connected with the call now ... Dustin? Is this Dustin Windworth?”

“Yes, th- is he. Whom am I speaking to n-w?”

“Dustin, Hello! This is Darla Darling with K-MIN News 5. Dustin, you are breaking up a bit, so we’ll need you to speak slowly for us, okay?”

“-kay.”

“Dustin, can you tell us a little of the why, how, and where of your amazing adventure in the sky?”

“Sure –arla. I’m on… mission to see someone, but I’m sorr- can’t tell y- who it is right now.”

“Can you tell us where you’re headed? We want to be sure we have enough fuel to follow you.”

"Sorry, Da—, can't tell you. It's top sec—t. They won't be able—follow me over the National For—. It's too far."

Someone in the room stifled a giggle. Then another kid belted out what many were thinking already, "Windworth is lost in some fantasy world, thinkin' he's a secret agent or something. I knew he was a total idiot!"

Melanie Welks turned around in her seat to face the accuser, "C'mon Zane! Look what danger he's in. Can't you cut him a break, I mean really, how rude!"

The TV droned on, "Can you tell us who made this flying craft you have? Where did you get all those balloons, Dustin?"

"I did res—ch online and f—nd most of—on the farm where I live. A friend did help m- but n- adults knew ab- it."

Morty gulped and sat still, trying to remain invisible. For the moment, nobody in class had made the obvious connection, but it wouldn't be long before somebody would.

"By the way, the smaller, blue helicopter below you is our own K-MIN News 5 Eye-In-the-Sky Gurdeep Canary, and he's got a cam on you now. Do you care to wave hello for us?"

Dustin leaned over and waved slowly. All the excitement was waking and warming him a bit.

"I realize we are slowly losing contact, Dustin, but we are all wondering if you are okay and if there is any way anyone can help you right now."

"To tell y—the truth I don- ... climbing too high t-breathe and lost my ability to descend."

Several students gasped in horror. Morty knew this must have something to do with the BB gun or ammo. He wished he could jump up and get on that phone to workshop with him, but he had to sit in silence.

"I know what mission that kid's on." Zane couldn't say quiet. "He's on a mission to see that blond girlfriend cousin chick he brought to school with him last week. Yep, it's a mission impossible for our own Wooddale flyboy!"

Next Harley chimed in, "The kid might as well strap on a clown nose and some size 22 shoes to go with that balloon carriage thingy ..."

They both broke out in a nasally snicker that lightly flew itself around the room, growing into random outbreaks of outright laughter.

Morty felt anger welling up inside, and it unlocked any caution he had left. "Zane, you know nothing, I assure you. What he is doing is totally noble, if you know what that word even means."

Zane mockingly masked his next outburst of laughter in a loud cough, "Uh, oh. Guess we just found out who the secret mission helper is, it's little Igor here. So, tell us, little man, what's the big secret?"

At that moment, Morty ceased to care about his reputation, his safety, or his future, "It's not a girlfriend, and yes, it's a real, true, life and death situation." Morty stood up, his disheveled 'fro adding to his limited height and frame. He walked up to Zane's desk. "Actually, if you must know, it's mostly about death, and he's trying to reach someone before it's too late—and whether you *choose* to believe it or not, the truth *you* need to know is this: it was the only way he could get there without someone trying to stop him, and I must say, it was pure genius. Just look at him, Zane, can you stop him now? Can you? You can't touch him, and your heartless, prejudice can't even slow him down. So, let me give you a tiny bit of advice, just shut up, watch, and learn, because besides praying, that's all we can do for him right now!"

Morty spun back to Zane's desk once more. "By the way…" He leaned his bespectacled face into Zane's with confidence. "If you want to get Harley to *beat me up* later, go right ahead. It really doesn't matter to me because we all know what you're about, Zane. The small stuff. That guy up there on the screen has figured out the big stuff you may never get to in your whole lifetime!"

Ms. Sandford was already on her phone to the office, her hand covering the receiver as she reported the situation and key witness. Morty glanced up and knew he was not going to be spending much more time in class. He walked back, collapsed in his seat, pushed his glasses back up his nose and waited for it. Within minutes, police officers were outside the classroom door ready to escort Morty to a place where they might gain more information from him.

"Are you going to cuff me, or can I just walk with you guys?" Morty asked as they began moving down the hall.

"Actually, if you cooperate with us, you'll be helping your friend and yourself."

"Can I make one final request while we are in the building?" Morty asked.

"Shoot," the taller officer said, while at the same time cringing as he realized that was a poor word choice right now.

"I'd like to share over the P.A. why Dustin is doing this, so kids can understand he's not an idiot or a crazy person."

The short officer was cordial. "Sure, we can stop in and see if they'll let you press the talk button. Maybe we can all learn a little more."

Flight time: 1042 hours. The phone in Dustin's fishing vest began ringing again. He had been keeping his fingers warm, so he was able to extract it delicately from his pocket and answer.

"Dustin Windworth, this is Captain Tiebor of the U.S. Border Patrol Authority. You are about to invade foreign airspace without consent. If you don't land now, the RCMP in Canada will need to place you under arrest, but we are most concerned with your safety and getting you back down on the ground. Are you capable of bringing your craft down or do you need some help from us?"

"No ... Can't get ... I guess you'll have to shoot balloo ... Just, please don't shoot me. Try- to d—thing really import—, and my mom may be watching. I dropped my BB g—, so I'm still rising hi—Getting ... to breathe now."

"Dustin, we can't get too close due to all the draft from the copter blades, but we may try to shoot out some of your balloons. However, we will have to keep moving around you because we cannot hover this high up. We want you to sit tight while we come up with a plan, and don't worry about getting down now, okay?"

"Alright, but can you prom—me you'll take ... to Th—Bay Hospital to see my mom bef—she dies? Then you can arrest m—fi—print me and ... that jazz."

"Dustin, we can't make any promises to you right now, but know we will do all we can since we can see what you're up to."

The co-pilot of the Blackhawk turned to his captain, "Cap, you know we can't do much for him at this altitude and we have to move around him so slowly that we're burning through fuel like nobody's business. We've got maybe ten minutes left before turn-around time. If he keeps rising, we're going to lose him."

Shivering with cold, Dustin hung up the phone and placed it back in his pocket, "Man, all these phone calls!

You'd think a guy could get a little peace and quiet all the way up here." He knew the helicopters would have a hard time tailing him above 10,000 feet and would run out of fuel before getting across the national forest, but now he realized this was to his disadvantage. The news helicopter had already turned back.

Another wave of dizziness swept behind his eyes. A terrific headache was starting in his forehead, and he knew he was beginning to build up dangerous fluids in his oxygen-starved brain.

The word of Dustin's mission spread from the Blackhawk helicopter to the K-MIN Radio police scanner and then like wildfire to other news stations. Meredith Windworth sat up in her bed breathing fast, but not in a panic. Nurse Abigail was still holding her, stopping every now and then to attend to her needs.

Several TVs in the hospice rooms could be heard broadcasting the story simultaneously. "We have now uncovered several new mysteries surrounding the sky traveler, Dustin Windworth. It has been confirmed that he is flying in a homemade lawn chair craft, not as a stunt or a dare, but as a love mission to see his mother in Canada who is now in a stage four cancer hospice ward in Thunder Bay. His father, who has been residing in Burlington, Minnesota, has not yet been reached for comment, however we have sources that have spoken with an uncle and aunt who have explained to us how he constructed the flying machine all of his own accord using materials, helium, and balloons from the family business, the Burlington Novelty Warehouse, which they own. An internet search tells us that this business has been online for only a day now and is receiving thousands of hits from all over the country."

Meredith, unable to speak or even smile, knew Dusty had set up that business using the computer she had purchased for him. She felt the pride well up inside, taking away some of the pain and giving her strength to stay awake, just like she recalled when Dustin was six and had pneumonia in the same hospital. That day she went thirty-six hours without sleep. Meredith determined to go one more sleepless round for her son.

The TV anchor continued, "A second mystery has just been solved as well. It appears a strange symbol has been artfully drawn on the bottom of his lawn chair. It looks like the symbol for infinity or the mathematical symbol for undefined, yet it also has a clearly drawn arrow snaking through it. It is most likely the Swedish symbol meaning: *You have to face setbacks to go forward.*"

Meredith glanced at Nurse Abigail and slowly lifted one hand with a thumbs-up.

22

The Face of Fear

Flight time: 1229 hours. The cell phone rang and rang without an answer. Another helicopter was coming in close for a rescue approach. Dustin awoke, startled by the crack of gunfire coming from the open door of the giant whining beast, its engines straining to slow the machine down enough for a few clear shots. The phone was ringing again, and as he held it in his numb fingers he saw the time and realized he'd been passed out for nearly an hour.

"Dustin ... is Captain D'Avion of the Canadian C— Guard. We can only ... more pass. You must ... prepared for extreme turbulence ahead. D— ... hear...? Tie yoursel— ...

"I can hear y— ... see the thunderclouds.—anks."

The mammoth twin-rotor flying tank banked sideways and turned away, the flapping sound of the rotors disappearing below him.

As Dustin's vision came into focus, he saw an enormous wall of cloud: a single, darkening mass that was slowly sucking his balloon cluster from the sunny blue sky into its vortex. Dustin was aware of the threat of thunderstorms forming this time of the year, especially as the weather approached Lake Superior, but he didn't think he would encounter one. The infamous storms of autumn on Superior that swallowed up ships were not to be trifled with, but neither was dancing inside a cloud so high he could see neither the top nor bottom.

Getting closer, he could view shafts of mist in the upper half, churning with fury as flashes of lightning began illuminating from deep within its heart. As fear set in, to his surprise, he was getting some gasps of good air that were helping him become more alert. The altimeter, still pegged at 12,500 feet, would go no farther. Suddenly he felt a jolt of movement from below like an invisible giant hand had slapped his chair; the turbulence was beginning.

Flight time: 1236 hours. Dustin took a sloppy drink of water and reached into the bag of pooper-troopers. He decided it was time to use Morty's messaging system. He got out the marker, pulled off the cap in his teeth and began to write on the yellow parachute: *"1236 hours: Going into a storm now. Still worth it!"* Tossing it over the side, he got out a second one: *"I love you, Mom! This is for all you did for me."* He tossed the second one over and grabbed a third: *"I love you, Dad. I already know you are a good man."* He wanted to write a few more to Morty or Asa, but the suction of the cloud and the jarring turbulence were picking up now. He could see the tiny paratroopers being drawn toward the white mass ahead of him as they floated down, and he had to be ready.

Dustin thought for a moment about using the mouse-nibbled fifty-year-old parachute he was sitting on, but then realized that the time to pull the cord should be only if he were indeed falling out of the sky, and that wasn't happening yet. He also knew from his research that a parachute trying to open in the swirling masses of air that lurked inside a thundercloud was most probably a fool's mission.

Looking up, he could see his giant collection of color begin to tilt ahead of him a bit, running toward the storm, all the many floating balls beginning to move about and bump into each other like a bunch of excited children on their way to the playground. He thought about the fishing line holding him to the balloons and tried to remember if Uncle Donny used fifteen or twenty-pound test for bass fishing. He hoped it was the twenty-pound test. Then he started to pray.

Uncle Donny and Aunt Myrtle sat on the couch leaning in, glued to the old console TV screen.

"This is the WMST weather for today. It's been an unusually warm Indian summer day here in northern Minnesota. There is the possibility of afternoon thunderstorms forming at our northern border which should be dissipated by Lake Superior winds as they move out towards Thunder Bay. We know as we report this that many of us are thinking about the well-being of Dustin Windworth on his amazing ride in the sky. The last reports were of him disappearing inside a storm cloud. To date, we know of very few people who have actually flown through a storm cloud unprotected from the elements, but we have Metrological Professor Dwight Wettonheimer on the line from Northern Minnesota University who can offer us some insight. Professor?"

"Good afternoon, Darla. The storm cloud we saw our balloon pilot fly into was actually the largest of its kind, called cumulonimbus, or 'king of clouds.' This massive storm cloud has a top reaching over 39,000 feet in the air, as estimated by experts. Although the lower part of the cloud is made up of water droplets, it rises so high in the air that the moisture in the upper regions is going to be in the form of ice crystals, which can form into hailstones. Hopefully our cumulonimbunaut is well-dressed for severe cold due to the average temperature ranging about forty degrees lower than surface temperatures. That means 65 degrees Fahrenheit on the ground will feel like 25 degrees at 20,000 feet. Basically, this cloud is like a giant mixing bowl of unstable air currents sending warm moisture from Lake Superior sweeping upwards at speeds exceeding 75 miles per hour. It is highly unpredictable, and can form into supercell storms creating lightning, tornadoes, hail, and all sorts of havoc."

The gnarly-haired professor leaned back in his desk chair and adjusted his heavy-rimmed glasses further up his flattened nose, snorting in a deep breath and pausing a moment before continuing. "Now, I'd love to tell you that I have good news for you all, but in this circumstance, I do not. We do have a small number of survivors of wild rides inside of thunderstorms, and I can share one of them with you. His name was Lieutenant Colonel William Rankin, who was forced to eject from his F8 Crusader jet at 47,000 feet during an engine failure, and within ten seconds he found himself entering a massive cumulonimbus thundercloud. Having pulled on his parachute, it finally opened inside the cloud after five minutes of freefall. He ended up cycling around inside the giant cloud, traveling at unknown speeds only to be spit out after forty minutes, bleeding from his eyes and ears from pressure changes, and pummeled by hail. In this boy's particular case, however, there is no history to go by. It has never been done before. A cloud of that size will be loaded with electrical charges as well, so we can only hope he will slip through without much harm, or—watch for a falling lawn chair, shorn of its birthday balloon flight system."

The camera flashed back on Darla, who sat frozen for a few long seconds with a look of horror in her eyes, not catching her first cue. "Okay, then ..." she replied after regaining her composure. "Thank you, professor, for your insightful analysis of the situation at hand."

Uncle Donny stared at the floor holding his peach soda. He started rocking back and forth again.

"Asa said they're holding an emergency prayer meeting over at the church," Myrtle whispered through her tears. "I think we ought to head over there, Donny."

The phone in Dustin's pocket signaled a new message. He quickly pulled it out and saw it appear on the screen for a few seconds before fading out. The number was labeled, Asa.

> ***Dusty, A verse for you:***
> ***The Lord is slow to get angry, but his power is great ...***
> ***He displays his power in the whirlwind and the storm.***
> ***The billowing clouds are the dust beneath his feet.***
> ***Nahum 1:3 NLT***

Dustin, I trust and pray you are safe in his storm because you're acting in love. Godspeed to you my brave friend.

As Dustin put away the phone and zipped up the pocket again on his vest, the colossal cloud swallowed him up. Backlighted mists began dancing mysteriously around him as if they were looking him over, deciding what to do with him. Within moments, the cloud turned darker, enveloping him in foggy shadows of grey and black. Then, without even a warning breeze, he felt himself falling downward at high speed into darkness, as if someone had just pushed him off a cliff.

"The stick says you're tall enough and you wanted to ride on this one, didn't you, Dusty?"

"Yes, but now I'm really scared. This is the biggest roller coaster that goes way up, Mom."

"That's true, but I've been on this ride already, so I can tell you that you're going to be okay. In fact, you might even find it rather thrilling. I know I do. But you've got to relax, let yourself go and know you're not alone. I'm right here with you."

23

Free Fall

Elise sat at the lunch table in the cafeteria of Thunder Bay Junior High School wondering how to eat her lunch. Her friends, Dustin's old friends, all sat around her joking, talking, and teasing, as usual, oblivious to what was happening to their old buddy. She couldn't risk telling them, though she wanted to. She just had to wait, and the waiting was beginning to drive her crazy.

"Elise, what is with you today, eh? You're like, way too serious," her BFF Willow said as she shot her a highbrow look. "Where's my endlessly positive, happy girl, huh?"

"I'm okay, mostly. I'm ah, just waiting to hear from Dusty. He's got something important to tell me, and I'm kind of worried about him. That's all."

"All that time with him kind of got to you, huh? Does this 'important' thing have anything to do with the fact that you told me you thought he'd gotten really cute and tall?"

Elise allowed a blush to hover in her cheeks and smirked ever so slightly. It didn't take away the worry and concern but talking about potential boyfriends certainly would do the trick to throw Willow off the trail of what was really happening.

"Maybe ..." Elise suggested back as she looked down at her phone. She had been following the story from a lower 50 news site.

"Did he just text you? Is he, like, texting you a lot?" Willow prodded.

"Oh—no ... Not as often as I'd like, I guess. I'm just doing a little research on weather patterns around T-B. Just wondering if our Indian summer will last or not."

Elise didn't think Willow was really buying it, but she didn't press any further. She wanted to just run out of the building and keep running westward until she got past the airport and out to the place he'd said he'd meet her. But she couldn't. It made no sense to make any moves yet, but she decided that when the time came, she was ready. For now, however, ugh! More waiting and hoping that she would see him alive again.

The wind sheers pulled Dustin down so fast his stomach felt as if it were choking off his windpipe somehow, which kept tightening, making it hard to breathe. Then just as suddenly, he leveled off for a few brief moments, buoyed from below by occasional upward gusts. From somewhere in the darkness, rain began pelting him, but not from above. The freezing droplets smacked at him sideways and then from below. All he could do was hold on and try to breathe but breathing soon became impossible as the rain in the air became the air itself, so full of moisture that every breath began to suffocate him.

He is in the whirlwind and the storm. Am I alone up here? Am I just a useless speck of dust on this planet ...? A speck of dust about to blow away and disappear?

The other voices returned.

"We're just standin' here waiting to see if you'll float away to where you came from," Harley's voice taunted. *"What do you think it would take, guys? Maybe five-or-so more balloons and a stiff breeze?"*

How ironic... Dustin mused. *It's like they already knew where I'd end up. How could they know that? Did they somehow have some great knowledge I don't have about life?*

He gripped the armrests of the chair though soaked gloves and considered their words again, and for a few more moments he searched for any truth in them.

After feeling as if he was rising a bit, and trying to hold his breath, Dustin began to see flashes of light flickering through the cloud. He knew it was lightning, but what it revealed was beyond what he could ever imagine.

Another downward surge grabbed him powerfully

and dropped his body so fast that he threw up, and as the flashes continued around him, he noticed the balloons were no longer above him at all, but instead leading the charge ahead of him, bumping and rushing past his chair and body, tangling in bunches around him. It dawned on him that either he was falling or being sucked, face down, toward the Earth somewhere below. The terror of the storm had met him, and he realized he was now a puppet to its any whim.

Asa's words returned, "... *It's the smallest bits that end up doing the most powerful things. What can one giant tree falling possibly do when compared to when one tiny atom splits!"*

"It's you, my friend. It is the mathematical symbol of infinity—for the undefined. It means your friends and enemies are trying to define you as one who is most apparently limitless. They just don't realize it!"

As Dustin approached the bottom of the cloud, solid light reappeared just in time to reveal his wild balloon gang being hijacked by an updraft of warm air, shearing upwards. Balloons, hundreds of them, hurriedly bumped past him, racing to the top of the cloud. He began to feel the jolting of the chair rising again, into the dark, angry mass above. Along the upward ride, amidst electric flashes, he began feeling tiny pinpricks on his face as the first legion of hailstones began pelting him.

"To be defined is to have limits, and to have limits is to be contained—and to be contained is to, in essence, be imprisoned, especially if one wishes for more."

"Your friends see it, your parents see it, I see it, and your enemies even confess it. Now the final question is will you embrace it yourself, and will you embrace it in others?"

Elise's voice piped in: *"You don't like the way they treat you, remember? So why would you want just to act like they want you to? Why? I'll tell you why. It's because you think you're a just a victim, like the stick in Corndog's mouth, just a plaything for their entertainment. You're letting them change you, aren't you? You're—not—a—victim, Dusty! Stop thinking the way they want you to!"*

Now Dustin began to hear himself speak. His own words came out in a small, horse, shaking voice, "No. No! Your words will not change me, I am *not* alone, and you *cannot* define me! I decide who I am. And up here, or down there on the ground, you—can't—touch—me—anymore!"

More painful smacking soon followed, assaulting him from every direction, popping balloons, bruising his shins and tearing at any exposed skin. Instinctively, he wrapped his arms around his face and neck as projectiles of all sizes smacked at his body and arms like baseballs out of a pitching machine. The hailstones were growing larger, smashing his head to one side as they exploded on his helmet. All he could do was howl in pain as he rose ever higher into the dark mass, jerking about like a marionette in the hands of a reckless toddler, before passing out in the thinning, high-altitude, freezing air.

"Walter, the issue is that it's not a matter of parental responsibility as much as it's about general upbringing, such as whether a kid is taught what's realistic and what's just movie magic. Obviously, this kid seems a little confused about safety and what happens if you fall from something higher than your rooftop," the TV news anchor argued.

"Well, Katie, my personal view is that this is an example of a child that didn't get enough healthy attention growing up, and now they've gotten themselves so into internet stunt videos to get online hits that we now have what we might call ego stunt extremists. This Dustin character is a prime example of where kids are going today."

"Walter, of course you may have already heard that a specific website was launched just in the last 24 hours by someone in the family connected to this stunt. It appears the site sells much of what is needed to make one of these dangerous flying apparatuses," she droned on. "I guess I just don't understand what a parent is thinking using their own son for a dangerous marketing ploy. I think it's downright disturbing!"

Flight time: 1251 hours. Dustin awoke with a loud smash to the side of his helmet. He wasn't sure if one of the gallon water jugs had just smacked him or a large hailstone. Either way, he was awake, soaked, cold, but breathing. He had gotten used to the constant extreme movements, the darkness, and the flashes of lightning, but the repeated bone-rattling vibrations of thunder unnerved him. The larger bursts jarred and shook his entire chair, making him worry it might come apart beneath him.

Dustin heard Asa's voice again, *"Sometimes we can't see the larger picture we're a part of, Dustin…a picture that doesn't belong only to you. We just have to wait, and trust things will work out."*

"Well, well, what do we have here?" Teddy's voice began. *"Ya goin' somewhere, Dust? Shouldn't you be on one of them yellow-colored busses? I thought school started for ya' already this year."*

"Dust, after years of wakin' up every day with that feelin' of guilt, trying to drink it off, joke it off, deny it, and nothin' workin', I've finally determined that I'm a lost cause at this

point. So ya know what I'm gonna do with what I've got left? I'm getting myself lost and seeing where that takes me. Crazy, huh?"

"No, Teddy! We're not lost! We're part of a bigger picture we can't see; that's all," Dustin croaked out of his bleeding lips before the cloud gripped him for one more ride, the one Dustin was going to enjoy—the one he was going to relish—the ride of his life!

The thundercloud sucked him back up into its upper lungs one more time. Dustin's ears and body were pressed in with rolling reverberations of deafening booms shaking his core, and he felt as if he were in the very center of the lungs of a giant mythical god, breathing with energy and power. As he neared the top, he noticed a tingling feeling all over his body. But this wasn't the kind you get from hours of feeling numb; it was an electric kind, borne out of the positive electrical current building inside the cloud, now enveloping his body. Light began flashing about him in an eerie, static glow and Dustin soon realized he was at the center of it.

He felt he was now outside his own body, no longer caring for himself at all, but happily thinking of all those he knew and loved, all the best of memories cycling through him like the winds in the cloud. The sick feeling was gone, and for some reason, the pain was suspended for now, and the only place he wanted to find himself was with family, friends, or in that coaster seat next to his mom one last time.

The final plunge literally took his breath away, but instead of fear for not having air, he just waited inside the darkness, spots forming before his eyes, until that moment when he could suck in real air and yell out a scream of thrill with all his voice had left.

Falling downward, so fast—so beyond ear-popping, and the falling wasn't stopping this time. Within a few moments, he began to sense light again. The phantoms of mist began to reappear, whizzing past him, kissing his face and body with their cool moisture. It was getting brighter and brighter, and he knew he was either going to exit the cloud or enter heaven itself.

24

A Second Escape

Flight time: 1320 hours. Dustin felt air fill his lungs again, clearing away the flashing spots inside his brain. He saw the clouds brighten and thin out and understood he was in a downdraft of colder air falling out of the cloud. He could clearly make out the shapes of the trees below him and glanced at his altimeter. The cracked glass face read 3,850 feet and was falling at an alarming rate. He looked up to see a much smaller cluster, with hundreds of shrunken or popped balloons hanging below the rest of the cluster. Countless pieces of fishing line from broken balloons were now slowly falling and resting all over his wet, bruised body, like a collapsing spider's web.

Looking towards the east, he could see the reward for his perilous flight on the horizon: Lake Superior. The buildings and suburbs of Thunder Bay created a light gray grid on the land ahead of him. He had made it over the national forest but was falling too quickly and would be on the ground long before Thunder Bay. He needed to jettison some weight, and fast.

Pulling up the plastic gallon jugs of water felt like a nearly impossible task. Every muscle in Dustin's bruised arms seemed to scream in complaint. He carefully unscrewed each cap and let the water drain out from all but one. However, the pummeled balloons above him kept bursting, giving up and falling all around him.

Checking the altimeter several times over the next few minutes he could see the needle slowing down some, but the chair was still falling too quickly. Descending to 3,300 feet, he could make out all the details on the ground below him, including the buildings of a town.

Getting closer, he strained his eyes and squinted to see whether he was near the airport or not. Even after slipping the smashed old goggles off his eyes, he could not seem to focus as well as he expected. He could make out what looked like a landing strip far in the distance, but it was not at all where he hoped it would be. While waiting, he decided to see if the phone still worked. It clicked to life, but the battery was at 15%, and a big red triangle on the screen warned that "roaming charges may apply." *This is it,* he thought to himself as he pressed the GPS locator app on the screen. *Let's see where this storm decided to spit me out.*

Dustin was surprised by what he saw. He was only 12 kilometers off his planned course but would end up on the south side of the Kaministiquia River instead of the north. "Well, at least I'm not going to run into planes at the airport," he croaked in a hoarse voice, "but probably too far for Elise to get me in time today."

His position was southwest of Thunder Bay, and what was worse, he was quickly approaching Rosslyn, a little suburb outside of town that was sure to spot him at this low altitude. He accepted the fact that there was nothing he could do but fly over it. It was too late to try to speed up his descent and try to land in the farm fields outside of it; he had already released too much ballast. He began to try to calculate whether the craft would reach the ground before flying out into Lake Superior because if he ended up landing miles out over the largest, coldest freshwater lake in the world, he was a dead man without help.

Aunt Myrtle and Uncle Donny were sitting in a small, white church up on a hill in the middle of a bean field, packed with locals for an emergency prayer meeting being led by Asa. Donny's phone began honking inside his pocket. He began fumbling for it, embarrassed at his noisy disruption, and now wishing he'd never asked Elise to set his ringer to Canadian goose honk while wondering why this never happened to anyone else.

"Donny!" Myrtle chided, "Don't you know to turn off your ringer on that thing before meetings?"

The phone got even louder with multiple geese now as he pulled it out and Myrtle began trying to grab it away from Donny in order to silence it. Their self-conscious panic soon turned into a miniature tug-o-war.

"I didn't even know you could turn it off!" Donny confessed in a screaming whisper as she got ahold of it, hung up, and shook her head at Donny in disgust.

As she stuffed it between one side of her ample rear-end and the church pew pad, it began making loud noises like that of an oversized bedspring being sprung. Donny just kept his face forward, his eyes darting over to her a moment with a knowing smirk, waiting for her to solve the problem. He leaned over and whispered, "That means I got a text. Maybe if you check it, it'll stop. You sound like you're breaking the pew, so hurry and give it to me!"

She quickly handed him the phone.

"It's Dusty!" Donny announced to the silent crowd. "Thank God! Oh, Yeah! *Woo-hoo*! He's still alive and flyin' over Slate River Valley right now! Asa, will you come with us?"

As Asa looked up to answer, he recognized the duck-lipped silhouette of Teddy, standing at the back of the church.

A well-smoked voice called out from the shadow in the doorway, "Preacher, got room for one more? I need to come with you all on this run!"

Flight Time: 1337 hours. Altitude: 2,800 feet. Dustin looked down at the subdivisions approaching below and could only hope that everyone stayed glued to their cell phones, big screen TVs, or dogs they were walking instead of looking up. It would only take one pair of eyes to rat him out to the media, or the RCMP, and his cover would get blown. The plan was to land north of the airport where there were only a handful of huge, mostly empty farm fields. One large cumulonimbus cloud, however, had changed all that for him.

He always wanted to live out in Rosslyn. Everybody had large lawns to play in, and there were lots of swimming pools in the neighborhood. He could see Markus Dalton's house with its rectangular pool and recalled Markus's 11th birthday swim party. It was now covered up for the cold, fall temperatures coming. His old friends were sitting in school buildings right now, utterly oblivious to what was happening, while he drifted silently above them. *How unreal this is*, he thought. He felt like a disembodied spirit floating above their little hamlet.

Dustin crossed above the rambling Kaministiquia River, Highway 130, and then passed over the Kaministiquia River again because of its rambling course, and, oddly, he crossed the Kaministiquia River a third time because of its snake-like, meandering nature.

Looking ahead, he could see he was heading into a more forested area; a perfect cover to make his landing. He was approaching the Loch Lomond Ski Area and pictured himself ditching the craft just beyond it, somewhere in the woods between the ski hill and the loch.

"Gotta say, this is my first road trip with a preacher," Teddy announced as they all piled into Aunt Myrtle's Buick. "Darkening a church door is hard enough after all these years, and now I'm sittin' right next to the reverend himself! It's makin' me a little jittery. You know, for some odd reason I'm findin' myself tryin' new things since I seen Dusty up there."

"Same here, Teddy," Uncle Donny agreed from the wheel. "Good thing you had that emergency travel bag, Asa. It was amazing how we're all packed and on our way in minutes; even Teddy showing up with his duffle in his hand. What'd you say to that?"

"I'd say someone's looking out for that boy besides us," Myrtle chimed in.

"I actually haven't been the preacher at the church in about six years, Teddy," Asa confessed as his eyes began to water at the potent cigarette odor coming from the passenger next to him.

"Yep," Teddy cautiously started. "I'd heard about your tragedy, and my deep respects to your late wife, Asa. I remember her bringing me and my ex, Laura, some delicious muffins the week my Andi was born. Funny how you remember that kinda stuff."

Asa just nodded silently, keeping a firm chin, trying not to get emotional.

Flight Time: 1348 hours. 1,800 feet. He knew he was going to be easy to spot now. Dustin began to drift over the Fort William Country Club, and unfortunately, the clouds had cleared. He could make out the tiny little golf carts moving about the greens and fairways directly below him.

Dang! Golfers have lots of time to look up at the sky and talk to people on cell phones, he thought.

Flight Time: 1350 hours. Before he even got to the far end of the course, Dustin could hear the wailing of RCMP sirens down below, and he knew it was him they were coming after. The chase began with two squad cars making their way down Feaver Road, catching up to his position in no time at all. The flashing lights reached the end of a paved cul-de-sac and then continued onto a two-track trail leading south just west of him. He rechecked the altimeter and saw he was beginning to fall at a faster rate due to more and more balloons failing from the battle in the clouds. He was at 1,100 feet and dropping like a papier-mâché rock as more balloons failed in the warming sunlight.

He tried doing some geometry in his head to figure the trajectory of his descent versus Loch Lomond, which lay before him. It appeared he would be landing somewhere just in front of the loch, which was a lot better than landing in the middle of the large, deep, sea-sized Lake Superior. However, this also left him landing into a nest of RCMP vehicles, which he could see were four in number now.

Dustin reached into the bag of pooper troopers again. If this was the way it was going to play out, he might have one more chance for escape.

Elise's Father heard her come in the front door after school.

"Hello, Elise. Can you come into the den here? There's something on the television you may want to know about."

Elise stared at the visuals flashing from one scene to the next of whom she knew to be Dustin, riding in a lawn chair in the sky. She crossed her arms and pursed her lips, anticipating the coming lecture.

"Elise, I know you may want to get involved in this. I realize he is your childhood friend, but I'm asking you to stay out of it and let the authorities take care of the situation. These are choices *he* has made, and as bright as he is mechanically, we need to keep in mind that he isn't always making good choices right now, and I want you to be safe."

Elise waited for more. There was usually more, but instead, he sat silent, pressing her to seal the deal with him. She knew he wouldn't understand. She decided to tell him anyway.

"Dad, I'm already involved. I was planning to help him get to the hospital, and I've already agreed to meet him there. I know that you may not understand why he did what he did, but I'm asking you just to trust me and let me be there for him."

"Elise, we already tried that, and it didn't go so well while you were there, now did it? Didn't you learn anything from that experience? He's adventurous, but not always reliable. You need to stay here."

"I'm sorry Dad, but I'm not staying here. It would be wrong for me to stay here. I'm his friend, and he is asking for my help. We help our friends, even if they aren't perfect. You can drive me, or I can get on my bike. Either way, it would really help if you'd please try to understand."

"You can ask your mother if she can take you when she gets home because I don't feel that it's right for me to take you. Either way, we need to do what's right."

"You know it will be too late by then. Why won't you help me? Have I ever given you a reason to doubt me? I think I've given you lots of reasons to trust me, and this is one time I need you to, even if it doesn't make any sense. Time is running out, Dad, and I don't want to miss what's really important in life, and I don't think you do either."

Mr. Cambry sat silent and thought for a long moment. Elise left the room and waited on the living room couch hoping and trying not to cry. Before long she heard the familiar sound of keys jingling. Popping his head around the corner, he motioned her toward the front door.

Flight Time: 1412 hours. Dustin could make out the equipment on the dashboards of the police vehicles through the windshields. Some of the RCMP officers were peeking out the windows of their vehicles as they made their way down the rough trail toward the Loch. The altimeter read only 250 feet, and he could see the needle moving on the dial. He was only twice as high as the tallest trees, and the sirens were loud in his ears.

By now, Dustin could not remember the exact weight

of the rubber chickens inside the three mail sacks still tied closed and hanging from the arms of the lawn chair. He guessed they might weigh about half as much as his body weight; probably enough to get him over the Loch. He already had three pooper troopers in his hand with messages on the parachutes.

Trooper number one carried the message: *RCMP, Sorry for the surprise drop. I mean no harm.*

Trooper number two read: *RCMP, I'm really not "chicken" to keep flying!*

Trooper number three carried the message: *RCMP, If something happens to me, take me to T B Hospital and contact Meredith Windworth (mom), or my U. Donny Windworth, Burlington, MN.*

He released all three, causing one of the vehicles below to stop alongside the dirt path. Two officers jumped out of the car and ran after each one.

"You'll soon know what I'm talking about," Dustin mumbled under his breath as he loosened the ties on the bags. They were nearing the Loch. Dustin knew that he probably needed to dump them all to get clear over Loch Lomond, beyond which lay one more stretch of land, wide enough, he hoped, to get to the ground before reaching Lake Superior. It was a gamble, he knew that, but he could see there was no way the RCMP cars could go around the loch. The lake was surrounded by rough, tree-covered land with no trails to chase him. Getting across the loch meant freedom again; a chance to finish the mission. Landing in Lake Superior, however, would be a disaster.

Flight Time: 1420 hours. 45 feet. The police vehicles were parked ahead of him, light bars flashing silently at the shore of the enormous loch. As he approached, an RCMP held a megaphone up to his face.

"Dustin Windworth, if you have means to land you need to do so now. If you have a rope, throw it down, and we can secure it to the squad car to keep you out of the loch. Please do all you can to cooperate for your own safety."

Dustin was unable to answer. He had no voice loud enough to do so. He thought about the 50 feet of rope he had with him. He could drop it, they could catch it, and this whole crazy flight would be over. He was exhausted, his eyes and ears felt like millions of tiny needles had poked them, and his body ached, but somehow he had to push all that pain aside; his body was ready to deny giving in just a little longer.

He began trying to signal them to clear out of the way, but they just looked up bewildered.

"Hey, the kid looks like he's trying to flap his own wings or something. I wonder if he lost a few marbles up ... Look out! He's dropping something on us!" one officer yelled, scrambling to this car for cover.

"Bombs away!" Dustin managed to screech out of a

dry throat. He released one load of rubber chickens as he approached the squad cars to see how much lift he could get. After a few seconds, he could see it wasn't enough; his craft was still descending. He pulled open the other two mail sacks and emptied them both on the patrol cars below, a sudden downpour of rubber chickens from the sky began smacking the ground, the cars, and nearby shoreline.

"This cannot be happening!" officer Sedgwick muttered as he picked up his microphone, smacking noises hitting the hood and windshield. "This is Officer Sedgwick. The flying suspect just released a bunch of ..."

"A flock, sir," a trainee officer sitting next to him suggested.

"...a *flock* of rubber chickens onto our vehicles and is proceeding with his flight over Loch Lomond."

"Roger that. Can you repeat? Did you say rubber chickens?" the dispatcher asked. "If they are *rubber* chickens, why can I hear them squawking through the speaker?"

"That's right ... Rubber chickens are raining down on our cars, and I guess they have squeakers in them ... maybe they're the deluxe kind of rubber chickens."

"Extra-deluxe, I'd say ..." the assistant murmured aloud, bringing on a look of disdain from the captain.

"No, I don't know how many, maybe hundreds! All I can say is it's a lot of chickens. Does that matter for the report? Please dispatch a helicopter to continue the pursuit."

Officer Sedgwick turned to the trainee next to him. "You can't call a bunch of rubber chickens a flock. Only real birds can be in a flock. These are not real, so I'm going to let you figure out what word to use for the report."

"That's what I'm talking about!" Dustin croaked as his dying balloon bird slowly began to rise in the air one last time.

He waved at the officers as he floated out over Loch Lomond. He was gaining quite a bit of height and was pleased with his plan. He decided it was time to update Elise on his current position.

Elise, I am OK but missed landing target!
Hope to land at Lake S shoreline near Pie Island.
Don't come for me. Cops follow me now.
Go to hospital. Find my mom. I will see you there.

Elise replied:
Dusty, I'm so worried about you. Please be careful!
I will do all I can to get to the hospital! Just land safely!

Flight Time:1438 hours. 380 feet. Dustin looked to the northwest. He could clearly see the buildings of Thunder

Bay and at this point, he wished he could just land over there. His body felt utterly spent, and his legs were beginning to cramp from dehydration. His new concern was his altitude. He was continuing to rise and had not leveled off yet. Dropping the rubber chickens worked a bit too well, and the breeze blowing from the northwest was pushing him along too fast, moving him toward the great sea-sized, dark lake. He could see the ideal place he needed to land pass below him and the shoreline of Lake Superior quickly approaching. He was still way too high in the air.

He looked off into the Lake, beyond the shoreline, out into the darker depths. He recognized the rocky upthrust of Pie Island. Perhaps he could make it over the water between them, but he no longer had any control of his craft. He had released all the extra weight except one jug of water. He began to wonder if he should have used the rope when the officers suggested he do so. He continued to workshop a quick solution in his head. *What if I dropped the 50-foot rope, climb down it, and drop into the water from there?* 350 feet was way too short to open a parachute but dropping himself into water from 300 feet would probably kill him too. Besides, he knew he did not have the strength to climb down the rope.

Teddy leaned his head forward into the front seats of the Buick. “Hey Don, can we pull over for a Slim-Jim before we hit the big woods? I quit smoking, and I’m getting a bad case of the shakes here and need a fix.”

“Hey, I love Slim-Jims on a trip! Sure, Sure, Teddy. I’ll look for a gas station. We need to fill up soon anyway, and we can load up on some road fodder,” Donny replied.

“Don loves any kind of non-health food on the road,” Myrtle added with an eye roll.

Donny leaned over and patted her on the knee. “Ya know it keeps me going, Aunty. I can drive all night if I’ve got me a food stash in the car. So, Teddy, when did you quit smokin’?”

“When I got in this car.”

“Mertie, you gotta quit watching all those video news feeds. You’re gonna use up all our data minutes!”

“Donny, I don’t care about silly data minutes or phone bills today! Do you know Dusty just started flying over Lake Superior? He wasn’t able to land. Oh, Lord! Well, maybe they can throw him a life preserver when he finally comes down. I just hope it’s before dark.”

The car got suddenly quiet.

25

Hanging in the Balance

Flight Time: 1455 hours. 320 feet. Dustin could hear the flapping of another helicopter in the distance. Thoughts of the old parachute beneath him returned, but realizing he was way too close to the ground for it to open in time, he abandoned the idea. Lake Superior lay before him, and the winds briskly pushed him beyond the shoreline, out over the crystal clear, cold waters of the deep. The view was beautiful and the air, fresh. The sun was beginning to sink in the sky, enhancing sparkle on the moving waters below, but the shoreline winds picked up, straining and picking off more of what was left of the balloons. Dustin's new hope was to land on Pie Island, a giant rock plateau surrounded by sheer rock cliffs rising out of the water. He knew at this point, if he landed out on the island, he wouldn't be sneaking back to the hospital. He would be going back in style to wherever "they" decided to take him, but it was all about getting down now ... just getting down.

As the island loomed closer, the winds picked up, rocking the lawn chair and cooling his body. Dustin stared at the rock cliffs and wondered if he had enough height to get over them and up onto the island. It was time to use up a little more data. He quickly opened the phone, battery 12%. “Yep, me too,” he whispered. After typing in “Pie Island, Lake Superior,” he couldn’t believe his eyes. The sheer rock cliffs rose over 800 feet above the waterline. The lake breezes were cooling his balloons and killing his altitude. He was going to hit the wall.

He couldn’t tell how fast he was moving. He stared at the rock wall swelling in size as he approached, rising out of the deep, dark, cold waters of the lake, coming toward him. As he gazed down into the water, it became apparent he was moving rather quickly, faster than he would on a bicycle. He had not designed a flying machine to land by smashing into a rock wall. This was not the plan at all!

A second helicopter approached, but Dustin just ignored it as he clicked on the screen and checked the GPS app on the phone for his speed and position: the lake breezes were moving him along at a brisk 27 miles an hour, 43 kilometers of speed. Dustin tried to gauge what the damages might be and how to minimize them. *That’s about as fast as you go on a bicycle on the biggest hill in town.* He imagined hitting a parked car at that speed. *What would that be like? No, a car would dent and break his impact. Oh, crap! I’m going to hit solid rock.* He felt his heart go into overdrive as he saw the breakers at the base of the cliff throwing sprays of water high into the air. The two helicopters took a position on each side of him, sliding doors open and cameras rolling. He loosened the seat belt and shimmied sideways to pull the parachute pack from under his butt.

“This is a TB News 13 live update on the lawn chair balloon boy. Right now, we are observing Dustin trying to pull out something from underneath himself. It looks like a large bundle of some kind, maybe a pillow? Our pilot says it looks like an old parachute. We are hoping he doesn’t attempt to jump as there is not enough space for the chute to open. Wait ... It appears he is going to use it as a cushion to mitigate his potential impact with the approaching cliff ...” the wall-mounted TV warned.

Meredith looked on with horror in her eyes, and Abigail offered to turn it off. Meredith did her best to shake her head “no” to keep watching. Abigail sat back down next to her, and they both held on to each other as if they were in the lawn chair themselves.

Dustin rehearsed the impact in his mind in several different ways, and from several different angles. He realized the most important thing to protect would be his head, even with the helmet on. The force of his neck snapping, or head smashing on the rock, may put him out for good, and he had to do whatever he could to reduce that impact.

Flight time: 1507 hours. 300 feet. A solid wall of crumbling aggregate rushed towards Dustin and filled his entire view. He studied the brown, gray, and gold streaks of color decorating the cliff walls like a giant painting illuminated beautifully by the setting sun. His eyes focused on a tiny rug of grass the size of a dinner plate, growing on a miniature outcropping, filled with late summer wildflowers, hundreds of feet above the water, only yards away from him. They happily danced and waved for him in the wind, oblivious of his plight. For a moment he thought about the beauty of it, maybe the last beauty he may ever see. He said a final prayer of thanks that he'd gotten so far, so close, as well as a plea to make it through this, too. He thought of all those he knew and loved, and as his chair spun around one last time, Dustin raised the parachute pack to his head to brace for impact.

"Oh, my Lord, my Lord!" protested Aunt Myrtle as she stared at Donny's smartphone screen in the car.

"What? What is it? What's going on?" Donny begged, keeping both hands on the wheel.

Tears began rolling down Myrtle's cheeks as she passed the phone back to Asa and Teddy in the back. She couldn't speak and put her hand to her mouth and looked out the window in silence, attempting to hold back a sob.

"Donny, he crashed into the high cliff face on Pie Island," Asa reported somberly. Myrtle's anguish began to get to him, but he fought the emotion back down, that is until Teddy piped up.

"All this stuff happening to Dustin, and I can't help but think of all I've lost, too."

Teddy turned and faced Asa with earnest hope in his eyes. "Preacher, you ever hear of a divorced guy actually winnin' back his ex before?"

Asa paused, holding back his own impending tears, then smiled and nodded. "Yes. I think it happens more than we know, and it's a brave and noble quest for any man to try."

"Preacher, it ain't your fault, you know ...losing her in that fire. I hope you don't blame yourself. You know what I'm known for, and I'm putting that behind me, too."

"Teddy, it's true. I've never really accepted what happened to my wife, and I've never been willing to forgive myself or accept that it happened to her. I have to admit that I've been angry with God about it. Imagine, the preacher being fuming mad at God. But you know what?"

"What, Preacher?"

"It's been too many years wasted waiting for a resolution to it all. I can see that now. It's not about me, it's about the glory; the bigger stories we're all a part of. It's about the glory we all have buried within to do great things—mighty things—brave things—truly beautiful things. It's imprinted but lost most of the time, and we all long for it, to see it, watch it unfold in others and experience it in ourselves. Dustin's found it and he's living it this very moment."

Asa turned and looked directly at Teddy; his eyes red with emotion. "It's okay for us to move on and do *all* the things we were made to do. It's okay, and it's time for action, isn't it? ... Life is going by too quickly to waste it."

"Yep, Preacher, I believe it's time to start living again, while we still got game."

Flight time: 1508 hours. 320 feet. Dustin heard the snapping of aluminum as he hit. The parachute pack he held against his helmet bounced off the rock face and fell out of his grasp, plummeting down and glancing off several rocks before splashing into the water below. Upon impact, he felt his right side and leg jerk downward, hanging over the chair. Sudden searing hot pain and ringing in his right ear followed, letting him know his helmet combined with the parachute pad idea worked, but barely so. After gathering his wits, he could see he was pinned to the wall, about 80 feet above a mess of huge boulders, below which were steep, rock-strewn slopes leading down to three-foot waves breaking over dumpster-sized chunks of stone. His chair had broken, and to keep his body from falling through the side of it, he had to place all his weight on his left elbow against the armrest. His right shoulder had taken most of the impact and was raging with pain. Something was broken, of that, there was no doubt.

As Dustin reached for the rope with his good arm, he felt the chair begin scraping along the cliff wall, occasionally catching on a chunk of protruding rock, spinning him around. He worked as quickly as possible to wrap the rope around and around the broken pieces, mending them as best he could amidst the burning shoulder pain, his body entwined in layers of spider-like fishing line, his vision a blurry haze. The wind below was pushing him upward as well as dragging the craft along the cliff to the east, smashing and bloodying his knuckles between aluminum and rock.

He had been meticulous and patient up until this

point. Dustin had accepted each of his circumstances thus far, and he was truly grateful to still be conscious, but this was just too much, and he felt himself beginning to feel anger rising inside him. He had tried his best. He had tried to plan carefully for as many possibilities as he could imagine, but this was over the top.

"I'm part of what larger story? A part of *who's* larger story? The one they want on the news for entertainment?" Angry curses, foul words of rage, expletives he'd never whispered before began streaming out as Dustin struggled to stay upright and hold the chair together, all while two helicopters hovered in the distance, watching his personal spectacle unfold.

"Katie, new information on Dustin Windworth has come in regarding his motives in attempting to fly a lawn chair 250 miles to Canada. Other news sources have quoted him as saying he was on some sort of mission to see his dying mother. Apparently, he really does have a mother in the hospital located in the city he has recently been spotted near. We have yet to verify this part of the story, but I am thinking now that it may be possible he did some of what he did with good intentions, at least in part. Katie, what's your take on this?"

"Walter, all I can say is, this kid, for whatever reason, hasn't given up on himself, and it makes me pause and think about how the reasons we do things can sometimes enable us to go farther than we believe we are capable of going, especially when we are doing something out of concern for someone else. I'm thinking that if these feeds we are getting about the dying mom are true, quite possibly this boy may be a hero of sorts trying to do what he is."

"Well Katie, hero or zero, we will eventually all find out, as he can't manage to stay aloft too much longer. We can see he is now pinned to the side of a cliff, and we are watching those balloons giving out one by one."

Flight Time: 1533 hours. 200 feet. Dustin was spent. Finishing off the last of his final gallon of water using his good hand, he promptly apologized to the Spirit that kept him safe through the storm in solemn, squeaky, dry tones. A quick check of the phone revealed that it was finally dead. *Well, no more harassing callers, for now,* he thought. It was getting hard just to think. He only wanted to sleep now, up in his chair, holding the rope that kept the chair from falling apart in his left hand. He took the mic off his helmet, leaned back and closed his eyes as the wind whistled around him. The muted flapping of the two news choppers began to lull him to sleep.

Dustin's napping was cut short as the sound of a third rotor flapping filled the ear that wasn't ringing. It was louder than the others, coming from a much larger machine that was heading straight for him as if it were coming in to attack. The red chopper flew at high speed between the two news choppers and then rose upward just as it reached the cliff, climbing over the top of the balloon cluster and disappearing. He knew it wouldn't be much longer now.

Tate Anderson had been waiting for a challenge like this his whole life. Growing up in a rock-climbing family had its benefits when working on a SAR (Search and Rescue) team, but this delicate procedure was going to call for all the skills he could muster. Pilot Dud Boyd banked the Canadian Coast Guard Bell 212 helicopter to the south, correcting his course directly toward Pie Island ahead of him. Flight mechanic Deborah Fox worked quickly to set up equipment behind them. Captain Boyd raced between the two hovering news choppers, ascended upward over the cliff, which was working with the wind to ensnare the young balloonist. Boyd promptly made a deliberate landing on the rocky surface above.

"This is Captain Boyd to SAR Coordinator. Our target is identified, and we have secured a landing area at the peak of Le Pate Plateau on the Pie, over."

The captain turned to Tate, "Hey, Rocky. Since you and Bullwinkle are going to have to rappel down, how about I send you a line on a winch to make it easy on you for the uphill climb?" the captain suggested.

"I'm the only one hanging on a wire today," Tate replied. "Fox is going to be my belay, and while we have the line out how about you just lower me and my basket down on my harness? I'll signal you when it's time to hit the brakes."

Dustin felt the first few pebbles hit his helmet and knew someone was coming down for him, but the strength to move escaped him now. He seemed to only blink a few seconds, and suddenly a voice was directly above him, emerging from somewhere inside the dying balloon cluster.

"Dustin, I'm Tate, and we're going to get you out of here. If you can hear me, nod your head or wave with your good arm."

At this point, waving was easier than nodding in a helmet.

"Alright, Dustin ... great! You've had quite a ride, so what do you say we help you with that last bit to get you on the ground? First of all, tell me where it hurts right now, then I'll tell you my plan ..." Tate continued talking as he dangled from a cable like Spider-Man. He was worried about Dustin falling into shock and tried not to look alarmed by his appearance. Small dried lines of blood ran down Dustin's face from his eyes and nose, as well as his left ear. His skin was a pale white-gray, and if anyone could guess his age, it didn't say teen right now.

"TB News 13, Okay, okay. I believe the EMT we are viewing out there is Tate Anderson with a Canadian Coast Guard SAR team and he is going to try to get Dustin into the life basket, but how? It definitely appears he has a broken arm or shoulder, but he does appear somewhat responsive, as we can see him talking with Anderson. He has now moved the life basket directly beside the lawn chair and is fastening the basket to the chair."

Flight time: 1601 hours. 180 feet. Tate looked down for a moment and thought about what he had to do. He wasn't sure how he was going to get Dustin safely into the life basket. They were still about 100 feet above a rocky slope, and the kid didn't have the strength left to lift his body into it. He tried getting a harness around him, but to do so meant releasing him from his seat belt, and judging from what was left of the chair, it seemed foolish at best to try that route.

"Tate here. We've got a situation with the chair he is in. It seems to be collapsing from the impact, and to do this safely we're going to need SARC to call in another team to assist ASAP. Also, the wind is really picking up along here, over?"

"Tate, we copy. We will call for a second team, however, we have a civilian on the line who says he can advise on the situation, and we're patching him in now. He says he has experience with rides like this one. He knows the victim personally and wants to confer. Patching in now ..."

"Dustin, can you hear me?" A unique, familiar whistle signal came out loud and clear over Tate's radio. "It's old Teddy! Listen to me. I need you to hang on because there are a lot of people wanting you back safe, including your mother, and maybe that blond you rode with on the Ferris wheel, too."

Dustin's eyes opened back up to the sound of that trademark whistle and voice he knew so well, "Hey Teddy, where are you?"

"Don't worry about me, Dusty. Listen, Tate, you gotta put the chair into the basket, and then tie him in. Do ya hear me, sir? Dump the whole chair into the basket!"

"Yeah, I copy you. Chair into basket. Wow, I guess you do have experience with rides like this! Foxy, drop me down a pair of tin snips, I'm doing some surgery on this lawn chair. We're going to have to amputate all its legs to complete this mission, over."

"Don't worry, Dustin. Everything on *you* is staying on and going to get fixed real soon."

Dustin slowly reached over with his bloody left hand toward the cliff face. He grasped a small handful of flowers as tightly as he could, yanked them out, stuffed them into his fishing vest, and fell asleep.

26

A Disappearing Act

As soon as the televised rescue was complete, Meredith's eyes closed in exhaustion, her head down on the pillow. Her slender fingers began slipping out of the man's hand in the bed next to her, and her heartbeat monitor began to slow to dangerous levels. Abigail had seen it before. She was failing. It was getting close to the end for her now, and the nurse knew there might be only one more wake up for her. She whispered to the man next to her where she was going and left the room.

Flight time: 1712 hours.

"This is Captain Boyd to SARC. The egg is in the basket, and we are headed for Thunder Bay Hospital. Please alert the helipad EMT for assistance, over."

"Roger, Boyd, we copy you. We have been advised by

RCMP that you are to drop suspect at RCMP regional center downtown for booking. Suspect is to be placed under arrest for flying in foreign airspace without consent or licensure, over."

"Copy that message, please forward to advising RCMP officer that this *suspect* is in need of urgent medical attention and I will be following my original plan to fly him to Thunder Bay Hospital, over."

"Copy that, and give our proud regards to Dustin from SARC for us, over."

"Roger, copy that. Cap out." The captain banked the helicopter toward the medical center, followed by the two news choppers.

Abigail headed down to the emergency wing, grabbing an empty wheelchair as she walked into the pre-treatment area. Speed-walking as fast as her feet would go without looking like an all-out run, she considered whether she had enough time to go through all the channels and red-tape of permissions. Reading tags outside each partition, the nurse easily found him lying on a gurney behind a curtain being guarded by an RCMP officer. She knew just how short her time was and wasn't going to let his epic act of kindness go to waste. She skimmed over his chart to quickly assess his condition.

"Hello, Dustin. What took you so long to get here?" Abigail sucked in her breath and swallowed, hiding her shock at how bad he looked. "Your mom really wants to see you! She knows all about what happened to you."

"Are you Nurse Abigail?"

"You guessed correctly," she said as she peeked behind the curtain to be sure the officer wasn't listening. Two other nurses were chatting at a nearby desk about the incident while watching news commentary on the wall-mounted flat screen. For the moment their backs were still turned.

Abigail leaned in and whispered, "Dustin, how are you feeling, really? I know they were prepping you for surgery, but they decided against it, and you need to know there isn't much time left now. I see you broke your collarbone, but they've already wrapped you up. Are you strong enough for this?"

"I need to see her!"

"You're going to get in this wheelchair and act sleepy with your head down. It'll work. People usually just glance at wheelchairs; they never stare. I'm going to get you there and give you exactly five minutes. Then I'm going to rat you out. Otherwise, I lose my job for sure. Once you're in her room, who knows? They may let you stay, or they may take you away. Be prepared for that."

She helped him off the bed and into the wheelchair and attached his I.V. bag to a hook on the chair. He was weak, and she knew it, but she trusted in his judgment.

“Wait, Abigail!” He croaked as she began pushing him toward the partition curtain. “I can’t leave without my fishing vest ... important stuff in there!”

She grabbed the vest without question and stuffed it in a storage pocket behind the seat. “Time for more X-rays,” she calmly declared as she scooted him past the RCMP officer. Abigail waved toward the reception desk and grinned as she wheeled Dustin toward the hallway.

“Your mother and I followed your whole journey on TV! Your big sky adventure wore her all out, so we are hoping to wake her up. You know, she’s going to look different from when you saw her over six months ago. Be ready for that, okay?”

“How?”

“Well, your mom originally wanted you to remember her the way she was, and she felt terrible about how things were with your dad, but she’s changed. Now she doesn’t care about anything except seeing you one more time. Just know, it’s still her.”

As she wheeled him down each hallway, she purposefully stayed on the wrong side, pushing into oncoming traffic, so no one got a good chance to look at him. She began to see more and more media people with cameras or tablets milling about, asking questions, or doing live reports.

Abigail grabbed a fresh blanket off a maid service cart and tossed it over his head.

"Dusty, keep your head down, like some old person on their way to the nursing home. At this point, we need to keep that head of yours covered."

She was about to ask him about the silver streaks of hair that ran down from the top of his head, but stopped short, realizing they were probably the result of the trauma from his sky voyage. It was then that Abigail fully realized what Dustin had really been through.

They reached the hospice wing and got into the elevator. Two reporters got in with them, eyeing the covered wheelchair passenger with mild suspicion.

A female wearing a PRESS badge turned to Abigail. "Did you hear they're all here in the same hospital? That's the word. I'd love to find the way in to get that reunion shot on camera, especially since we flew all the way from his hometown. What an amazing story!"

Dustin recognized the voice. It was the voice that first interviewed him up in the sky. He had seconds to decide whether to reveal his identity to her or not. Would she blow his cover, or would she help him reach his goal? He decided to trust her, but just in case, he'd play the invalid role a little longer.

"Darrla?" Dustin mumbled from under the blanket. He tried to sound as much like a dying old man as possible.

Abigail smiled at the two reporters. "He's suffering from dementia ... Near the end, you know. We're taking him up to the ..."

"Did he just say Darla?" the reporter asked aloud, turning to her partner. "Gurdeep, I think he just said my name!"

"Darrlaa Darrling ..." Dustin mumbled again as the elevator stopped.

Gurdeep pressed the hold button to keep the door closed for a moment.

"Dustin," Darla questioned, "is that you under the blanket? May we have a peek and talk for a moment?"

Abigail had a look of horror in her eyes as Dustin revealed himself. He took a good look at his new personal press crew. Darla was a bit shorter than on TV and her eyes, framed by a soft face and bobbed brown hair, looked even bigger in real life. He looked up at Gurdeep, whom he had never seen before. He stood in a dark tweed sports coat, towering over all of them, his head covered in a magnificent bright yellow turban, sporting a full beard framing a big smile.

"Is Canary really your last name?" Dustin squeaked out in exhaustion.

"No. It is my pseudonym, or 'on-air name' that I use in my traffic reporter profession. My real last name is Singh. I chose to use the last name, Canary, because they were the birds that sang happy songs in the mines to let the miners know the air was okay to do their work. If they ever stopped singing, it was a warning sign of danger.

Dustin looked up at the nurse. "Don't worry, Abigail.

I know these guys, and I think they can help us. Besides, it may help clear up questions people have. I only ask that you don't do any video, okay? Out of respect for my mom ..."

"Agreed," Darla stated. "Now, how can we help make this happen?"

"Well," Abigail started, "this kid has a broken clavicle that may still need surgery. He's recovering from exposure, exhaustion, mild shock, and his mom may only have a few more hours to live, at best. There is a warrant out for his arrest, every news team is trying to get access to him, hospital security is raised to high level, and his mother's whole wing is being guarded. By the way, I'm Abigail, his mother's nurse. I'm not supposed to be here either."

"Okay then," Gurdeep began. "As usual, I will be the expendable crewman on this mission. How about I create a terrific diversion to get as many of the security guards distracted as possible, then you guys go in for the sneak pass when I give you the signal?"

"Sounds good, Gurdeep. What's the signal?" asked Darla.

"You'll hear me screaming or singing from the other end of the hallway near the stairwell. Just don't ask any questions later about any weird stuff I do or say before the signal. I can't be held accountable for that."

"Gurdeep," Dustin whispered out into the elevator, "You're a brave man."

"Dustin, I'm just doing for you what needs to be done today. Besides, you haven't heard me sing yet," Gurdeep said with a grin. His tone stayed calm but got more serious. "Okay, I'm going to hit the 'open' button. Stay inside against the back wall until you hear me shout, 'go.'"

The elevator door opened on Meredith's floor. All appeared calm except a few reporters lining the walls outside the room along with several security guards. One stood by Meredith's door, one at the end of the hallway, and another at the nurse's desk. Gurdeep closed his eyes for a moment, took a deep breath, removed the press tag from the lanyard around his neck, and pranced into the hallway like a trained ballerina.

"Gentlemen," Gerdeep shouted down the hallway, "Mary Kay Ash once said that, 'aerodynamically, the bumble bee shouldn't be able to fly, but the bumble bee doesn't know it, so it goes on flying anyway!'" he declared at the top of his voice as he pranced down the hall toward Meredith's room.

"Do you believe I can fly?" he asked a security guard as he danced past him, grabbing the hat off the guard's head and skipping toward the second guard, collecting his hat as well.

"Look, I've got wings now!" Gerdeep declared while flapping both of his arms with the security guard hats. "It's time to go through the window and fly away *free*. Who's coming with me?" he asked, dancing his way toward the windows at the end of the hallway.

The guards were already running after him as the remaining press reporters followed, hoping for a good picture for a crazy story they could sell.

Just as Gurdeep reached the window and began climbing onto the sill, he was tackled by two of the three security guards. "No! Let me *go*! I want to *go* fly! I want to *go* sail across the blue, blue sky! Ouch! That kind of hurts! Hey buddy, you should try out that hold on yourself before doing it to someone else ..."

Nurse Abigail's heart was pounding in her chest. Dustin stayed under the blanket in calm anticipation. He was just about to see his mom again—just about to reach his goal.

27

Reunion

Abigail bolted out of the elevator, pushing the wheelchair toward Meredith's unguarded doorway. Another nurse from the floor reception desk recognized Abigail and signaled that she knew what she was up to by giving a hearty thumbs-up. Abigail signaled back by tipping her head to the side toward the door she needed open. The desk nurse ran over, opened the door, and in a moment all three were inside, the door closing behind them.

"Well, this wasn't exactly my plan, but then my plan probably would have never worked anyway," Abigail confessed. "So, let's wake her up now, Dustin."

"Abigail, do you have Dusty with you?" A deep voice questioned from behind a partition curtain next to the door.

Dustin used what little strength he had left to stand up. He recognized the voice.

"Dad? Are you in here with Mom?"

Abigail pulled back the curtain. Dustin just stared for a few moments trying to understand it all in the silence of the room.

Everyone could hear the voice of Gurdeep out in the hall whining, yelling, and carrying on, along with the scuttle of many feet trying to drag him down to the elevator.

Except for the heart monitor beeping painfully slow, everything fell silent. Darla stood in the corner near the door with Abigail, careful to not interfere with what was about to happen.

Dave's eyes just stared into Dustin's for a long while, tears beginning to stream down. He was sitting up in his own hospital bed next to bale, emaciated woman who slept peacefully next to him. Dave's arm was plugged into an IV tube, his head wrapped in a large gauze bandage, bruises on both cheeks swelling his eyes partly closed. He sat up in a fixed position, a body cast around his rib cage.

"Dusty, I can't ..." Dave started but had to stop for a moment. "I can't tell you how happy I am that you made it," he said before beginning the work of holding back a sob to regain his composure. "You made it, Dusty, and I'm so proud!"

Dustin walked over, pain still searing his broken clavicle, and reached for him with his good arm for a hug. Dave was equally shocked at the sight of his own son. He stood with dark circles under bloodshot eyes, silvery spikes of hair sticking up from his head. He glowed with calm confidence.

"Dad, what happened?"

"Don't concern yourself with me right now, Dusty. She's still with us. We need to wake her. I'll be fine. We can catch up in a bit."

His father's eyes moved to the frail woman in the bed next to him.

Nurse Abigail stepped toward Meredith's bed. Darla stood silent; her own eyes wet with tears.

Dustin turned to face her and reached out to touch her hairless head. Bandages covered most of her lower face, her mouth, neck, and upper shoulders. A tube protruded from under her nose where her mouth should be. It did not appear she had a chin anymore, just a neck that reached up to her nose. It confused Dustin for a moment. Tubes were stuck into her arms, her wrists, and came out from under the sheets. Her skin was a pale grayish yellow, so different from the tanned summer face he always remembered. But he knew it was her because of her eyes. They looked the same as they always did when she was napping, like a sleeping Ojibwe princess. Yes, it was her, his beautiful, kind, sweet mother, and he had made it to say goodbye.

"Yes, ma'am, I understand, but Mrs. Windworth is my old neighbor, and I am expected by her son, Dustin," Elise reasoned with the desk nurse.

"I'm really sorry, but in this particular case, there is absolutely no one allowed but family or clergy. I'm just following orders. Again, I'm sorry. You can wait to see family in the waiting area, but that's the best we can do for you."

Elise wondered if her dad's advice to let him come in with her was really what she should have done, but she had insisted on going in on her own.

"Excuse me nurse, but we *are* family, and this girl is coming with us!" called a familiar voice beside her. "I am Donald Windworth, and this is Dustin's Great Aunt Myrtle, and this here is our clergyman, Reverend Asa Wilmington, also a lifelong friend."

"...and you, sir?" The nurse asked as she pointed to Teddy.

Teddy whispered into Donny's ear, "That's okay; I can wait outside with the rest."

"Oh, this fella's a key player in Dustin's life too, and he's like kin to us all here back in Burlington. This'd be Dustin's Uncle Theodore Russell," Donny added with a wink and a grin.

Teddy, not being a tall man to begin with, stood up straight, a proud smile on his scruffy face. "That's right, sister. Now, how about we get past all the pleasantries because time's tickin' away, and let me tell you, these minutes we got left ain't the cheap ones!"

Asa's huge eyebrows flew up in approval of Teddy's boldness as he rocked on his heels, arm on Elise's shoulder completing the group.

"I just need to see your I.D. sir, and you may all go ahead," the nurse complied.

At first, Dustin couldn't figure out why in the world thoughts of a canoe trip filled his head, but they did. It was the last thing they ever did together as a family and the last thing they ever would. It was a pristine fall morning, perfectly still, the peak of color, no wind at all; the river ahead of them reflecting the sky like plate glass until broken by the bow of their canoe. It had been cold enough for frost the night prior, so Dustin's mother decided to get up before sunrise.

Meredith had planned this event. She insisted they go on the morning of the first heavy frost knowing about the show they would get on the Kaministiquia River that morning. Only Meredith understood the magic of a morning like this, how to see it coming, how to time it, so it happened just right. She knew what would happen the moment the sunrays warmed the top leaf stems on the trees.

As they floated silently down the river, the leaves began to release in the morning rays. At first, Dustin could hear upper leaves colliding with the ones beneath, knocking off even more leaves as the collisions multiplied, like slow-motion fireworks. Sometimes they would watch an entire tree covered with leaves become nearly bare in a matter of moments. On several trees, only a few leaves would start the event inside it, creating a cascade of colorful red on the oaks, yellow on the paper birches, and orange from the sugar maple; heavenly confetti, paratrooping into the calm river below. Then the leaves would gently float on the glassy surface that had just perfectly reflected their fall in the morning sunshine. They would quickly gather, like a flotilla of a thousand glowing ships, spinning on the surface and finding their places, until the bow of the canoe parted them, and moved beyond.

Everyone knew it was magic and poetry only Meredith could find. Now the sun was shining on her leaf's stem, warming it up. It was time for her final, glorious flight into the waters of eternity.

Nurse Abigail reached into her apron and pulled out a small vial of liquid she had ready. "I'm going to put a little something in her IV to help wake her up now. It may take a few minutes, so let's be patient."

Dustin bent down and kissed his mother's forehead. That's all it took. Her eyes opened.

The moment Meredith focused on her son's face, her

shoulders relaxed, and her heartbeat picked up speed again on the bedside monitor. She couldn't smile, that part of her had been removed and wrapped in coverings, but Dustin could clearly see the joy in her eyes, which began to sparkle with gratitude for the moment she had been given. She began to shift her eyes from Dustin's, then down to her hand.

"She wants you to hold her hand, Dusty," his father coached from the other bed as he leaned his own body onto its side to get closer.

Dustin looked down to see her slender hand open with all the strength she had left. His right arm hanging from a shattered shoulder, he placed his own bandaged left hand into her IV-wrapped hand and knelt down, face to face.

Meredith slowly reached out and touched the battered eagle feather still hanging over Dustin's shoulder. Her mind, as exhausted as she felt, still raced from frame to frame with all the memories of thirteen years with her son: Dustin's first birthday, the time he helped her change a flat tire when he was six, his unique Lego creations, his invention lab in the basement, the jokes and laughter, and all those wonderful trips into the wilderness of Cameron Falls, including their final family canoe trip on that crisp, fall morning. It was all she had left, treasured movie clips in her head that still played just fine, little memories worth more than gold because they really happened. Bits and pieces of the life she would take with her into forever.

There was a knock at the door. “May we enter?” Asa whispered from the now empty hallway.

Dave turned his head to see his trusted neighbor and brother poking their heads in like curious chickens. “Yes—sure, you may all come in!” Then he turned his head to Nurse Abigail, “They’re family.”

“Dave!” Uncle Donny shouted.

“Shh!” Everyone else hissed back.

“Dave!” Uncle Donny whispered. “How the heck did you get in here? What in tarnation did you do to yourself? The truck ... it’s gone?”

“Shhh!” Everyone else hissed more loudly. Aunt Myrtle smacked Uncle Donny on his arm and stood in front of him, sweetly smiling to everyone to smooth things over.

Meredith’s finger pointed to Aunt Myrtle and gestured for her to come over to the bedside. She slowly reached for a pad on her table. Dustin quickly grabbed a pen and placed it gently in her hand. She began making letters on the paper.

You are finally a mother. Your son, Dustin, beside you. Thank you, Myrtle.

Meredith put down the pen and rested her arm. She closed her eyes for a few moments and tried to take in a deeper breath to gain more time.

Elise watched with wet eyes from between Uncle Donny and Teddy, her hands holding onto Teddy’s arm.

“Mom, thank you for all you did for me. I’m going to

miss you so much. I wish we had more time. I promise I'll never forget your smile," Dustin got out between rising sobs. "I'm so sorry this happened to you! I'm so sorry we can't go on more adventures now."

Meredith slowly reached for the pen one more time, her hand beginning to tremble.

No loss. We all gained. Tomorrow, I start over.
My last adventure is about to begin!
I love you all!

Meredith closed her eyes again.

Dustin read it aloud to those in the room. The pen dropped to the floor and rolled under Dave's gurney, but no one went after it. The heart monitor beeping had slowed way down now, and Asa made a step forward.

Unable to move, his mother opened her eyes one more time and looked at Dustin, then winked. She then looked over at Elise and winked again. Slowly, she made her way around the room to each family member and did the same, except when she got to Dave, she raised what was left of her eyebrows several times before winking in his direction. With her son holding one hand and her husband the other, she closed her eyes for the last time, and the breathing and the heartbeat slowed until they came to a stop.

Nurse Abigail unplugged the heart monitor. All was silent in the room again. Asa said a prayer and closing blessing.

"Oh no ..." Dustin began, his eyes turning red with tears. "The flowers ... the flowers I picked are still inside my fishing vest, and I forgot to give them to her!"

"Dustin." Nurse Abigail started as she pointed to an empty vase filled with water next to her bed, "She saw everything on television. She saw you pick them. She knew they were for her. She asked me to get that vase ready. Would you like to get them out now?"

Teddy bent down and pulled out the green fishing vest life preserver, shaking his head in amazement. He handed it to Dustin, who pulled out the flowers and tenderly cleaned them off. Dustin lifted his mother's hand, kissing it before wrapping her warm fingers around the tiny, rustic and rare bouquet, hand-picked off the side of a cliff.

28

Reunion Redux

Two weeks later Dustin found himself climbing the steps of Wooddale Middle School once again. He paused, his good hand on the door handle and his right arm bundled in a shoulder sling to isolate his healing bone. Letting go of it, he looked back to wave at Uncle Asa in his old truck, who told him it was okay to start the day during the third hour because his dad had called in already. Dustin thought about how it was going to go for him, and he knew that no matter what happened, or what was said, he was determined to remain unmoved.

When the RCMP tried to come to arrest him after his collarbone was set, he didn't care. He didn't worry. It would all work out. When some government people threatened to take him away from his dad and uncle, he trusted it would all work out okay, and it did, after a lot of phone calls and emails sent to child protective services from all over the U.S. and Canada. When he told his dad and uncle just how much of their inventory he used for his voyage into the sky, he wasn't nervous; he only wanted their forgiveness. He could see himself in that bigger picture now. He occupied a place in that picture—an important place.

For some odd reason, he thought of Uncle Asa's heavy, rusty, iron sculptures. That was him now. Solid. Grounded. No more wind blowing him here and there. It was going to be better than fine. It was going to be whatever he could make it every single day, and that felt great. If he still couldn't stay focused enough to keep up in school; that was okay too. He would do what he could do and do well what he could do well. Coming home to find out the Burlington Novelty Warehouse site had over $10,000 in orders to be shipped out was evidence of how doing what he did well was paying off. The fact that his father hired Teddy to run the shipping in the warehouse now was a priceless bonus.

Still, that familiar feeling of being an idiot nagged at him. It was weaker than ever now though and was quickly snuffed out by his determination to care about people more than about what was in his head. Everyone *needed* everyone, somehow, and every little thing counted, like a pebble in a pond.

As he walked into the school office, Dustin found it odd how the secretaries all greeted him by name. "Dustin, before you head to third-hour class, I need you to drop off this little note to Mr. Pheut in the gym. He's expecting it," one secretary said with a strange grin on her face.

Walking to the gym, the halls and classrooms were strangely quiet. *Lots of reading going on today, I guess,* Dustin thought as he could hear his own sneakers squeaking along the tile floors.

Principal Henderson was standing by the gym door with his arms crossed when Dustin arrived looking like a naive rock star with his long, silver-streaked hair standing on end. “Let me get that door for you, Dustin. We’re all really glad you came out of your trip okay. How’s your arm doing?”

“It’s my clavicle actually—broken in two places, ya know. Cliff faces can be hard on clavicles!” As Dustin finished his small talk the door opened and he could see the entire student body sitting on the bleachers, bunches of colorful balloons all around the gym, tied to everything, including the drinking fountains. A small group of news media stood off in a corner with their cameras readied, poised to capture an event.

The crowd erupted in a roaring cheer, clapping, whistling, and stomping their feet on the wooden bleachers until the principal led Dustin over to a microphone stand in the center of the gym.

Principal Henderson turned away from the mic and cupped his hand toward Dustin’s ear. “Sorry about all this, Dustin, but the media called and kind of expected a set-up of sorts for your return. You know what I mean, right? Just say what’s on your mind. Speak from your heart." He then turned back toward the mic, "Alright then, Wooddale students..."

The cheering, clapping, whistling and stomping continued for another half minute.

"Okay, then, Wooddale students, we thank you for your enthusiasm, but now we'd like to hear a few words from Dustin before we move on with our day. Dustin?"

Dustin had not been warned. He had not expected this at all, and he wasn't sure how to react. Panic began messing with his emotions at first, but he got outside of his head and thought about how to care about the crowd in front of him more than himself. The humbled sky pilot decided to start with a simple mock bow, an easy move with his arm in a sling, which only razzed up the kids into another frenzy of cheering again. He stood and waited for the screaming and whistling to calm down.

Dustin scanned the students looking for Morty and found him in the front row, arms in the air cheering, joyful confidence on his face. Behind him, about five rows up sat Zane, and several of his groupie girlfriends. Zane's arms were crossed, and he stared straight-faced as their eyes met across the room. Nearby, Harley seemed uneasy, glancing between Zane and Dustin. Melanie Welks was standing and waving a sign painted with the same Malin symbol Morty had taped under the seat of the flying lawn chair. He looked out at them all. What were they cheering for? For him? Maybe. Was he a celebrity? Probably not for long. They were cheering for an idea, a dream, a risk he took worthy of celebrating. They wanted to know more about that kind of courage. How would he tell them?

Dustin leaned his skinny body forward, balancing his shoulder sling away from the mic stand. He cleared his throat and it echoed across the suddenly silent gym.

"Hey, I'm ..."

Dustin thought briefly for a second about how much he hated his name. It seemed like a silly concern now. He was Dustin Tecumseh Windworth, semi-successful sky pilot, contributing comrade of Wooddale Middle School, Burlington, Minnesota, a proud Ojibwe First Nation son who had just survived his greatest battle with the sky. That was who he knew himself to be and it just had to be good enough for everyone else.

"...I'm Dustin Windworth. It looks like most of you know what I've been up to lately. I guess I'm standing here today, in front of you during third hour, for several reasons. One reason is because I was told to bring this note to Mr. Pheut."

Dustin looked left and right for the gym teacher while holding a piece of paper up in front of the mic. Principal Henderson gingerly removed it from Dustin's good hand.

"I didn't expect more balloons. I kind of thought I was done with them, but I guess I was wrong. I realize you probably thought I was crazy to do what I did, but I needed to say goodbye to my mom before she died.

I really did try to find other ways to get to Canada, but none of them worked. So, I decided to fly on my own, as insane as it seemed. I knew it was possible for me to do it in the short time I had to get to her, and sometimes *time* really counts for a lot, every second of it. Now Melanie knows the real reason I was sketching balloons in class.

"I guess some kids might be asking whether I knew what I was doing before I launched. The answer is yes, I had done a lot of research, but it still didn't prepare me for what happened. The thing that pushed me over the edge to take the leap was someone helping me realize that I had the stuff inside me to make it happen ... What do they call that in science? The potential—I have an infinite potential!"

The crowd began to stir at his outrageous claim. First, it was a few disappointed moans, followed by a few boos, then random chatter. Dustin knew he had said the wrong thing and was losing everybody. Morty's head was looking down at the floor.

He took a deep breath and leaned back into the mic. "Okay, before you all decide I'm hopeless up here, let me tell you where I started from, eh? I came here from Thunder Bay, not because I wanted to, but because my family got turfed out due to my dad getting downsized. So, I walked in here, and a few of you decided you didn't like the way I looked or spoke and did a darn good job of convincing me each day that I was worthless and pointless. You know, I didn't *think* I believed any of it at first, but funny thing, I start feeling it instead. So, I had this bad feeling about myself going on in my head, I'm having to come to this school where I'm told I don't belong, and I'm waiting for my mom to die all alone, 250 miles away, where I'm not allowed to go, either. But a real friend convinced me of a few important things: first, *everyone* has this infinite potential. That everyone includes you all out there, too. The problem is that many of us don't believe that what we start will ever go anywhere or make any difference. Well, when I heard about this potential inside myself, I wondered if it was really true. I tended to believe it because my friend, Asa, always tells me the truth. I decided to see what I could do with my own gifts, starting with helping my dad and uncle's business. One thing led to another, and it wasn't long before I was finding a way out of my own problems by using the skills I already had. When I learned my mom had only a few days to live, well the next thing I know, I'm flying at two miles up.

"Another thing I ought to say is that the stuff you choose to say and do really makes a difference, even if you don't believe it will. You might be thinking that hateful words won't really destroy a life, but they can. Or you might think some silly little plan to help someone else isn't worth trying because it's just forgotten the next day. I think that everything we do and say is like a pebble being tossed into a pond. Every splash and plunk makes something—a wave, a ripple, and it keeps moving out until it reaches the shore. I needed to make one more splash in my mother's pond. She deserved more than that, but you know I had to at least say goodbye.

"Here's a third thing I learned: we are all tied together into some bigger picture that I don't think we usually see, but everyone gets a place in it, even people who feel kind of small. Small people can accomplish big things too. What we see might look messy and unclear because this world is full of troubles, but I choose to trust in the goodness of a higher power seeing to us all somehow. So, I guess I've learned that when you have make a hard decision—like whether to strap yourself into a lawn chair tied to balloons—things like faith, hope, and love, work better than fear, depression, or anger to steer us in the right direction. In my case, I guess it was the wind that steered me pretty much the right way, except for that storm cloud.

"Oh yeah, um—if you ever decide to try go out for a rip the way I just did, you ought to know that it can get more complicated than it looks. Fluffy clouds can get downright moody when you're in their space; I suggest you stick with planes."

Someone toward the back of the bleachers cupped their hands to their mouth and yelled, "Who's that mystery girlfriend of yours? Who is she?" Cheers, whistles, and catcalls started streaming out of the crowd.

"She is a friend from my old neighborhood, a true friend if you can get past your hormones and imagine that. I've known her since we were little, and she came to cheer me up before my mom died. All I can say is I hope you all find at least one person like that someday."

He began to turn away, stopped, turned back and leaned in one more time, waiting for quiet to return. "Um, thanks for all this, you know, for showing you care today. I'm grateful to the rescue team that peeled me off that cliff, glad to be alive, and I hope you are too, because no matter who you are, you matter a lot more than ya might think."

Dustin stepped away from the mic, and the crowded gym erupted again, standing this time with more clapping and whistling, all except for several who remained seated. Principal Henderson leaned toward Dustin, said something and motioned for him to walk back to the door. As Dustin approached the exit, the gym door opened with Asa standing, grinning from ear to ear. Elise ran from behind him and threw her arms around Dustin, nearly knocking him over. His father, Uncle Donny, and Myrtle squeezed through the door just in time to hear a second round of cheering and shouting at the two of them hugging near the gym entrance. Turns out Dustin got the rest of the day off school.

After going out to lunch, everyone drove back to the farm for dessert and some final goodbyes. Dustin insisted on riding alongside Asa in the Power Wagon with Elise and Morty stuffed into the cab with him.

"Well, Dustin, do you remember that giant snail idea you came up with for a sculpture?"

"Yep, I do. You got it done?"

"I delivered it to a local elementary school this morning ... my final delivery." Asa revealed as he shut off the truck in front of the house.

"What do you mean, Asa? What are you going to do now?"

"Going back to preaching. Life is short, and it's time to be about the business I'm best at."

"But you're a great artist, too. What about your art?"

"Dustin, I've learned a lot from my art, and it's helped me work through some big things. I'll still do my art, just not as my main thing anymore. I'm taking the lessons that I've learned from it back to the people as best I can," he said with a grin on his face. "This truck is for your daddy. It's his to keep until he can get a replacement. It will get him into town, anyway."

Asa tossed the keys to Dustin, got out, and shut the door. He leaned into the open window. "Dusty, you might think about tinkering with the engine on this thing a bit, so it won't quit on him." The reverend then turned away and began walking down the long gravel drive to his home. When he reached the road, he stopped, turned around to look up at the silo with its painted "Burlington Novelty Warehouse" sign, and gave Dustin a kind of waving salute before disappearing behind the tall rows of corn that lined the road.

"Morty, did you know about this?"

"Nope, but I suspected it was coming. Dust, take a look at what's leaning against your porch."

Dustin got out and walked up to a blue mountain bike, the tags still attached to the handlebars, blowing in the breeze. One of the tags had some writing on it.

Dustin,
I told people you were stuck with your aunt's lame bike and put the word out for you and took a collection. I promise not to paint this one. But no more "borrowing" my orange bike without asking! By the way, what you did up there was really cool.
Not your friend, but not your enemy anymore,
H.D.

While the adults ate their ice cream and peanuts, going on and on about how freaked out they were when this happened, or when that happened, Dustin excused himself to go outside with Elise and Morty.

"I need you guys to help me out with one more thing. Follow me to the barn."

Dustin had something in his hand and passed it to Morty. "I can't climb the latter to the loft with only one hand and the altimeter. Can you take this up for me? Elise, can you hold the flashlight for us?"

He climbed one step at a time, his right arm hanging in the sling. The other two watched him struggle from the ground floor and then followed him up the ladder and through the hatchway door into the barn loft. By the time Elise got up on her feet, she found Dustin standing by the plane, silhouetted against the setting sun rays streaming in from the upper window.

"I need you to help me get this altimeter back into the plane."

"Now? Does it really matter, Dust? I mean, the thing has a cracked face now, and we can do it later," suggested Morty.

"Morty, this altimeter helped keep me alive up there, and it belongs to Great Grandpa Ash. This is still his plane, and it's not complete without it. I borrowed it, and I just can't sleep tonight until I put it back. Can you help me? The tools I got it out with are still there on the seat," Dustin said.

"I get it." Elise whispered, "It's about respect."

Morty's small body easily slipped under the seat, and he went to work bolting it back in while Elise held the flashlight.

Dustin stood away from the plane in the dark shadows, admiring it. "I know how it feels now, Grandpa. Thanks for taking me up there. It was amazing, and I got to say goodbye to Mom! I brought it back like I promised."

Later, after Morty left, Elise's parents arrived to take her home.

Dustin turned to Elise and gently took hold of her arm to look into her sky-blue eyes. Even though she kept smiling for him, he wiped one of her tear-soaked cheeks with the back of his good hand. "Thank you ..."

"Thank you for what?" she asked, confused.

"For helping me see the possibility of what looks impossible, and then telling me to reach for it."

"I guess I really don't know how I did that, Dusty," she sincerely confessed.

"Neither do I," he agreed. "Maybe it was about you just being there for me, you know, so I wasn't alone, and you just being—you, in my life. I guess it's not really explainable, but it's real, and it helped me get through." He wanted to say more but dared not risk ruining a good thing.

She was okay with his words. She knew him and believed they were much more about trust and friendship than any romantic ideas flying around, though she wasn't entirely opposed to those either. It's just that their friendship was more important than a crush, and it always would be.

Once more, he watched the minivan lights disappear into the dusk, but this time felt joy as he watched her go. She was a true friend who stood by him in the worst weather, and always would.

~ *Beginning today, treat everyone you meet as if they will be dead by midnight. Extend to them all the care, kindness, and understanding you can muster, and do it with no thought of any reward. Your life will never be the same again.*

Og Mandino

EPILOGUE

It was a sunny afternoon in mid-November when Dustin's shoulder sling finally came off. He got out of the car and walked directly to the silo. His arm was weak, but it didn't matter. He was going to climb it anyway, and nothing Aunt Myrtle said was going to convince him to wait. It had been over two months since his feet had left the ground, and he had missed something he loved. Great Grandpa's biplane had been on his mind and in his research for weeks now, yet he didn't know why. Something about the plane called out to him, but it was trapped inside the belly of an old barn, and he was too young to even ask. Questions dogged his mind. *Would the engine start after all these years? Would it fly? How did it feel to fly it? What really happened to Great Grandpa?* He needed to test out these thoughts he had in a place more fitting, in a place of peace.

One step at a time, relying mostly on his good arm, he slowly made his way to the top, breezes tangling his silver-streaked hair. He needed to meet with the sky and the Spirit who made it, face to face. He wasn't quite finished with whatever he needed to do up there, beyond his understanding, and he suspected the sky wasn't finished with him either.

Credits and References

Chapter 15 Quoted References:

1. Anne Frank. *Anne Frank: The Diary of a Young Girl;* Bantam Books, 1993.
2. Og Mandino. *The Greatest Salesman in the World;* Bantam Books, 1968.

Chapter 16 Online References:

1. Balloons and Helium FAQ, 17 May 2011. Facebook.com, http://www.facebook.com/note.php?note_id=10150249891521554.
2. Katherine Neer "How many regular-sized helium-filled balloons would it take to lift someone?" 1 April 2000. HowStuffWorks.com. <https://science.howstuffworks.com/science-vs-myth/everyday-myths/question185.htm>.

Music Reference:
Dust in the Wind
Words and Music by Kerry Livgren

Made in the USA
Middletown, DE
22 July 2019